# Duty

First Novel of Rhynan

# Also written by Rachel Rossano

### Wren
(A Romany Epistles Novel)

### The Mercenary's Marriage

### The Crown of Anavrea
(Book One of the Theodoric Saga)

### Exchange

### Word and Deed

# DUTY

FIRST NOVEL OF RHYNAN

WRITTEN BY

RACHEL ROSSANO

ISBN 978-1482360110

Cover by Rossano Designs

First Printing

This novel is dedicated to
Abigail, Elizabeth,
Alyssa, JoAnna,
and all the readers
who love the adventure
of the written word.

# Chapter One

"The red one is mine," he said.

I didn't raise my head although instinct urged me to. Father had called me Red. He said I was born screaming, skin deep red like the beets in the garden and hair fiery like the setting sun. The man who spoke was not my father.

I glanced at him from beneath my cloak's hood. Arrogant in his size and superior mass, his eyes picked me out of the writhing mass of captives. Early morning sunlight glinted off plain armor and an unadorned helm, yet the unwashed barbarians treated him with the respect due a commander.

The crowd of women around me parted for the soldier fulfilling his order. Mothers moved back with babes in their arms, toddlers clinging to their skirts. Their fingers clutched older children's hands or shoulders. A living mass, their voices silenced by the army surrounding them. Their faces spoke eloquently of their fear.

The soldier, smelling of sweat and sour wine, grabbed my left arm and dragged me out from among them. I didn't want to bring harm to the women around me. The soldier would injure many before subduing me. I allowed him to pull me toward the commander with only minimal resistance.

Once free of the captives, however, I yanked from the man's grip in an attempt to run. Three pairs of rough hands caught hold of my arms before I managed more than a few steps. The stench of their unclean bodies turned my stomach. I gagged as I fought them. They dragged me through the dust and dumped me at his feet.

I struggled up only to be brought down again. Pressure behind my knees forced me to kneel.

I lifted my face to glare at the commander.

"Remove her hood."

Someone pulled my cloak half off my shoulders in his enthusiasm. Red curls fell free in a wild mass about my shoulders.

Silently I cursed the color. If only I had been blessed with plain brown or even blond tresses, I could have hidden in plain sight.

"My Lady Brielle Solarius, I presume."

He had the audacity to meet my glare. His eyes were only glimmers beneath the beaten metal and leather of his helmet. He made no bow or any show of the honor due me. I was a noblewoman. I didn't claim the right of deference often, but still the fact remained.

"Might I know your name, barbarian?"

His reaction did not change his posture. I could not read his emotions.

"Lord Irvaine is no barbarian."

The soldier at my left, a young man barely my senior, shoved me between the shoulders. I resisted, pressing back against his hand despite the burning in my thighs from the effort. Finally I shrugged him off.

Anger filled me, blinding my reason. Caution, a weak flicker of light in the night of anger, wavered and almost went out. The darkness like a living thing, growing ever stronger, pressed me more closely every second I lingered, waiting to hear my fate. I could not lose control. My people were counting on me. Their families were under my watch.

"By what right am I treated like this? I am a noble of Rhynan, born of an ancient house and loyal to King Trentham."

"Trentham is dead." Lord Irvaine lifted a gauntleted hand and pointed off to the south. "He fell in battle a fortnight past. Mendal of Ranterland is now king."

Panic clutched my chest. Old stories of the unrest that followed a coup flooded my mind. Allegiances sifting with the wind and the death toll rising despite the end of hostilities as the loyal were killed off and the loyal rewarded.

"My cousin, Orwin?"

"Sworn allegiance to my liege, but his sincerity is suspect. You are King Mendal's guarantee from Orwin that he will remain faithful."

I laughed, a bitter sound despite my efforts to quell it.

"I am a worthless pawn for that purpose. Orwin cares not for my safety. My peril will not hinder his plans a hair's breadth."

"Your peril is not my goal. I seek your submission."

Before I could seek clarification, another helmeted soldier approached. This one moved like a man with a purpose. The sudden silence and tension of the men around me clearly marked his importance.

3

"All are accounted for, my lord, thirty-five women of marriageable age, twenty-five dwellings with potential to last the winter."

"The lord's hall?"

"Usable also, given time for cleaning and repair."

Lord Irvaine nodded. "Take the quartermaster and assign wives. See to it that the men show respect and offer the women the option to purchase refusal. Give care to look up the fate of their previous mates before presenting them to the officiate for vow recording. Warn the men that I will suffer no abuse. If such is discovered, the offender shall lose his share of spoils and suffer further punishment based on the crime."

The soldier bowed and retreated.

"By what right do you do this?" I demanded. "We are citizens of Rhynan, not cattle to be divided and claimed. These are free women not slaves."

Lord Irvaine's displeasure at my words was evident in his stiffened stance. I savored my small victory.

"They, you, and this land are tribute to King Mendal from your cousin, part of his measures to convince the king of his shift in allegiance."

"You take pleasure in raping women and possessing land not your own? You are no better than the robber barons over the border. They take what they wish without compensating us. You defile the title of noble, my lord!" I spat the title into the torn earth at his feet.

Answering anger tensed his left arm as his fingers curled into a fist. I lifted my chin and awaited the blow that would reveal his true nature. Instead, he pulled his helmet from his head. Dark, sweat-matted hair plastered his head and dirt streaked down his hollowed cheeks from dark circles around his eyes. He dropped

4

his helm to the ground at my knees. It rolled to rest against my thigh. He stepped forward and leaned down so close I smelled his sweat. I noted the lack of sour wine on his breath.

"Look in my face, Lady Solarius, and see the truth. I take no joy from this task. But I am a loyal soldier. I do as my master bids."

His dark, haunted eyes bore into mine. Something deep inside my chest stirred. However, anger still possessed my tongue.

"I see only a monster intent on unleashing his pleasure-seeking men on a village of unarmed women and children."

He flinched, a barely perceptible movement in his features.

"Enough." Rising to his feet with more grace than I expected, he strode away. "Antano!" A burly man, helmetless and carrying more visible weapons than the other men in the group, answered the call.

"My lord?"

"See that she observes the operation, but doesn't interfere. Then escort her to my quarters by nightfall."

"Aye, my lord." Antano approached respectfully. "This way, my lady."

I watched Lord Irvaine stride away among his men. As I rose from the dust, I picked up the helmet. It was heavy, but well made. The leather felt worn and supple. What kind of man hid behind its surface?

I offered it to my escort.

"Nay, bring it with you, lady." Antano loomed over me. "You can return it to him tonight. For now, we must go. He wishes for you to see how your women are treated."

5

He crossed the now empty village center toward the lord's hall, due east. I followed him, dreading the hours to come. Despite the fleeting inclination to leave it behind, I carried Lord Irvaine's helmet with me.

# Chapter Two

Taltana, the village midwife and wise woman, took the news of her only son's death without the release of tears. Her face stilled, the light in her eyes dimmed, and she stared at the mud wall over the record-keeper's shoulder.

"Marriage status?" he asked.

"Widowed last spring." Unmoving except her mouth, Taltana's life withered before my eyes.

"Age?"

She flinched and shook her head as though dispelling a dream before looking at the man bent over the leather-encased tome. "Thirty-seven summers."

His pen scratched the parchment. "Do you own property?"

"I maintain the western most hovel, the garden beyond, and a one day's plow in Lord Wisten's fields."

The recorder grunted and wrote. Then without lifting the tip of the pen, he asked, "Do you wish to marry or pay the price to remain unwed? Either choice requires you house three men under your roof for the winter season. They shall contribute to the household. If you marry, your husband will protect you."

"What is the cost of saying nay?"

"A month's measure of grain or an animal from your flock or herd."

"How can you put a price on her..." Antano's grip on my upper arm silenced me.

The record-keeper's pen paused, but he didn't lift his head.

"No interference," Antano reminded me softly.

Taltana spoke. "I will marry."

The record-keeper nodded. "Proceed through that door." He flicked ink-stained fingers in the direction of the far doorway and the sunlight beyond. "Your choice of mates will be presented to you."

As she passed, Taltana bowed to me. "I don't blame you, my lady. You had no hand in sending my son to war. Tell Orwin that he owes me a life. I spared him at birth when I convinced his father that he would thrive despite his curved back. Now he has taken my son. Should we cross paths, I'll claim his life."

The cold death in the woman's eyes froze me to my core.

Taltana turned away and walked through the door into the stable yard as though she had just discussed the weather. Beyond the opening, her voice greeted the men. I released the breath in my chest.

"I would warn your cousin, my lady," Antano advised. "That woman has revenge in her heart. I believe she will kill him as soon as she lays eyes on him."

"I know." A shiver gripped my spine.

A quiet, feminine voice interrupted. "Am I to come in now?"

At the sound, my chest constricted. "Not Loren."

Loren, my sister of the heart, stepped into the room. She had no brother, husband, or father to ask after and no land in her possession. She lived in the hall as a companion for me. Willowy and fair, she embodied most of the village men's ideal. Over the years, she had discouraged all advances. My chest ached at the waste, saving herself only to have the choice taken from her in the end.

"Spare her."

Antano acknowledged my plea by gripping my shoulder.

"Nay, my lady. None will be spared between eighteen and forty. Your men were wiped out in the final confrontation. The king ordered us to settle here, set down roots and replace the male population. We will till the land, maintain the holdings, and defend the border."

In the background, Loren continued to answer the recorder's questions.

I asked Antano, "Is the king doing this elsewhere?"

"Yes, though many commanders are far more brutal than Lord Irvaine. The tales are not for feminine ears. Be thankful Lord Irvaine is your new master."

"What of me, Antano? What will my fate be?"

"That, lady, is not for me to say. Ask Lord Irvaine."

"I shall."

Loren replied to the recorder's final question. "I will marry."

He directed her toward the door into the yard.

As Loren passed us, I caught her hand.

"My lady, no..." Antano protested.

"I request to accompany her."

He frowned at me, but listened.

"I nursed at her mother's breast, learned to toddle holding her hand, and shared every step of my life with her. I wish to walk beside her now."

Antano studied our faces for a moment. "No interfering."

I squeezed Loren's cold fingers and received an answering tightening. Antano spoke with the record-keeper. While his back was turned, Loren pressed against my side. I drank in the familiar warmth of her presence. "Thank you," she whispered.

"I will see this is stopped. I will speak to Lord Irvaine." I wasn't sure what I would say, but the Kurios would give me words. Surely this wasn't His will.

"Nay, Bri, I have had more time than most. Marriage was my fate. I have delayed long enough. It is time for a husband and children."

"I wish the circumstances were otherwise."

Loren turned her face toward the only window in the room. "Wishing won't change reality."

I preferred the tears to the silence of raw emotion petrifying the heart. I witnessed too much dull acceptance, resignation to circumstances. I wanted to scream, fight, rage against the injustice.

Antano led us out into the yard. Forty-five men stood and lounged about. Loren's entrance caused a stir. Men straightened their shoulders and stood to their feet. A bald man licked his fingers and smoothed the few hairs remaining on his crown. I scanned the gathered crowd, at least twenty strong. Tall and short, all broad in the shoulders and muscled, they bore scars and signs of their craft. Though, some were more weathered than others. Loren focused on her feet, blind to all but the dirt beneath her bare toes.

I nudged her elbow. "You need to at least look at them."

"I can't." She trembled.

In desperation, I turned to Antano. He had been decent, considering the situation. He knew these men.

"Who will be a gentle husband, Antano?"

"Nay, lady."

"Please, we don't know these men. How can she choose on appearance alone?"

Antano held against my pleading gaze for a moment only to give in with a sigh. Despite the grim lines of his features, I found kindness there.

"Choose the one without a left hand."

I frowned up at my guard, but something in his voice made me look again at the man he indicated.

The man stood at the back of the crowd, a solid and unmoving island among the shifting men. He held his shoulders square, but his manner remained loose and comfortable. He allowed those around him to move first.

"Quaren has a child, a girl of four summers, who needs a mother, otherwise he wouldn't be here. He was a good husband to his first wife. Your friend will be safe with him."

"He appears to be a man of patience, Loren." I pressed her shoulder. "See how he waits."

Finally lifting her fair head, Loren peered at the group. As though sensing someone spoke of him, Quaren turned his face toward us at the same moment. The two's eyes met.

"I will take him." Loren pointed at Quaren.

The officiate grimaced. "He has but one hand, miss. Surely you wish a man who has all of his parts."

"He lost the hand honorably, I assume." I glared at the balding man. He listed to one side himself, suffering from a twisted back much like my cousin.

"Aye, my lady, saving Lord Irvaine's life."

"Then I don't see how that would be a disadvantage in anyone's eyes."

"But, my lady, some women prefer..."

"She wishes to choose him, Ryanir." Antano's voice cut off any future protest from the officiate. "Unless you wish Lord Irvaine to hear of how you are interfering with the choices of the women, I would recommend you witness their vows without fuss."

In answer, Ryanir motioned Quaren forward. Within moments the new couple exchanged vows, were allotted a living space, and dismissed. I hugged Loren tightly.

"You will still see me," she protested.

"I know." I still didn't release her. "But from now on it will be different." She was no longer going to be constantly near. I wasn't going to be her responsibility now, he would, he and his child. "If he ever lifts even a finger to harm you, come to me."

"You will be as helpless as I, Brielle."

"Promise me." I pulled back to lock gazes with her.

"I promise."

Only then I let go. I watched the pair leave the yard and grasped at hope. The gentle way Loren's new husband touched her shoulder reassured me, but the sour sensation in the depths of my stomach refused to be ignored. I lifted the helmet I still carried and frowned at it.

"Antano, take me to Lord Irvaine."

"He didn't wish you to return until nightfall."

"I have seen enough. If you don't escort me, I shall find him myself."

Antano eyed me warily before pointing toward the lord's hall.

Contrary to my keeper's obvious concerns, questions not anger burned in my gut. Only Lord Irvaine could answer the most pressing one of them all. What did he mean to do with me?

# Chapter Three

The familiar dim shadows of the lord's hall during the daylight hours comforted me. All remained as it had been the night before though it was now well past midday. Trestle tables leaned against the stone walls, the noon meal forgotten in the chaos. A smattering of pallets still littered the floor. The daylight falling from the single smoke hole illuminated little except the center of the room. On the edge of the light, Lord Irvaine slumped in the steward's chair. His fingers lost in his shaggy hair, he groaned.

"That is hardly enough to last us through the first few months of winter." The thin man to Irvaine's left waved a sheet of parchment for emphasis. Dressed in a simple tunic and leggings, he stood just beyond the touch of the light. His other hand clutched a parchment roll.

"Brevand, I can count. I surpassed you at figuring when we studied under Master Tarn. I know the provisions are inadequate."

"I was just..."

"I know. Sorry." Irvaine rubbed brutally at his face. "This whole confounded situation is a nightmare."

Antano cleared his throat.

Brevand's cold eyes fell on me from the shadows. An icy tingle tensed my spine as his bored gaze assessed my lack of attributes. Lord Irvaine didn't bother to lift his head.

"What news do you bring?"

"Lady Solarius insisted on speaking with you."

"I told you, Antano, I..." Irvaine finally lifted his face. He still hadn't washed away the dirt. It ringed his eyes and stained his cheeks. He rested his elbows on his knees. Beneath the grime, he appeared haggard. He sighed. "Very well, my lady, what do you wish to say?"

"I have questions, my lord."

He closed his eyes, resting his head against his fisted hands. "Leave us."

The men exchanged a glance of confusion.

"But, my lord..." Brevand protested.

"Leave us, Brevand. You have provisions to recount and divide. Expect the worst and then return with the details."

Brevand's thin features flinched in anger before arranging into an expression of indifference. Unease tingled along my forearms, but I brushed it away. I needed to focus on the man with the answers.

As Brevand and Antano retreated into the sunshine outside, I studied the man who held all of our fates. His rough hands and muscled limbs were not the markings of a noble. He moved like a warrior, quick and purposeful.

My cousin Orwin's hands were lean and weak. Despite his attempts to appear a strong man among men, his face remained permanently flushed from excessive wine and his belly soft.

"You have not been a noble long," I observed.

"That is not a question."

"Very well, what did you mean when you said I was yours?"

He lifted his head and regarded me intently as though weighing my reaction before breaking bad news. Finally he let out a sigh and thrust himself to his feet.

"We were married by proxy before King Mendal a month past in the presence of your cousin and the full gathering of nobles. The land, the village of Wisenvale, and your hand were given as gestures of loyalty by Lord Wisten, accepted by King Mendal, and imparted to me as gestures of peace."

My head swam and the room tilted. I forced air into my lungs and closed my eyes. This stranger was my husband.

"I was given orders to marry you publicly before my men and take possession of this land."

I was not alone in this. A fact I could not forget. All the women I witnessed that morning, forced to make a choice, were no better off than me. Nay, I preferred their lot. There was no selection before me. He already owned me.

"And the portioning out of the women?" I asked, hoping for more information.

"It is by order of the new king. He needs a resident force here at the border. There have been reports of activity among the robber barons on the other side of the river."

The Varvail River marked the easternmost border of Rhynan. Only three days ago a hunting party stumbled through an abandoned campsite as close as the first ridge beyond the river. Soon winter would come. The

17

snows and wind should keep any raiding ruffians at home. This far north the weather was a curse and a blessing. But come spring, the situation changed.

"Back to the matter at hand. I am honor bound to fulfill my duty, Lady Solarius, but you are not."

Pulling myself from my thoughts, I focused on him. His dark eyes met mine as though he had never looked away, his expression unreadable. Intense and probing, his gaze left me no room to shy away.

"Are you suggesting I am without honor?" I pulled back my shoulders.

"Nay, lady, I suspect your measure exceeds most. I only wish to say I will not hold you to a promise made by another. If your father, or brother perhaps, granted your hand, I would feel more…at ease. But your cousin makes this whole scheme smell of deceit."

His scrutiny made me want to squirm.

"I am nothing like my cousin, my lord. I do not scheme or plot. I have lived the simple life of a peasant. My hands bear callouses from laboring alongside the humblest in our village. I am not a delicate woman to be cosseted."

"I can see that."

I lifted my chin. Men frequently took exception to my height and direct manner. Bracing for a biting summation of my lack of virtues, I met his regard.

Instead he smiled. Well, not really. It was more of a lift to the left side of his mouth, as close to a smile as I had seen so far. The slight change warmed his eyes. Looking away, I grasped at my train of thought.

"I am not the kind of woman a rising noble should have by his side."

He stepped closer. The smell of leather and dirt filled

my nostrils. He was two handsbreadths from me.

"I am not a noble."

I opened my mouth to protest the obvious, but he stalled me by raising his hand.

"I am a soldier, a man accustomed to grueling marches, meager fare, and long, cold nights sleeping in the dirt. Alive by the strength of my sword arm and the speed of my feet, I need a wife who can stand at my side, not cower behind me. The more I know of you, the better suited you appear, my lady. Should you have me, I would willingly take you to wife."

"You are giving me a choice?"

"Aye."

"And should I choose nay, what will happen to me?"

"You can marry your sweetheart."

"I have none."

"You nurse a secret yearning for one of the youths of the village? Or perhaps your beloved died?"

I peered at him. Was he jesting? "I have no romantic attachments."

"Do you object to men?"

"No. What are you driving at?"

He flashed a balance-skewing grin. "I didn't think I was that ugly."

"You aren't."

I spoke truth. He wasn't handsome, but I had never been inclined toward men proud of their face. He was tall, gaining on me by at least a handsbreadth. He possessed all of his hair and teeth, remarkable considering his line of work and his age. Judging by the creases in his face, he was at least thirty. I eyed the traces of silver highlighted by the sunlight. Perhaps he was closer to forty-years-old.

"Then I suggest a solution. We marry. I will give you protection, children, and companionship. I believe we can hope for at least friendship, but..." He studied my face. "...I haven't completely given up on the possibility of more. What do you say?"

In light of the sacrifice of the other women in my village, I had a duty. It was the obligation of every noblewoman to set an example. Mother lived the lessons she taught me until her death. Always gracious and supportive, she even accepted the introduction of Orwin into their household, never speaking a word against him. Orwin saw no reason to still his own tongue, however. I blackened his eyes a few times before he learned to not speak his insolence in my hearing.

This man would not be so easily directed. His life spoke to his skill with a sword. His position indicated he possessed some ability to learn. Memory of his control when I prodded his temper that morning reassured me that I would not be constantly warding off his blows. Still, his character remained untested.

I boldly studied his face again. A mask of indifference kept him guessing, I hoped.

"What is holding you back from decision?" he asked.

"What I do not know about you," I answered. "I lack even the questionable reliability of second or third-hand witnesses."

"I promise to never strike you in anger, if that is your fear. The rest, I am afraid, you are going to have to discover later."

I could ask for more, but nothing at this point would completely reassure me. Closing my eyes and releasing a prayer to Kurios, I took a step of faith. "Yes."

I didn't really have many expectations for his response, but he defied the few I considered. He kissed me.

Rough, calloused hands held my head still as he took my mouth with his. There was no other way to describe it. Warm, commanding, yet gentle, and brief, he stepped away before I could respond. My heart thundered in my ears.

"Thank you. I will send Antano to guide you through the preparations for tonight."

Then he was gone.

I stared at my cousin's chair, once my father's chair and now Lord Irvaine's, and wondered what manner of man I agreed to marry. Nay, I was already his. What I just handed to him was my consent. Something he apparently valued very highly.

"My lady?" Antano waited just inside the outer door. "I am to take you to choose a marriage gift to give Lord Irvaine during the ceremony."

I nodded numbly. *Kurios, have mercy,* I prayed. Only then did I realize I still carried Lord Irvaine's helmet.

# Chapter Four

Torches flared in the breeze, transforming the familiar village square into a sea of shifting light and shadows. Music—lute, tambourine, flute, and pulsing drum—stirred the spirit. My feet moved in time to the beat without volition. The mixture of familiar and foreign faces among the revelers set my instincts on edge. I never knew if the next person I met would leer or smile. It didn't help that I no longer dressed as one of them.

A full skirt swished elegantly about my ankles with each step. The diaphanous emerald silk whispered against itself. I missed the reassuring warmth and weight of my rough linen and wool. Finer clothing, thinner shoes, and birth set me apart from them. I walked alone. I no longer belonged to the dancing crowd around me. I was his.

My stomach twisted. I swallowed with caution, suddenly thankful I had eaten nothing since early morn.

"Brielle!"

Loren plowed into me, wrapping her arms about my shoulders, pulling me down four inches to her level.

"I am so sorry, Brielle. Quaren just told me. You weren't even given a choice." She drew back to study my face.

"She has forgotten to tell you I also said Lord Irvaine will make a good husband." Loren's new husband stepped out of the crowd pulsing about us. His mild eyes smiled slightly at me in the flickering light.

"Are you a wife to evaluate such things?" Loren asked him sharply. "Besides, Brielle is hardly a typical woman. She rides, brawls, and works like a man. She doesn't need a husband."

"Unlike you?" Quaren tilted his head slightly and watched Loren's features with amusement. A smile tugged at his mouth, lightening his features.

"Exactly." Loren turned to mouth words missed. I didn't catch the sounds in the din around us. The gleam in her eyes and heightened flush to her cheek gave me hope she would be happy with her new life.

"Have you met his daughter yet?"

"No. She will arrive in a few days with the supply wagons." She grabbed my shoulders. "Bri, are you going to be alright? I can help you run if you want. I know where they are keeping the horses. It is only a few miles to the river. Once across it and into the hills, you would be free."

"Nay, Loren, I have given my word."

Her eyes grew round. "He didn't hurt you, did he? Did he touch you? They say you were alone with him for an hour, more than enough time to..."

I stopped her with a sharp shake of my head. Her husband stood close enough to overhear if the volume of the merrymaking slackened unexpectedly.

"This is my choice, Loren. I have given my word."

"But, Brielle, will you be happy?"

"I have as much a chance at happiness as you, Loren." I smiled at her and jutted my chin toward her spouse. "You seem quite settled already."

Loren blushed to the tips of her ears. "He has been very sweet so far."

"You chose well. Now wish me happy and go with him. It is almost time."

The music stopped. Around us, voices hushed. The crowd parted, making a path for someone. Lord Irvaine strode toward me. A gold edged tunic of emerald emblazoned with the figure of a hart covered his chest. His dark hair, now dry, curled to his head. He had finally washed his face. He stopped at the edge of the open circle that hastily formed around Loren and myself.

"My lord." Quaren bowed his head.

Loren curtsied.

I remained standing, meeting his inky-eyed scrutiny. "My lord."

He lifted his right hand, extending it palm up toward me. "It is time. Are you ready?"

I felt Loren's gaze on my face, but I didn't lower my own to meet it. *Kurios, give me strength*, I prayed. Stepping forward, I laid my hand in his.

Together we walked toward the dais outlined in the glow of ten flaring torches. My hands trembled when I realized we would be standing on it before the village and his men. The officiate, the man with a twisted back from before, stood at the dais edge dressed in a heavily embroidered gray robe. The few hairs on his head danced in the breeze.

Irvaine squeezed my fingers. "I would prefer

something more intimate, but the king decreed a public speaking of vows. He intends there should be no mistaking the validity of our marriage."

"A bedding ceremony then." I faltered at the thought.

His fingers tightened around mine. "Leave that to me. I will not see you humiliated."

I opened my mouth to ask how he intended to accomplish it, but our arrival at the dais interrupted. We climbed the single step together and faced each other before the company. The old man wrapped our joined hands with a length of white silk. Beneath the fabric, Irvaine's fingers cradled mine, warm and strong.

"Speak your vows after me. Make sure they are loud enough for all to hear." The old man faced Lord Irvaine first.

"I am Tomas Nirren Dyrease, Earl of Irvaine." Irvaine's rich voice caught me off guard. I frowned up at him in surprise. The officiate had not spoken yet. "I do willingly speak these vows to Brielle Solarius." His eyes locked with mine. An emotion I couldn't name grabbed my attention. "I pledge my sword to your protection, my hands to your comfort, my shoulders to your provision, my children to your body, my heart to your heart." With each phrase, he squeezed my fingers. My stomach tightened. His gaze, black in the torchlight, never wavered from my face. "I take you as my wife." A shiver shot through me. He meant every word.

"Repeat after me." The officiate led me through my vows.

"I am Brielle Solarius, daughter of Tyranen Solarius, late Lord of Wisten. I do willingly speak these vows to

26

Tomas Nirren Dyrease." His name came surprisingly easy to my tongue. "I pledge my hands to your comfort, my body to your children, my loyalty to your cause, my means into your control."

My gaze lost focus. I was handing my future to this man. Cold gripped my core as I realized the full implications of my words. I could not speak against him or deny him anything he desired of me. Everything I possessed belonged to him. My hands shook as my thoughts filled with visions of our children. He now held their lives in his hands as well.

"Brielle?" Irvaine's suddenly painful grip on my hands brought my gaze up to meet his. Worry bracketed his eyes in wrinkles. His dark brows lowered, but concern, not anger shone in his eyes. "Breathe slowly and focus. One sentence more."

"I take you as my husband," the officiate prompted.

I only whispered the words, but it was enough for the officiate. "Bring forth the gifts!" He waved dramatically.

My middle ached and darkness edged my vision. I blinked. Perhaps I should have eaten something.

"Brielle?" Irvaine's voice came from far away.

My knees gave out. Someone caught me as I fell, but oblivion took over before I figured out whose arms held me.

# Chapter Five

"I can't believe you forgot to feed her!"

The man's voice resonated in my head, jerking me to awareness but leaving my sense of balance behind. I took five steadying breaths before opening my eyes. By then, Irvaine's voice grew soft with restrained anger.

"I gave her into your care, Antano, because I trusted you. I thought that you of all my men would know how to treat a lady. Now I see that I was wrong."

Silence stretched as the tension in the room thickened the air. I blinked up at an intricately woven tapestry, my mother's work, suspended over the bed by the four thick posts. It was my parents' bed. Heavy curtains fell to the floor drawn back by thick loops of the same fabric. When closed, they shut out the rest of the room. The mattress beneath me gave more than it had the last time I slept there half a decade past. I turned my head cautiously to the left.

The gold of the firelight cast the two men in high relief. Irvaine's leaner form loomed over Antano's bent head.

"It wasn't his fault. I wouldn't have been able to eat even if food was offered."

Both men straightened at my voice.

Irvaine glared at Antano. "He still stands responsible for not offering it." He dismissed Antano with a flick of his hand. "See to it we are not disturbed."

Antano turned toward the door just as it opened. A young man entered and bowed, not lifting his eyes from the floor the whole time. "My lord, the officiate wishes to speak to you."

"What about? His duties are finished. I have already ordered he be supplied for his return journey."

"It is about the...bedding, my lord."

I bit back my own protest when I glimpsed Irvaine's face. Tight control hid his emotion, but his eyes glinted brightly in the light. An impatient twitch flicked the fingers on his right hand. "Have him come. Antano stay." He crossed to the bedside as the boy left. Pinning me with his gaze he asked, "Can you trust me?"

I began to ease myself up onto my elbows, but he stopped me with a hand on my shoulder.

"Answer the question?"

I grimaced up at him. "To a point."

"That will be enough. No matter what I do or say, don't protest. Can you do that?"

I eyed him warily. "I will try."

"Fair enough."

The bedroom door opened and the officiate entered. The edges of his gray robe were brown from the dirt outside. Drunken laughter wafted in through the open doorway behind him.

"The witnesses are prepared, my lord." The officiate bowed.

"I already told you earlier, Ryanir. There will be no bedding ceremony tonight."

"But the king..."

30

Irvaine cut him off. "She is in my bed." He gestured to where I lay. I tried to look submissive, an easy feat lying on my back on a massive bed.

"I intend she not leave it 'til the morrow. Considering the events that brought her there, I doubt she will have the strength to resist. I gave my word as a loyal subject of the king. I shall attempt to produce heirs. It was part of my vows. Besides, I have to consider my lady's delicate nature."

Antano coughed before regaining control of himself. Irvaine's attention never wavered from Ryanir's face. The older man shrunk under the noble's stare.

"I refuse to invite a crowd of drunken men into my bedchamber. I will do my duty to her and my king, have no fear."

"But, my lord, the king's instructions were very clear. You are to…"

"King Mendal intends to validate the marriage so Lord Wisten cannot make claim on the land through her." Irvaine gestured toward the scattered parchment littering the top of the table next to the fireplace. I recognized the heavy trestle table from the kitchen. "I have been in communication with him too."

Irvaine's feature tightened. "A crowd of drunken men witnessing me climbing into the same bed with her while you recite words over us hardly validates our marriage more. Many of those men will not remember the events of this night come morning. No, Ryanir, there will be no bedding ceremony."

Turning from him, Irvaine unpinned the brooch at his shoulder and threw his cloak so it draped the chair before the fire. The metal clasp skittered into the shadows beyond. He pulled the emerald and gold

31

surcoat over his head and dropped it at his feet. His undertunic of green looked almost black in the shadows.

"Go, Ryanir."

Ignoring the officiate's mumbled response, Irvaine strode toward the bed. I choked on the protest swelling in my throat. I instinctively slid my hand to where I usually carried my eating knife and found nothing.

Irvaine's gaze moved from my hand to my face. His expression a blank, only the rich depths of his eyes reassured me that he played a part. "Antano, show him out."

After a brief scuffle, the door thumped closed behind our unwelcome guest and his escort.

Sagging forward, Irvaine dropped his palms to the mattress and let out a heavy sigh. "I am sorry about that." He lifted his head to look at me.

I scrambled awkwardly from the bed, careful to exit on the side opposite from him.

He crossed to the table and picked up a log book. A tap on the door stayed his hand before he opened it.

"What?" he demanded.

"Food."

"Come."

The door opened and a middle-aged man entered, limping heavily on his left leg and carrying a tray. Two jugs swung on hooks on his belt. He paused long enough to close the door tightly behind him. Then he crossed to the table, managing his limp with the ease of practice.

Irvaine didn't even glance his way. Instead he proceeded to open the log. He scanned the surface of the table and groaned. "Where did the letter go?"

"I moved it, my lord."

"What?" Irvaine straightened and dropped the book to the table.

"Here." Jarvin slid the heavy tray onto the table, causing an avalanche of parchment. I lunged to catch the ink well before it followed the sheets to the floor. He lobbed something at Irvaine, who caught it deftly.

I set the ink well far from the table edge and knelt on the stone floor to gather the scattered pages. Many of the sheets were filled with ranks of numbers in flared handwriting with figuring in the margins in a tight clear hand. Two men, one recorded and the other did the sums. Out of habit I scanned down to the totals at the bottom. My stomach sank as I realized their meaning.

"Only two months?" I whispered.

"Pardon?" Jarvin asked, pausing in transferring items from the tray to the table.

"Nothing." I swept the pages into a stack. According to the figures, we had only two months of provisions. My head reeled. With no harvest left to gather, no money, and nothing to trade, I could see no way we would survive until spring, let alone the first harvests. The game of the forest wouldn't support us all.

"Yes." Irvaine's voice directly behind me startled my heart into my throat. "We only have two months before the villagers all starve together, but I have a plan." Kneeling down, he picked up the last three sheets of parchment just beyond my reach. "I see you are familiar with keeping accounts and figuring."

"My father taught me since Orwin showed no interest in such menial work. Someone needed to see we weren't cheated."

"That sounds like Orwin." His smirk lacked humor.

I offered him my stack, but he pressed his pages into my hand. Surprise brought my eyes up to look at him truly for the first time since waking in my parents'— no, his bed. His eyes, still dark and unreadable in the firelight, seemed to see into my soul without giving any insight in return.

"Keep them, look over the accounts, and tell me if anything seems off." Rising, he turned toward Jarvin. "Now where is that letter?"

"Under your sword on the chair, my lord." Jarvis plunked down two heavy mugs and pulled the larger jug from its hook on his belt. "What do you wish to drink, my lady?" After pouring a generous measure of liquid into the larger mug, he paused and waited for my answer.

"I will have what he has." I could use a bit of wine after this day. Besides there was much left to come.

"Water then, my lady." He filled the second mug from the same jug. I watched in confusion. A warrior drinking water and not wine on his wedding night?

"I require your signature on the dower agreement." Irvaine approached suddenly

"On what?" I gained my feet faster than my head wished. The world tilted a bit and the black haze threatened my vision again.

"Steady." He crossed to me in two strides and enfolded me in warmth. "I thought you understood. You are of age. Your agreement is required for me to claim the dowry."

I shook my head in protest. "I have no dowry." This was all moving too quickly.

"She needs food," Jarvin pointed out.

Not even bothering to assist me, Irvaine simply picked me up like I was a flour bag and deposited me in the only chair with surprising grace. "Eat," he ordered, shoving a hunk of bread into my limp fingers as he removed the parchment from my other hand. "We can talk after."

Ripping a piece of bread for himself, he claimed a mug and strode away to study the linen again. We all ate in silence. No one spoke until I had consumed two hunks of excellent bread and a trencher of stew. I finished my last bite and reached for my mug only to encounter my new husband's watchful gaze.

"Better?"

"Yes, thank you." The bread sat a bit heavy in my stomach, but my hands had steadied.

"Good. Now we can discuss details. I don't intend to press you tonight. You've endured enough as it stands. However, I do insist we share the same bed and act in all other ways as a married couple. I will be giving you demonstrations of affection in public and I expect them to be welcomed or at least accepted. Understood?"

I nodded.

"She isn't one of your troops, Tomas. You cannot command affection."

"I am hardly doing that," Irvaine protested.

"What am I to call you?" I asked before the argument could continue.

Those unsettling eyes regarded me again. Heat filled my middle and a pleasant tingle teased the back of my neck. He studied my features so long I began to wonder if he would answer me at all.

"Tomas. And you? What should I call you?" The way he said it made me wonder if he wanted an answer.

35

"My given name is adequate."

"Brielle." He said my name as though he were testing the taste of it on his tongue. "Yes, it suits you."

"I am happy you approve." I stifled a yawn as best I could. My head's weight, suddenly awkward, listed to the side.

"I think it is time we slept." Before I could protest, Irvaine lifted me into his arms again. My weary body sank against him, eagerly seeking sleep. He strode toward the bed. "Jarvin?"

"Yes, sir?"

"Clear the meal and see that Ryanir gets his evidence."

He laid me on the bed. Exhaustion pulled at my senses. I needed to stay alert. My body betrayed me, relaxing into the feather softness.

# Chapter Six

Chaos ruled the village center. Horses, men, gear, and a wagon commandeered from a local farmer crowded the open market square. From the back of the wagon, a small, round man handed out rations to the soldiers assigned to travel with us. The charred remains of the previous night's bond fire still smoked on the edge of the square. Hangover-shortened tempers flared as the men raised their voices to be heard over the sounds of the horses.

Village women moved among the men, new wives making sure their husbands had all their gear. Children tugged at their skirts and tangled in their feet. Half-grown boys dashed underfoot. They sought a bit of the excitement. I wanted to wish it all away. I didn't want to leave, but I must. I was no longer mistress of my own decisions. I belonged to another. Rubbing a soothing hand over my mount's neck, I turned my attention to my husband.

The eye of the storm centered on Irvaine. He sat astride his stallion, dark eyes observing all and ears tuned to the voices around him. When one of the soldiers walked by complaining about his rations,

Irvaine intervened.

"You there." He motioned the soldier over and indicated he wanted to see his provisions for the trip. After studying the bread, cheese, dried meat, and skin of ale, he sent the man on his way. "Brevand," Irvaine gestured to his quartermaster. "I want to see the ration plan for the next month."

Brevand's chin rose. Defiance glinted in his gaze for a moment before he obeyed.

The furrows in Irvaine's forehead deepened as he scanned the parchment. "This isn't enough."

"It is all we can spare."

"The supply wagons will arrive in a matter of days."

My gaze followed Antano as he moved through the ranks calling out names from a list of his own. When each man answered, he directed them to form ranks. However, my ears were still tuned to Irvaine and Brevand's conversation.

"I am taking over half the company, Brevand. The wagons should provide enough to keep the remaining company for a few weeks at least. Surely there is enough for full rations for the villagers and our escort while we are gone. There is no profit making anyone starve."

"More troops will arrive with the wagons. More mouths to feed."

"Bringing more food."

"I ran the figures thrice. We used up a week's rations of wine last night." Brevand glared up at me as though it were of my doing. The fact he had to look up to find my face diffused his power. Still, something about the intensity unsettled my calm.

"King's orders. I had no choice." Irvaine handed back

the lists. "We will have to make do with less. Have our escort give back half the supplies. I need to speak with Antano."

Half the men now formed ranks. I counted seventy-five mounted warriors standing at attention. They presented a fearsome sight with the early morning sun glinting off their armor.

"Reclaim half of the rations!" Brevand called to the nearest unarmed man. Most of the crowd stopped moving. The soldiers glanced at each other, but didn't break ranks or speak. Instead, as one, they looked to Irvaine.

Anger flickered over his features. He glared at Brevand, who ignored him.

"We will hunt to supplement our meals." Although Irvaine spoke loudly, not a trace of anger crept into his voice. "Once the rations are gathered we leave." He pulled his stallion closer to my gelding.

"Is Brevand always so testy?" I asked.

"On occasion he can become peevish." He squinted at the rising sun. "He announced the change in plans brazenly to annoy me, nothing more."

"Why would he wish to irritate you?" Despite his control thus far, I didn't trust a man of the sword to keep his temper.

"His second accounting of supplies came a quarter short of his first. Unless someone moved a significant amount of grain and vegetables from the barns during the night, Brevand botched his figures severely. He did not appreciate me taking him to task over it."

"Why do you keep him as your quartermaster if he is so lax with his duties?"

"He isn't normally so careless." He studied my face.

"Antano mentioned the nature of your relationship with Quaren's new wife. My ties to Brevand are similar. His father took me under his wing, overlooked my illegitimate birth, and gave me a chance to prove my worth. Brev and I shared tutors, sword masters, everything. We are brothers in all but blood."

It sounded like a relationship strong enough to bear a bit of incompetence. Brother or not, Brevand held too much hate behind his eyes for my peace of mind.

"Ready, my lord." Antano approached. His sat on his solid chestnut mare as though molded to the beast's back. He acknowledged me with a slight dip of his head.

"Then let us move out." Irvaine heeled his stallion and led the way west. Antano and I flanked him a pace behind while the crier bellowed orders to the waiting men. The villagers who had not gathered in the square stuck their heads out windows or paused in their work as we passed their houses.

Loren hurried out the door of one of the last cottages we came past. Behind the house, Quaren worked at preparing the kitchen garden for spring. He came around the front of the house to stand at her side. She wiped her hands on a floury apron before waving farewell. I waved back.

A crowd of villagers and the remaining soldiers followed us to the village edge. As I looked back one last time at the village of my birth, I spotted a face that didn't belong.

Tyront? One of my cousin's henchmen from childhood, Tyront and I squabbled enough times for me to lose count. He used his mouth more than his brain. I recognized his broken nose.

A horn blast from our crier brought my attention forward again. Something was wrong. I felt it in my gut. Tyront belonged with my cousin. Orwin should have been far from here, enjoying his ill-gotten freedom. Why would one of his cronies be among the villagers?

As we tramped the last bit of village road, we came in sight of the healer's cottage. A middle-aged man worked on a broken wagon wheel in the front yard while a younger man bent over a churn. Taltana straightened from clearing her garden to watch us pass. I waved, but she didn't acknowledge my gesture.

By the time we reached the forest edge beyond the last field, we were flanked by four additional men. A young squire charged ahead and disappeared among the shadows between the trees.

Irvaine came alongside. "He carries word of our impending arrival."

I jumped. My mount shied with a whinny of protest. I tightened my hold on the reins until he resumed his leisurely pace.

"I am sorry. I didn't intend to startle you."

"My mind was on something else."

"What?"

I glanced his way, encountering his interested gaze. Turning to watch the trail ahead, I debated telling him. I could be worrying about nothing. However, if something came of it, I would regret not mentioning it.

"I saw a face in the crowd as we left the village. He could be harmless, but ..."

Irvaine tensed. "Orwin?"

"No."

"Then whom?"

"Tyront, one of Orwin's childhood companions."

"How close are they?"

"Inseparable. He rode out with the rest to defend King Trentham."

Irvaine grunted. "Have you seen him since?"

"No."

"Could you describe him?"

"Shorter than I by a hand's span, his brown hair is thick and straight. His nose has been visibly broken twice and he has only one eyebrow."

"I appreciate you telling me about him. Giving up information about friends can be difficult."

I laughed. "Tyront and I have never been friends, my lord. More like enemies who tolerated each other's existence. I broke his nose, both times."

"And the eyebrow?"

"Loren."

This time he laughed. "I shall have to warn Quaren not to wrong his new wife; a spitfire lurks beneath her serene surface."

I watched the play of his laughter cross his face with fascination. He appeared almost boyish in his mirth. His whole face eased away from its usual hard lines.

"Tyront deserved it."

"I am sure he did." He grew sober again. "Any associate of Orwin most likely deserved worse."

"You speak as a man who has had dealings with my cousin."

"Orwin lives to torment anyone he can. Of late he wishes me to incur our new king's disfavor."

"Why? No, disregard that question. Orwin needs no motive."

"No." Irvaine's expression grew serious. "Never

assume an enemy simply hates. He always has a reason to hate. Illogical or not, he has motivation. Seek out the reason behind the hate. Understand your enemy. Only then can you truly defeat his hold over you."

"Why does Orwin hate you?"

He weighed the question carefully. "As he fell from favor, I rose. He attempted to win King Mendal's ear and I stood in his way. I believe he despises my role, not me, but I am not certain. Why does he hate you?"

"I was born. If I had not lived, my father would have accepted him into our household sooner. Growing up, I refused to submit to his schemes, partake in his cruel games, and stop undermining his plots."

"Did you break Orwin's nose too?"

"No, but I did hit him once. He rammed me into a fence post, lamed my favorite horse, and then refused to put my horse out of her misery. I asked him. He laughed in my face." I could still hear my mare's agony, the whinnied screams ripping at my heart. Her leg, contorted beyond repair, thrashed across the bloodied grass.

"What did you do?"

I had forgotten Irvaine was there.

"I slapped him, took his knife, and did the deed myself."

"How old were you?"

"Twelve."

The forest deepened around us. Trees, some as thick around as my horse's girth, arched twisted branches over the path. Their barren hands darkened the way despite their lack of leaves. The weak autumn sun cast their lacy shadows over the trail.

"I have a question." Irvaine guided his horse so close

43

that our knees almost brushed. "Who used to call you Red?"

Grief crawled from nowhere and clawed my chest. I forced the words past my constricted throat. "My father." The memory of his vigor for life warmed my middle as the agony of him being gone ached in counterpoint.

"I am sorry." He sounded genuinely regretful. "How long has he been gone?"

"Three years."

"The pain is still fresh then."

I wrestled the storm back behind my defenses. "What about your father?" The question slipped past my lips before I remembered his illegitimate origins. He probably didn't know who his father was.

"My father is well and healthy. I have seven half-brothers and a half-sister. They don't know it, of course. No one knows of our connection." He turned and pinned me with his gaze. "I won't call you Red again."

Then he heeled his stallion forward, signaling simultaneously for the crier to approach. After a few moments of conversation, the crier fell back. I suspected one of his men would be heading back to the village to investigate Tyront before the noon meal.

I retreated into my own thoughts, remembering a happier time when my parents lived, the holdings prospered, and Orwin was nothing more than a distant annoyance I dealt with once a year for a week.

# Chapter Seven

Evening fell quickly. As the shadows lengthened and my limbs protested their long time in the saddle, my anxiety rose. The men carried nothing that looked like a tent. Kyrenton lay another two days away. I would be sharing Irvaine's bedroll tonight.

Despite his profession of restraint the night before, I doubted any man would continue that way. To do anything less than share a bed would demean his manhood before his men and expose me to scorn. Still the thought of lying within his arms all night knotted my stomach. Fear and anticipation twisted me with equal pull.

My fingers sought my eating knife at my waist. Would I have the strength to use it? Should I use it? I had promised him. To hold him off would be a denial of that vow. I pulled my hand from the worn hilt with determination. I honored my vows. Duty bound me. I must submit. Kurios' law and my own conscience demanded it. I groaned.

Irvaine rode with Antano. He listened to the older man, the tilt of his head betraying his interest. Not that he had anything to hide among his friends.

Loud voices brought my attention back to Irvaine

and Antano. Irvaine threw his head back and laughed without shame. Shoving playfully at Antano's shoulder, Irvaine grinned broadly.

The crier called for a halt. Men broke formation in all directions. I guided my mount to a nearby tree and climbed down next to its trunk.

Pain shot through my thighs. Muscles protested first at the movement and then the lack. Blood rushing through my limbs brought a third kind of sensation, prickling agony. My knees wobbled and threatened to give out. A deep ache spread across my already sore back. I closed my eyes and concentrated on remaining upright. *Kurios, please give me strength.*

"Need help?"

I didn't need to look over my shoulder to know it was Irvaine. I gripped the saddle, straightening my back despite its piercing protest. The horse shifted and I wavered.

His arm encircled my waist and pulled me back against him.

"I can stand on my own." I attempted to push his arm away, but encountered a solid band of muscle.

"Not likely. When was the last time you rode for more than an hour? You were hurting when we stopped for the noon meal. I suspect your knees quiver like jelly now."

I refused to admit my weakness. "At least let me try." His solid warmth began to penetrate my cold body. The refreshing nip of the morning air had long ago lowered into a biting wind. Part of me yearned to just lean back and let him carry me. I ached in places I'd never hurt before. "If you hold my elbow, I am certain I could walk."

After grunting his disbelief, he slowly released me so I stood alone. Only the vise grip of his hand on my elbow connected us. "Take it slow."

I took a tentative step. My limbs obeyed my command with screaming protest. Knees feeling like noodles, by some miracle my balance held.

"Where are we headed?" I scanned the campsite more closely. Men moved with purpose around us. Some built fires and others worked on small frames of wood. I blinked. It looked like they were erecting little tents.

"Over to the left. Jarvin is setting up our tent and Antano will see to the food."

"It is good to be a noble."

"A title has its purposes, yes. Don't let your expectations get too high. We will eat the same food as the rest of them."

My stomach rumbled. "Most anything would sound good right now." Noon seemed so distant.

"Bread, cheese, herbed broth, and mulled wine, lean fare for now, but by tomorrow morn, we will have meat. Our trackers find game even in the leanest times."

"I will be content with whatever we have."

He settled me on a fur-lined cloak someone spread on the ground. He left, striding over toward the nearest fire. After adjusting my legs into the least painful position, I looked around. I counted twenty tent structures, each barely high enough off the ground for a grown man to crawl into on hands and knees. One structure would contain two men lying full length with squeezing. After the closest tent appeared completed, a series of men approached it, tossing saddlebags between

47

the flaps.

"What are the tents for usually?" I asked Irvaine when he returned.

He spread our feast before me, scarred wooden bowls of steaming liquid, metal tankards smelling strongly of wine and herbs, hard rolls speckled with bits of green and brown, and two hunks of cheese. I reached eagerly for a bowl.

"Careful, the pot was bubbling when I filled them."

I breathed in the steam, savoring the scent as it warmed my face. I tested it with a finger and found it too hot.

When I looked up to ask him again about the tents, I found him watching me. His dark eyes invited me to lose myself in their depths. I resisted, moving my gaze lower. The choice proved just as dangerous. His strong mouth, scruffy cheeks, and firm chin reminded me of the sensation of his kiss. It had only taken one. Quick, unexpected, and fiery enough to make me wonder what another would taste like. I shook the thought away.

"So, are any of the others going to be sleeping in a tent?" I reached for a roll, examining the strange flecks. They were baked through the bread, not just sprinkled on top.

"It is only parsley, garlic, and pepper."

I shot a glare at him. "Are you going to answer my question or is it some state secret?"

He chuckled deep in his chest. "Not many of the men will sleep in the tents. They prefer the open unless it is raining, snowing, or blowing. Then we erect a tent for every two men."

"We will be sleeping in a tent?"

"Yes. I figured you wouldn't like the whole world to

48

know we are not acting as other married couples do."

My cheeks flamed with heat. I bit into half my roll to hide my embarrassment. A wondrous medley of tastes blossomed on my tongue.

He laughed again. "Never tasted anything like it, right?"

"It is so delicious. And fresh."

"It still tastes good stale, trust me. It is Antano's recipe from his travels. He picked up some spices when he spent time in Ratharia and brought back samples and recipes. When I first encountered it, I ordered all our waybread be spiced. It makes even the stalest of rations a bit more palatable."

He bit into his own roll with vigor. "The broth is his creation as well."

"I will make a point to thank him." I tested my broth again before drinking. The fragrant liquid soothed my throat and warmed my middle. "What do you plan to do once we reach Kyrenton?"

"Assess the situation." He swallowed a gulp of wine and explained. "You might as well know, your cousin is a terrible land manager."

"I lived with his neglect, remember."

"True, but even then, I was stunned at the level of his laziness. The ground is fertile. The clerk's records indicate you had more than adequate rain for four years, yet for some reason the village barely scraped by each winter. I haven't figured out why."

"Orwin." Anger pressed against my breastbone. "For the past four years, he and his men came immediately after harvest, removed a quarter of our provisions, and left. We ate some of the seed stored for the spring planting to make it through the winter months. When he took our men with him last spring, I knew the end would come this year. We didn't have the seed or the hands to plant enough crops to make it through the winter."

He stilled. "What did you plan to do?"

I stared down into my bowl. The broth resembled the gruel we consumed the last month before the first harvests last year. Without the supplement of bread and cheese, it provided inadequate fuel for the hours of labor necessary for bringing in the harvest. A familiar pinch of hunger came with the memory. "The only thing I could do. I taught the boys and able women to hunt. We went out daily. Your arrival came just as we were assigning hunting rounds for the week."

"That explains the freshly smoked meat. You would have driven off the game for miles around by midwinter."

I lifted my chin. "We would have lived one more year."

After a few moments of silence, he asked, "Who taught you to hunt?"

Unexpected emotion choked me. "My father."

"Because Orwin wasn't interested?"

"No." Memories of my father's hands guiding my ten-year-old fingers into position on the bow almost brought tears to my eyes, but I willed them not to fall. "'Every woman should know how to fight and hunt. Men are not invincible.'"

"Was this before or after Orwin entered your household?"

I choked on my cheese. Coughing violently, I gasped for breath. He whacked my back abruptly, jolting the bit free. It flew into the grass beyond the cloak.

"Are you alright?" He rubbed my back infusing warmth and tension with each stroke.

I nodded, blinking away tears, not all brought on from choking. "It was after Orwin came to live with us."

"Your father was a wise man."

"He had no other choice. Orwin became his heir by law. My mother could bear no more children. She was young enough, but after seven stillbirths neither of my parents possessed the heart to try again."

"I don't blame your father, Brielle. He did the best he could by you. You are a strong, wise woman, a worthy wife for any man."

"I fight, figure numbers, and hunt. I don't dance or flirt. I am not a noble's wife."

"I am not a noble." The tone in his voice sent shivers along my spine. I didn't dare glance his way.

"My lord?" Jarvin's voice came to my rescue.

"Yes?"

"There is a disagreement over the watch rotation and the men request your guidance."

"I will join you in the tent, Brielle." Irvaine rose and strode off.

"Let me clear the meal, my lady, and then I will guide you to your tent."

"Just point me in the right direction."

He indicated the tent and cleared away the bowls and tankards. I waited until he had turned away before beginning the painful process of gaining my feet. My thighs protested every movement. With great relief, I crawled into the tent and sank to the fur covered ground. Pulling the thick blanket over me, I curled up and fell instantly asleep.

51

I dreamed of mother and father before Orwin entered our lives. Their love caressed me. I woke to dawn lightening the canvas inches from my face. Warmth from the fire radiated at my back. *Loren must have stoked the fire early.* My blanket lay heavily against my ribs. Shoving it aside, my hand encountered resistance, not of wool but the weight of a man's arm.

Instant full awareness dawned.

Irvaine shifted. His hand moved to my hip. My fully clothed hip, I reminded myself. The small fact slowed the panic in my throat.

*Calm. He won't hurt you. This is his right.*

His breath stirred the hair on my neck. It tickled. The regularity and slowness of his respiration reassured me he still slept. I cautiously rolled over, easing his hand off me as I turned. Finally free, I contemplated how to extract myself from the tent without waking him.

"First call!"

The crier's voice startled me so that I brushed Irvaine's chest.

His hand caught mine before I could pull it away. Powerful fingers gripped my wrist, the pressure painful for only a second before his eyes focused on my face. Recognition filtered through their depths. The intensity of his grasp eased.

"Good morning, wife."

"Good morn." I silently praised the Kurios my voice didn't break.

"Sleep well?" His thumb stroked my inner wrist. An answering tremor shook my fingers.

"Aye."

He smiled. After placing a lingering kiss in the palm

of my hand, he released it abruptly. "We have a full day ahead." He rolled away to reach for his gear.

"When will we reach Kyrenton? How soon?"

"Tomorrow. Shortly after noon should we travel at the same pace as yesterday. Then we shall discover the true state of our holdings."

The closest town, our destination, was the previous Earl of Irvaine's seat of power. Before the war and endless death, he and his sons ruled as quiet neighbors. They remained on their side of the border stones and we on ours. Only tradesmen passed between us and a dwindling number of those as Orwin's abuse impoverished us. Our village, Wisenvale, struggled to keep mind and body from starving. We offered little to entice a man selling goods and services.

Feudal law kept us from seeking help from them. We were of Lord Wisten's domain thus none of Lord Irvaine's concern. Until now.

"Come, wife, we have miles to cover before our noon meal. Best get to your feet and seek out your breakfast before they put out the fires."

I scrambled awkwardly out of the tent behind him. All the aches from the night before had stiffened to dull pain during the night. A bitter blast of air whipped the loose hair of my ruined braid into my face and pressed frozen hands against my back. The wind howled in my ears, momentarily blinding me and stealing my breath.

"Here, I forgot to give this to you yesterday." A heavy cloak settled over my shoulders, blocking out the assailing wind. He fastened the ornate clasp beneath my chin. "It will help you stay warm until I can warm you again tonight." He spoke slightly louder than necessary.

My cheeks burned despite the chill.

Then before I could protest, he smoothed my hair back from my face, effectively trapping my head between his large hands. "Don't freeze up, Bri." His obsidian eyes scanned my face, fire in their depths. "Remember our agreement about showing affection." Then he kissed me.

The firm pressure of his mouth on mine brought unexpected heat in contrast to the frigid air around us. Then he tilted his head and deepened the kiss. Liquid fire filled me from head to toe. My knees threatened to give way and leave me hanging from his hands by my head. I grasped the front of his tunic out of pure self-preservation.

He drew away.

Leaning his forehead against mine with his eyes closed, he simply breathed for a moment. My blood pulsed. My mind frantically went everywhere and nowhere at once.

"You are enough to drive a man mad," he whispered harshly. Then suddenly I stood alone. He strode away in the opposite direction as the campfires.

# Chapter Eight

"'Tis bitter cold, my lady. You should be wearing gloves." Antano's voice startled me out of a half-slumber. My horse snorted at my abrupt movement.

"I have none." My eyes watered. The wind bit at my fingers, the parts I could still feel. I glanced to check they still held the reins. I feared I would never be able to straighten my fingers again. Should I try, they might not clasp the leather leads again.

Antano grunted. "Fine way to treat his wife."

"Pardon?" I glanced around, encountering the setting sun in all of its blinding golden glory through a break of trees. It took me a few moments of careful blinking before I could see again. By then Antano moved away.

I shifted slightly in the saddle in an attempt to ease the sharp ache in my lower back. I gasped at a flare of pain and dared not move again. Thankfully, my mount docilely plodded on, following the soldiers' horses before it.

My respect for the men around me grew as the morning waned. Until their appearance in our village, travel filled most of their days. Hour upon hour with a horse between their knees, backs aching, armor chaffing, they rode in all weather. Only a bit over a day on the trail and I ached for home. I craved the luxury of sitting on something that didn't move.

The pair of men to my left drew closer as the cleared area around the trail narrowed.

"I got a spirited woman," the darker of the two commented.

His companion whistled appreciatively.

"No, not that kind of spirited. She threatened me with a hot poker should I attempt to touch her, ever."

"At least she shows life." The blond lowered his voice. "Mine doesn't even look me in the face. She mumbles her words and stutters horribly. If I so much as sneeze, she turns white and scurries off. After the third time, I tracked her down behind the forge. Apparently her father was the village blacksmith before–"

His voice whipped away on the wind. The darker one nodded in understanding. They stared before their horses, lost in memories of shared horror.

The dark one shook off his thoughts. "We have our work set before for us."

"No more than Irvaine."

"Did you see the anger in her eyes? Now that is a woman of spirit."

"I don't envy him the task of taming that fire."

I focused back on my stinging hands as they glanced my way.

They fell into discussing the advantages of the long bow over the crossbow. I lost interest.

"I have been accused of neglect." Irvaine's deep voice interrupted my thoughts as his knee brushed mine. "Show me your hands, Brielle."

"They will survive. I have suffered worse." True, but

not for such a length of time.

"Brielle!" The harsh tone of his exclamation brought up my pride.

"It isn't that bad."

His hard glare clearly indicated his disbelief. He drew off his left glove with his teeth while reaching for my reins. After pulling my horse to a standstill, he tugged off his other glove.

"Give them here."

I attempted to release the leads. My fingers uncurled, but fire spread from the tips to the knuckles. Tears escaped my eyes, but I bit my lip to hold back the cry that clogged my throat.

"Why didn't you say something?" Claiming my right hand, he enclosed it in his warm palms. "Give me the other one too."

I obeyed.

"Have I been so boorish that you feared asking?"

"No."

"Then why?" His dark gaze raked my face, seeking—no, demanding—an answer. "I told you I would care for you." He swore. "Didn't you have gloves yesterday?"

"No. My last pair became useless last fall. I hadn't replaced them yet."

The day before had been mild. I saw no need to point out the inadequacies of my gear. Today, however, had passed differently. Since morning the temperature dropped steadily as the wind grew stronger. Our breath grew misty in the air and the stream we crossed at midday boasted ice along its edges.

"Brielle, I can't read your thoughts. I need you to speak up when you need something. Your hands are freezing. Much longer and you would risk losing fingers." He rubbed them. Burning pain flooded through my hands.

I cried out. I couldn't stop the sound. I bit down hard on my lip to prevent another protest.

"I will stop rubbing them." He pressed them between his palms instead. Bringing our clasped fingers to his mouth, he breathed on them. "From now on you are using my gloves."

"But what about your hands? You need protection as well."

"I will seek out a spare pair."

In his silence, I realized three men had stopped with us. Lingering at a discreet distance, they conversed among themselves. Two of them were my previous companions. I caught the blond one's gaze. He dipped his head.

"What must I do to earn your trust, Brielle?" The hurt in the tone of Irvaine's voice irritated my conscience. His strong fingers worked warmth into my frozen ones.

"You were preoccupied."

A lame excuse, but it remained the truth. He spent the travel time with many of his men, listening and conferring. Interrupting him then required drawing attention; something I loathed doing, especially in the company of so many strangers. Besides, the business at hand seemed so much more important than a bit of discomfort on my part.

I lifted my eyes to find him studying my face.

"You are more important to me than my men, Brielle. I carry a duty to them, but I did not swear my hands to their comfort and my shoulders to their provision as I did to you. You cannot convince me that this is comfortable." He squeezed my hand gently. Exquisite heat emanated from his rough skin, easing the cold's hold on my fingers.

Shame burned my cheeks. I lowered my face to hide the moisture in my eyes.

"Now don't hide. I didn't mean to make you cry." He brushed away an old tear with the back of his fingers. The cracked skin of his knuckles caught at my cheek. "I am just disappointed you didn't come to me. Next time, ask. Promise me you will ask."

I nodded without meeting his dark eyes.

"I mean it, Brielle."

Before I could nod again, a male voice tore the winter stillness. "Traveler riding fast."

Irvaine dropped my hands and reached for his sword. The three men arrayed themselves, weapons drawn, between us and the road.

"Stay behind me." Irvaine maneuvered his mount between me and the approaching rider. "If this goes poorly, ride for the rest of the company."

My knife was strapped to my thigh. Despite the temptation to reach for it, I didn't. My hands wouldn't be able to grip it effectively. Instead, I wound the reins around my hands and watched the road.

The pounding of hooves on frozen ground filled the unnatural silence. Fear thundered in my ears as each breath came fast and shallow.

"He wears our colors."

"It is Kuylan."

The horse came to a clumsy halt several feet beyond our gathering. The soldier listed dangerously in his saddle as he turned to greet us. Face white, he pressed his free hand to his side as though he had a cramp.

"We have been betrayed, my lord." He coughed, wincing in pain with each spasm. "Three hundred soldiers arrived at dawn."

"Wisenvale?" Irvaine asked.

Kuylan swallowed with great care. Sweat beaded on his brow. Crimson oozed between his fingers.

I laid a hand on Irvaine's arm. "He is bleeding, my lord."

"Fetch Muirayven," Irvaine ordered. The blond man set off at a gallop. "Let us get him down."

Irvaine and the dark-haired soldier lifted the messenger from his horse while the third man held his horse. I managed to dismount, despite my aching thighs. I pulled a clean tunic from my saddlebag. They eased Kuylan to the grass beside the path. I pushed past Irvaine's shoulder as he backed away. My cold, clumsy fingers managed to unbuckle Kuylan's pierced leather breastplate on the first try. But they fumbled over the lacings of his padded jerkin.

"Here, let me." Irvaine pushed my hands aside so he could cut the lacings.

I peeled back the stiff, quilted cloth to reveal the wound. After wrapping my clean tunic around my right hand, I pulled the skin together with my left before applying pressure. His blood soaked the cloth with alarming swiftness.

"What did this?" I asked.

"Arrow, my lady."

"Come, Kuy, surely you were not the only man they could send." Irvaine knelt at my side, offering a small measure of shelter from the biting wind.

"Nay, my lord, I volunteered and rode off before they knew. There were many worse than I. Someone needed to catch you before you reached the gates of Kyrenton."

"Why?" My mouth spoke before I thought.

"When the invaders discovered you were not among our number, Lord Wisten hinted someone in Kyrenton would deal with you. He named no names and perhaps spoke more than he should have. The foreign baron seemed ill pleased with his loose tongue."

"Is that what you meant when you said we had been betrayed?"

"Nay. Brevand betrayed us. While we faced the main company in the fields before the village, he led the others into the village and gathered our women."

"Loren." My breath caught in my chest. Anger rose despite my inability to breathe.

Kuylan grunted. "Aye, Quaren's wife as well as the rest. They threatened action against them should we not withdraw." He coughed. "Not so hard, my lady."

I eased the pressure slightly. He laid his head back and closed his eyes. The pallor of his face worried me.

Nudging Irvaine's shoulder with mine to catch his attention, I nodded toward Kuylan. "Keep him talking."

He nodded. "Did we outnumber them?"

"Barely. We maintained the upper hand until Brevand marched out of the village. He held Quaren's wife before him with a knife against her throat and ordered we retreat." He coughed again. "My lady, not so hard." He lifted his hand to move mine away.

Irvaine intercepted the movement. "She is preventing you from bleeding out. Focus on your tale. I need to know every detail. How did Quaren take the threat to his wife?"

"Poorly, sir. We retreated though he gave no order and rode after you. He didn't wish to leave her with the traitor. Those cowards sped us on our way with a volley of arrows. I gained this dragging at Quaren's reins." He waved weakly toward my hands.

The thunder of approaching horses brought all of our attention to the trail toward Kyrenton. Irvaine stood to greet them. Five men burst upon us.

The foremost rider, a thin young man with wild yellow hair, dismounted before his steed stopped. His feet hit the ground at a run as he clutched a satchel to his side. "Where is he?"

"Here." Irvaine pointed to me and strode on to meet Antano and the other men who accompanied the healer.

The healer wasted no time assessing the situation. "Arrow to the gut," he muttered as he lifted away my hands and ruined tunic. "You are a fool, Kuy. That ride might have been your last." He glanced at me. "My lady, if I might?"

I pivoted back onto my heels to give him room. Surveying my blood stained hands in dismay, I tried to ignore the panic constricting my chest. Loren, Taltana, and the rest of my village were at the mercy of a lawless robber baron, my cousin, and Brevand, not to mention their army. I closed my eyes against the images, but they pressed all the harder.

A hand closed on my shoulder. "Come, let me clean you up." Irvaine helped me to my feet.

Sudden exhaustion pulled at my bones. The wild emotional ride of the past few days pressed against my temples. I wanted to do nothing more than find a warm quiet place and sleep. Perhaps if I slept long enough, the world would right itself again.

I closed my eyes as Irvaine doused my hands in water

and rubbed them briskly with a rough cotton cloth. When he finished, the skin remained red, but no longer from blood.

"We will go and rescue them." I searched his face. I needed hope.

"I won't abandon them." He met my gaze. "But we won't return yet. We are closely matched in number. The baron will send for reinforcements from across the river. We must do likewise."

"From Kyrenton?"

"And possibly beyond. It depends upon what we find."

*But Loren....* I forced myself to breathe. Images of her resisting Orwin's caress turned my stomach. I remembered well the leer in his gaze last time he passed through the village. *Kurios, please protect her. Protect them all.*

A gentle touch to my cheek brought my thoughts back to the present. Irvaine lifted my chin so I gazed up into his dark eyes. I couldn't tell if they were black or brown. Even in the bright light of the midday sun, I couldn't be certain of their color, only of the sorrow in them.

"If I had the slightest chance of victory, I would leave now to challenge Orwin and his allies. I will do everything in my power to reclaim Wisenvale and its women."

"Before...." I couldn't put it into words. To do so would make it reality.

"I can't promise that." Pain etched creases about his eyes.

Though my heart screamed at the injustice of it all, I held my tongue.

63

"Come, we need to move forward."

I followed him numbly to our horses.

Hours later after nightfall, we made camp. No one settled down for sleep, though. A watchful restlessness roiled beneath the calm activities of the men. Irvaine moved among the soldiers, speaking quietly with the healer, consulting with Antano, and arguing with Jarvin.

Dinner was comprised of roasted rabbit and waybread. Jarvin's seasoning did a great deal to make the stringy meat and stale loaf palatable. I ate alone. Irvaine didn't join me until I was picking the last of the meat from the bones.

"Morale is poor." He set his wooden bowl full of meat and waybread on the cloak before lowering himself down next to me. "I don't know whether to be encouraged that the men took to their wives so quickly or discouraged that I can't improve the situation more than I have."

"We reach Kyrenton tomorrow," I reminded him.

"Aye. Should Kurios will it, we will find provision enough to turn and reclaim what was taken." He moved his food about without eating. "Until then, we wait." He dropped his bowl and rubbed his forehead. "I am not hungry. I think I shall bed down." He rose to his feet and offered me a hand up. "We both need our rest."

We settled in under the tent. For the first time I was thankful for his presence at my back. His body heat kept the growing cold from overwhelming me.

The defeated appeared at dawn as we gathered up

our gear for the day's travel. They arrived in a cloud of dust white with sleepy sunlight. The healer plowed into the fray seeking wounded.

The leader rode straight to Irvaine. Not bothering to dismount, he inclined his head. "My lord, Quaren has deserted."

"What?"

"After sending Kuylan ahead, he ordered us to find you. He took only a water skin and three day's rations. Last we saw him, he was moving south."

"Wise man," Irvaine muttered. "He intends to intercept the supply caravan. Someone needed to do it. I wouldn't have chosen Quaren to accomplish it, but he most likely needs a task to occupy his mind."

"My lord?"

"Nothing of consequence, Ryon. You have been granted a temporary promotion until Quaren returns. Go see to your men."

Ryon bit down on a protest and saluted with two fingers to his left brow. He then prodded his horse back to his company.

Irvaine resumed his interrupted task, lifting me onto my horse.

"You don't consider Quaren's action desertion, do you?"

"Going up." He hoisted me up into the saddle.

I settled myself. He handed me the reins.

Once mounted himself, he guided his horse to my side.

"No, Brielle, I don't consider Quaren a deserter. He saw to it that his men were safe. Once accomplishing his duty, he turned his energy to his more important

65

duty of protecting his daughter and our resources. We don't want our rations and loved ones riding straight into the enemy's waiting arms. I hope he reaches them in time." The distant focus of his gaze planted a revelation in my mind.

"You have someone in that caravan too." My tone accused more than I intended. His back tightened and his shoulders came up. He didn't meet my gaze.

The horn signaling for us to move on tore through the tension. In the following cacophony of shouts and horses' hooves, snorts, and whinnies, I almost didn't hear his response.

"My son."

My world shifted.

"I will answer your questions." He studied my face. Wariness tightened his shoulders as though he expected me to be angry.

I was, but not a large measure. Despite my disquiet, my brain proceeded to process everything. It made sense for him to not tell me of his son at first. Still so much about him remained a mystery to be discovered. I still felt awkward about the idea of being his wife. Motherhood carried a whole new set of responsibilities. The most pressing thought, though, was for the woman who gave him the child. "What was she like?"

"My wife?" His focus shifted inward. "She was vibrant."

I noted the lack of emotion in his voice. My relief at the boy's legitimate origins quickly transitioned into shame. I was a fool to think Irvaine immoral enough to produce otherwise. If there was one thing I had learned about my husband, he valued the marriage bed.

"How old is the boy?"

"Five summers. She succumbed to fever shortly after giving him life." His features aged at the memory.

That made the boy a year older than Loren's step-daughter. Just placing his age in relation to her made him more tangible. Tempted to visualize him, I resisted. Regardless of how I viewed his father, I wanted to see him for himself. Others always judged me by my connections. I was the former lord's daughter, Orwin's cousin, the remnant of a great family left among the ashes of once vibrant traditions and power. Now I was Lord Irvaine's wife...a mother. Simply the word made my heart swell in anticipation and fear. *Let me guide with wisdom as my mother before me.*

"What is his name?"

"I named him Darnay, after my maternal grandfather." He didn't meet my gaze, watching the men as they moved about us. "We must send word to the king about the invasion." He urged his mount forward to speak with Ryon.

I kept myself apart. Heart heavy with fears and questions, I traveled in silence.

# Chapter Nine

Kyrenton spread beyond its own walls. I eyed the rise of stone above with a twinge of envy. Cottages speckled the landscape about the town, but few looked large enough to house more than a small family. Hills spread with fallow and harvested fields spread out from the town to the forest's edge.

As we approached the walls, the gates lumbered opened. Irvaine lifted his left hand. Two of his men rode forward and unfurled a banner between them, a golden hart leaping on a field of green. The cloth snapped and flapped between their fisted hands, but the emblem remained clear.

A single man strode out from the gate. The green and golden cloth of his tunic and the badge on his chest of the same leaping hart declared his allegiance. His thin, gray hair whipped in the wind. He approached on foot, scanning our front lines for a sign of his new master. His gaze fell on me, the only female, and then flicked between Irvaine and Antano flanking me. Irvaine wore the same plain armor as the day he arrived at Wisenvale. With no way to identify his new master, the man weighed his options.

"My Lord Irvaine?" He bowed tentatively in my direction.

I glanced at Irvaine.

"Who wishes to know?" Antano asked.

"My lord." The man bowed deeply to Antano. "I am Horacian, steward of Kyrenton."

Irvaine kneed his horse forward a step. "I am Tomas Dyrease, Earl of Irvaine."

Horacian paled at his mistake.

"This is my wife, Brielle Solarius of Wisenvale."

Horacian bowed hesitatingly to me. I could see his mind working as he processed my identity. Whatever he thought of my origin, family, or village, he kept it from his features.

"Welcome to Kyrenton, my lord. If you would follow me, we will make you welcome." Shoulders squared and head held high, he led us through the gate and into the town.

I clamped my jaw closed, but I couldn't control the rising anxiety in my gut. A cobbled street wound between picturesque houses complete with freshly whitewashed faces and straight rows of shingles on their roofs. Each structure stood in sharp contrast to Wisenvale's thatched cottages of worn stone. Only the interiors of our buildings were whitewashed and not often.

When we rounded the last turn and passed into the shadow of the vargar's keep, I wanted to cry in despair. With thick stone walls and heavy wooden gates, the fortress offered protection and security to its new master. Add in the visibly well-maintained town and Irvaine would be a fool to return to Wisenvale after the crisis passed.

Where he lived, I must live.

The portcullis bared its teeth at me as we passed beneath it. *Kurios, I want my home. My people.*

A party of servants waited on the staircase into the keep and my heart sank further. Even the lowliest of the servants wore clothing richer than any I had ever owned. *Simplicity, Kurios, I long for simplicity where we are all equals sharing in the burdens of survival.*

"My lord, may I make known to you my daughter, Rolendis Briaren. She is the widow of Kolbent Briaren, late Earl of Irvaine."

Irvaine tensed at the man's name.

A young woman stepped forward to take her father's extended hand. She curtsied deeply, dropping her head so a cascade of brunette curls fell about her face. The longest loops grazed the neckline of her low cut gown and the bosom beneath. She lifted doe-shaped eyes of golden brown and my heart froze in fear. Offset in a gown of rich blue, her skin glowed with health. The flutter of her thick eyelashes as she smiled winningly up at my husband made my palm itch to smack her.

Startled at the strength of my reaction, I turned my face away before she could look my way. I needed to give her a chance. Appearances could be deceiving.

"You must be mistaken." Irvaine's brows drew together. "She is too young for Kolbent. Surely you mean she is the widow of one of his sons."

"Nay, my lord," she answered. "I was Kolbent's wife. Welcome to my...your new home."

Irvaine studied her features. She smiled at him, returning his examination from beneath lowered lashes.

My stomach turned over. My inadequacies grew ugly in the splendor of those perfect features.

71

The steward laid a hand on his daughter's arm. "If you would come this way, my lord, Sirs Jorndar, Rathenridge, and Landry have gathered to swear allegiance."

Irvaine caught my arm the moment I gained my feet. My gratitude for his steadying touch dissolved into concern when I met his gaze.

"Do not allow them to separate us."

"What do you suspect, my lord?"

He held my cheek for a moment. His rough leather gloves hurt my cold skin. Emotion flared behind his mask. Fear?

As I searched his face, questions flooded my mind. Had he seen something I missed? Did he suspect something? Surely Rolendis' flirtation hadn't disturbed him as it had me.

By the time he released my head, Rolendis had disappeared. Horacian ushered us forward with a sweep of his arm. "My lord?"

Irvaine straightened his shoulders, smoothed his cloak and tugged his metal breastplate into place. His emotional armor settled about him with the movements. When he turned to face his steward, all traces of the man disappeared beneath a neutral facade. He offered me his arm.

"Do you wish for some of us to remain behind?" Antano asked.

"Bring five."

I rested my hand on Irvaine's forearm, fingers light. He caught them and pulled my arm through his. "Don't believe everything you hear," he whispered.

Liveried guards opened the doors to the keep. We followed Horacian up the stairs and through two sets of

72

doors into the great hall beyond.

The hall rose to twice the height and thrice the length of our lord's hall in Wisenvale. Three heavy iron torch rings hung from the ceiling, suspended there by thick ropes. Unlit, they menaced over us like dark guardians, their clawed undersides splayed for the kill.

"Tomas the mongrel!" A male voice, grating in its false jocularity, pulled my attention to the dais on the far end of the hall.

A broad-chested man with beefy arms straining his velvet sleeves sneered at Irvaine from the head table. If hatred could murder, my husband would have breathed his last then and there. Two men sat with the speaker at the head table. They rose almost as one to greet us. The scrape of wood on stone echoed with our footfalls in the empty room.

Irvaine's steps never faltered. Invisible to our audience, though, the muscles of his arm coiled as he tightened his fisted fingers. He stopped abruptly at the base of the stairs to the dais and returned the man's glare.

"I see you have grown older but not wiser, Jorndar."

Jorndar spat in the rushes. His brief mirthless grin transformed into a scowl as he focused on Irvaine's unchanged expression. "Your lofty height reveals your soiled linen in all its glory."

"Be still, Jorndar." A bear-sized man with wild hair black enough to absorb light laid a massive hand on the first man's shoulder. "He is your liege lord now. Best not begin on the wrong footing."

Jorndar laughed without humor. "What will he do? Go whining to King Mendal that his knights are misbehaving."

"One of his knights." The third man stepped around the end of the table. His hair flared red in the sunlight streaming from the high windows lining the walls. "I do not share your opinion. I doubt Landry does."

Irvaine's arm relaxed slightly at the redhead's voice. Not even a flicker of recognition leaked into his expression, though.

"What, Rathenridge, afraid to tarnish your family name?" Jorndar turned on the red head. "Or is it too late? That rough wench on Tomas' arm looks like she hasn't fallen far from your family tree."

Antano stepped brazenly between Irvaine and the knights. He cleared his throat and began reading from the sheet of parchment in his hands. "In recognition of exceptional loyalty and sacrifice in the service of the crown of Rhynan, Tomas Nirren Dyrease is awarded the title, properties, and fealty rights of Kolbent Briaren, late Earl of Irvaine. By His Royal Majesty Alfren Riond Mendal's decree all knights who refuse to honor the assumption of his choice to the title shall be deemed treasonous and subject to the full extent of the laws of the land."

Jorndar snorted. "Swear fealty to a baseborn, never." He proceeded to describe Irvaine's mother in terms that burned my ears. My stomach turned at the images.

One moment Irvaine's arm looped mine. The next, Jorndar stopped speaking mid word. Irvaine's sword tip rested against his throat. They locked gazes along the length of metal.

"Leave." The clipped tone of the single word echoed in the sudden silence.

Jorndar's fingers sought the hilt of his sword.

The bear man, Landry, caught Jorndar's elbow. "I

74

might not have spoken the loyalty oath, but that will not slow my sword arm should you draw that blade."

"Nor mine." Rathenridge hooked a thumb on the belt next to his own weapon. "You are no longer welcome here."

Jorndar released his grip on his blade. Otherwise, he made no sign of acquiescence.

Irvaine lowered his arm, but not his glare.

The silence pressed in as everyone waited for one of the men to move. The changing colors of Jorndar's face starkly contrasted the cold stone of Irvaine's.

"This isn't over, Dyrease." Jorndar spat toward Irvaine's boot. "You are fools to follow him." He shoved Irvaine's shoulder as he strode past.

We all listened for the heavy thud of the outer door.

"Antano?" Irvaine's even tones broke the awkwardness.

"My lord?"

"See that he and his cohort are escorted from my land."

Acknowledging the order with a salute, Antano handed the parchment to the steward and quick-stepped after Jorndar.

"I take it you are acquainted with Jorndar," Landry commented. He studied Irvaine's face with mild amusement.

"A childhood playmate," Irvaine replied, his eyes still on the distant door.

Landry roared with laughter. "I doubt anyone called him playmate then. Tormentor, bully, or oppressor would be more believable."

"He was all of those and more." Rathenridge laid a hand on Irvaine's shoulder. "Why does he worry you so, Tomas? He is only a man, and one of little status or consequence now that you have a title."

"How many men does he command?"

"One hundred fifty, hardly an army. Why do you ask?"

Irvaine sheathed his sword. "Because we are at war. Any inconvenience, no matter how small could be enough to decide the result." He fell into the closest seat.

"War?" Rathenridge met Landry's gaze.

Horacian's gasp pulled my attention to him. "We just accomplished peace."

Irvaine explained without lifting his head. "A baron from the west took Wisenvale two days ago."

"What were you doing there?" Rathenridge asked.

Irvaine shot him a weary frown. "Claiming my bride and establishing a resident army to prevent just such an action."

"Wife?" Rathenridge's attention transferred to me. "My condolences, Lady Irvaine. King's orders?"

His strange mixture of humor and seriousness upset my equilibrium. "So he told me." My voice sounded strange in the huge room.

"I would believe him, my lady. Marriage is one topic Tomas takes very seriously."

I peered into his face struggling to ascertain what he meant. So far, my husband took most things with a large measure of gravity.

"If King Mendal ordered you to establish an army presence in Wisenvale, why are you here?" Landry asked.

"Supplies." Irvaine sighed.

"My cousin has been draining the village dry for

years," I explained. I didn't like the way Landry had looked at Irvaine. It was as though he thought the worst of him. I reminded myself that Landry didn't know him as I did.

"My wife speaks the truth." Irvaine briefly outlined the situation. "I left behind half the men to defend Wisenvale and prepare the village for the winter. Which reminds me...Horacian?"

The steward stepped to my side and offered a bow.

"I need the account books, harvest records, and the latest census logs."

Horacian's face drained of color. I was tempted to lay a hand on his arm to steady him.

"My lord, I did not expect you to ask for them so soon.... I mean, we didn't–"

Irvaine's gaze narrowed on his steward. "In whatever state they may be, I need the records."

The steward took a shaky breath, wavering slightly with the effort. For an apparently healthy man, he appeared suddenly ill. "I cannot, my lord."

The air thickened. Irvaine stood and stepped down off the dais. After crossing the short distance separating him and us, he asked, "Why?"

The single word, uttered calmly, wrought a singular effect. Horacian sank to his knees. "Sir Jorndar took them. He claimed them as his right as the late Lord Irvaine's heir apparent. He showed me King Trentham's decree. It had his seal. He said Mendal would honor it because of the child. I believed him or I would have never–"

"Aiden?" Irvaine turned to Rathenridge who was already trotting toward the back of the room.

"Enroute." He called over his shoulder as he forced

the heavy outer door open and disappeared into the sunlight beyond.

Irvaine looked down at the man before him and asked the question burning my tongue. "What child?"

"Rolendis is with child."

My hands grew cold. Another innocent life had been thrown into the mess. I wanted to cry.

"Is the child her husband's?"

Horacian's head snapped up, fire flaring in his eyes. "Are you accusing my daughter of unfaithfulness, my lord?"

"No, I am asking the question that every man, woman, and child will ask for the rest of the child's life unless we can prove beyond doubt that the child is legitimate. Have no fear. I mean her and the babe no harm. I simply must know. The answer determines how we proceed."

Wary trust flickered in the steward's features. He swallowed carefully. "Four months past, Lord...my late master sent for Rolendis. She traveled to join him at the battlefront and returned a month later."

Relief lightened the lines around Irvaine's mouth. "Good. Then it is his." He met my gaze briefly before moving toward the dais and the waiting Landry.

"My lord?" Horacian scrambled to his feet. "What will happen to my daughter?"

Irvaine looked at me, a question in his eyes. I answered it.

"We will make sure she and the child are cared for and protected."

Horacian relaxed into relief. "Thank you, my lady."

# Chapter Ten

Horacian led Irvaine, Lord Landry, and me to a barren room. A massive table hunkered beneath the single window. Stacks of books, parchment, ink, and candle nubs crowded the surface as though the master only stepped away for a second. A chair, the only one in the room, stood against the wall opposite the door.

"My lady, let me." Horacian dusted off the chair. After bowing me into it, he bowed to Irvaine. "The late Lord Irvaine used this room for conducting business, but we haven't used it recently. Do you wish for refreshment, my lord?"

"Yes." He raised his brows to Landry.

"Not for me, my lord."

"Repast for two then."

Horacian bowed once again before ¹ Landry moved to the corner opr leaned back against the stone.

Irvaine paced the length ⸗ and then the breadth, fo⸗ faced Landry. "How proceed?"

"I say we wait for the crossed his arms as though to

79

his stance.

"We can't," I said.

Irvaine leaned back against the heavy table. Arms folded across his chest and shoulders hunched, he studied the floor as though it would reveal the solution to the quandary before us.

Landry's gaze flicked between us. "Why?"

"One of the captives is my best friend." I met Landry's piercing gaze with more strength than I felt. "Lord Wisten has taken a special interest in her before. I fear for her life and…" A sudden lump pressed against the back of my throat. I choked on the words.

Irvaine straightened. "The king commissioned me to marry, settle in Wisenvale, and see that the eastern border was defended. Those women and children in the invader's grasp are the wives and families of my men. I intend to move against this invader the instant it is feasible." He crossed to confront Landry. "Can I count on your men?"

"All four hundred of my men are yours. Only seventy-five of them attend me now, but I can summon the rest in a matter of days."

"How many days?"

"Three at the most."

Irvaine frowned. "Did you notice how many henridge brought with him?"

ndry grunted. "I counted eighty plus his wife and ompanions. I would expect him to send her home is departure. She prefers her own hearth. Also, three young children behind."

laughed. "Rathenridge has children?"

three daughters."

t be a sight to see." Irvaine shook away the

80

thought. "How many does he command?"

"About five hundred last I knew."

"With my three hundred, we will have twelve hundred. What about Avenhege? He should be on the road here as we speak, answering the call to pay honor to my arrival, right?"

"Only if he answered Jorndar's summons. Avenhege's holdings can only be reached in three days if one rides hard."

Irvaine's head snapped up. "Jorndar summoned you?"

"Four days ago a messenger reached my gates demanding I appear at Kyrenton Vargar to do my duty to my liege lord. I learned after I arrived that Jorndar sent messengers to each of us. He was attempting to claim right of inheritance based on Rolendis' widow's rights."

"She has no rights. Mendal removed the title from the line and heirs of Kolbent Briaren in light of his loyalties."

"Jorndar didn't count on Rathenridge knowing you personally or your arrival so soon after your marriage. I believe he hoped you would linger in your new wife's arms longer before venturing to claim more."

Irvaine looked over at me. His expression lightened slightly. "As diverting as my wife is, she expects to be fed. Lord Wisten handed over a starving village as a show of loyalty."

"A shabby gesture."

Irvaine pushed away from the table to pace. "It indicated the true value of his allegiance. He led the invaders across the border."

Landry swore. "Sorry, my lady, please pardon my rough tongue." He bowed to Irvaine. "When do we march?"

"Summon your men and ask them to meet us west of Wisenvale. We will not wait for them."

"I shall do so immediately." He strode for the door, pausing just before it to bow to Irvaine. "My lord." Then to my utter astonishment, he bowed low to me. "My lady, I hope we free your people soon."

"Thank you, Sir Landry."

He left. Silence settled over the pair of us. My thoughts and prayers strayed to Loren.

"Are you feeling okay?" I jumped at the sound of his voice, so loud in the small room.

Irvaine stood before me, a tower of familiarity in my drastically changing world. How had he become so important to me so quickly?

"I was just trying to figure out how you were going to manage three hundred men when you only have half that with you."

"You forgot the caravan."

I blinked at him in confusion.

"The rest of my men are coming with the caravan of supply wagons." He rubbed his face distractedly.

"I am not ready for this."

His soft chuckle brought my chin up. "Those very words circle my thoughts twice an hour, sometimes more."

"How do you quiet them?"

"I ignore them. I was put in this position for a purpose. I plan on doing the best I can under the circumstances." He offered me a hand. "Come, this is no place to eat. Let us wait for Aiden and Antano in the hall."

We met our meal in the passage. The servant women

who carried it led us back to the great hall. They settled us at one end of the head table. Mutton, pork, and a rack of lamb roasted to perfection lay on a bed of cabbage. Beet leaves, carrots, and a selection of dried apples accompanied a fresh loaf of bread still warm to the touch. My mouth watered at the smell.

We set to work on the bounty. But before I managed more than a handful of bites, the outer doors burst open.

Five men tromped in the room. Rathenridge led them up the center of the room. I spotted Antano near the back. Two hefty men pulled a resisting Jorndar to the foot of the dais.

"Kneel!" Rathenridge commanded.

Jorndar spat at him.

Antano kicked the prisoner's legs out from under him. "Show proper respect to your superior, fool."

Yelling curses, Jorndar attempted to gain his footing again, but the two men restraining his arms kept him on his knees. After a few moments of struggling, the guards simply pinned him to the floor, face down.

"Sir Jorndar, you are accused of sedition against the crown. How do you plead?"

"How do you think, idiot? Not guilty. You shame the house of Loineir and Irvaine. Your mother should have smothered you at birth. I demand my right to plead my case before the king. I refuse to accept any ruling you hand down, pretender. You hold no law over me."

A twitch in the muscle below Irvaine's left eye was the only indication he heard Jorndar's rant. He stood frozen in his effort to contain the anger burning behind his dark eyes. His left hand clenched his eating knife in a death grip.

Dissatisfied with the reaction of his target, Jorndar changed his tactic. Straining his head around so that he could just see me out of the corner of his eye, he grinned crookedly. "How does it feel to be bedded by the son of a demon and a witch? Didn't know his mother was a witch did you? Watch him. He will remove your soul and feed it to his master. He is well versed in the ways of--"

Irvaine lunged forward.

I caught his arm, throwing my weight against his momentum. "No." My intervention spun him around so I encountered the full blast of the fury behind his mask. He trembled with the effort, but he didn't turn back toward his tormentor.

Rathenridge unceremoniously laid his foot over Jorndar's face. The man's ranting dissolved into a wordless yowl.

I reached up to caress my husband's face, anything to distract him from the liar on the floor. "Whatever you want to do to him, you will regret it later." Thankfully it helped. He focused on my features.

He closed his eyes, breathed in, and held it. He rested his forehead against mine. His hands encircled my head, thumbs resting on my cheekbones and fingers buried in my hair, destroying the remains of my braid.

Antano spoke. "I request permission to throw him into the dungeon, my lord."

Without opening his eyes, Irvaine replied. "See that you treat him humanely."

"My lord?" Antano's protest filled every tone of his query.

"Give the king no reason to doubt my character, Antano."

"Yes, my lord."

Irvaine waited only until Jorndar's protests faded to a distant murmur. "Thank you." His dark eyes, still glinting with rage, seemed to soften as they met mine, warming to a different emotion.

"Not a bother," Rathenridge replied, throwing himself into the nearest chair and helping himself to some of the mutton. "Just make sure that the next villain you send me out after has a cleaner mouth. I have never heard so much talk about refuse since I last ordered my men to dig privies."

Irvaine smirked. He gently released my head and retreated before turning to face his friend. "I appreciate your longsuffering service, Aiden."

"I haven't even sworn allegiance to you and you are demanding I track down a pompous fool and his foul-mouthed minions."

"Lord Jorndar is not a fool. He is not wise, but never mistake him for a fool." Irvaine pulled out my chair for me as we resumed our places at the table. "How many of his men did you detain?"

"Seven. Three discontented striplings, a middle-aged weakling, and three ancients too old for the saddle. I wonder at his choices for traveling companions."

Irvaine pushed away his unfinished meal. "I am more concerned about where his prime warriors are at the moment. If they aren't with him, he has them otherwise occupied."

"Terrorizing the countryside and collecting rents?"

"More likely serving a new liege lord." Irvaine rubbed his temples and closed his eyes. "Did you find the records?"

"We confiscated a crateful of ledgers, rosters, and lists. If they aren't the missing records, I would be very interested in what they are." Rathenridge rose abruptly to his feet and plucked an apple from the middle of the platter. "If you don't need me further, my lord, I wish to seek out my wife. I need sweet conversation to distract my thoughts from the mire of Jorndar's ravings."

"First, send word for all your able-bodied men to meet us at Wisenvale. We will be riding out tomorrow."

"They will be there."

"Where did they put the records?"

"Delivered to your new study, my lord." Rathenridge offered a jaunty bow. "Ready and waiting for your perusal."

"Then, be off. Say hi to Moriah." Irvaine dismissed him with a wave of his hand.

I waited to speak until the door blocked my view of Rathenridge's loping gait. "How long have you known him?"

"Aiden?" Irvaine glanced my way, but didn't truly focus on my face before returning to his thoughts. "Twenty years."

"Since childhood?"

"Hmm…" He nodded absentmindedly.

"You think Lord Jorndar is connected with the invasion, don't you?"

He nodded again. Leaning his forehead on his fisted hands, he closed his eyes. "I think the root of this invasion runs deeper than we suspect. I am going to have to get word to Dentin and the king."

"Who is Dentin?"

"He is the commander of the royal guards and general of the garrison. He also keeps tabs on everyone's whereabouts and loyalties."

"He sounds like the man to know."

"He is. Giving him the task of security of the realm was the best move Mendal made."

I studied my husband with new eyes. "You are an intimate of the new king."

He eyed me over his clasped hands. "You just figured that out? I thought the world knew."

"Remember where you found me? We didn't even know the war was over, much less we were subjects of a new king."

The left corner of his mouth lifted slightly and a glimmer of amusement flashed in his eyes before worry clouded them again. "Someday I will fill you in on all the details." He leaned back with a groan. "Right now a crate worth of documents awaits us. I hope your recordkeeping skills are as good as you claim. It is going to be a really long afternoon."

I pushed back my chair. "Then we should get to work."

Irvaine signaled a servant. After requesting a second chair be brought to the study, he offered me his arm.

# Chapter Eleven

A bathtub! I stared in wonder at the luxury. Not a quick wipe down with tepid water from a bowl before the fire. The metal tub came to my hips and steamed even in the radiating warmth from the hearth. My aching joints and muscles called out in a chorus of joyful anticipation.

"Where is my tunic, Jarvin?" Irvaine shoved the bedroom door closed and promptly began undoing his armor.

My face burned as I hurriedly looked away.

"I laid out the best for you to choose from."

"They brought the bath. Good."

"The pitcher and basin you requested came too, my lord. Lady Rolendis sent gowns and soap for Lady Irvaine. She also included some of her husband's personal effects so that you might use whatever you wish."

"Come and choose what you wish to wear, Brielle." Irvaine's order was punctuated by the clunk of his chainmail hitting the floor. I turned in time to see him pull his tunic over his head with his back to me. Scars crisscrossed his shoulders, faded with age, but deep enough to never heal completely. A gash across the back of his left ribs spanned the length of my forearm. A third, more recent, scar cut an angry crescent around his right shoulder blade. Despite the obviously whole muscles moving beneath the marred skin, I shivered to think of the events that had scarred him.

A mixture of fear, nerves, and pity churned in my belly. The indelible markers branded forever across his back spoke of a man who had fought his way through life. I tried to reconcile them with what I had witnessed of his character over the last few days.

The rough, calloused hands that rubbed warmth into my fingers were also hands that weilded a blade with skill and deadly finesse. They were the hands of a father. I tried to envision them cradling a child.

"Brielle?"

I blinked.

Jarvin had left. We were alone. Irvaine gazed at me quizzically. I must have missed his question.

"Pardon? I didn't hear you."

"You should choose a gown and begin washing. We have to be down in the hall in an hour or so."

"Yes." I nodded, but made no move toward the silks cascading over the far side of the bed. Instead my mind wandered back to the tidbits of his past I discovered today. I could see him as a slender child with no father to protect him from the world and with a mother to defend. I wondered how he had dealt with Jorndar then.

"Brielle?"

"Hmm?" I pulled my thoughts together and focused with effort. Exhaustion fought back.

"Are you going to make it through the meal?"

I jumped at the brushing of his fingertips under my

chin. When did he move? He now stood over me. The musk of his sweat filled my nose. It was laced with a scent I could not name.

"Brielle, go to bed." He eased my face up so our eyes met. "I can face them alone if you need the rest. I know these past few days have been difficult for you. They..." He hesitated. Raw emotion tightened his features. "None of us have had an easy time of it. I understand if you prefer to rest here instead of facing a host of strange faces."

After an afternoon of studying documents, consulting with the cook, and supervising the organizing and counting of supplies with Horacian's help, I did long for bed. However, when I looked into Irvaine's face, I hesitated.

Dark circles and dirt ringed his eyes. New creases marred the bridge between his eyebrows. The brackets around his mouth deepened with worry as he scanned my face. Somewhere behind those searching eyes he still faced the world alone.

"No. I can make it. I want to help."

"I have Rathenridge."

"You need me to show them your domestic side. I represent hope for a peaceful future."

He tilted his head. "Who told you that?"

I smiled up at him, hoping to cover up the weary grief that swelled behind my words. "My mother epitomized nobility and duty."

"She was a wise woman."

I nodded and turned away. He let me go. I walked toward the tub, untying my surcoat. A few tugs at the laces and the neck opened enough for my head to slip through. My belt followed, the worn leather slipping

91

easily through the buckle loop once I untied the excess.

The scrape of wood on wood halted my undressing. Irvaine dragged a screen across the floor. As tall as me and six arm lengths wide, its elaboratedly painted panels blocked the tub from the rest of the room.

He stepped back, studying the screen. "I will use the water in the bowl; you take the tub. You need it more."

"Are you saying I stink?"

He smiled. It wasn't a laugh, but it lightened the lines of his face slightly.

"No more than I do." He walked toward the basin of water resting on a heavy table along the wall.

Taking that as a sign to tend to my own washing, I slipped behind the screen and began undressing in earnest.

The bath lived up to all my expectations. I didn't emerge from the water until my fingers resembled the walnuts my father once purchased from a foreign traveler. My muscles no longer ached and the tension in my back eased. My return to comfort brought a fresh burst of energy. Familiar hunger grew urgent now that pain no longer claimed my foremost attention.

A midnight blue gown of soft wool hung over the screen. It slid on with ease but fit loosely through the chest and hips. An inch of the silver-trimmed hem lay on the floor. I needed a sash so I could loop it up a bit. Thankfully the fall of the material and the ties at the back allowed for adjustment from bust to hip. Though, I needed help to lace it properly. Gathering the excess skirt in one hand and my damp fall of curls in the other, I stepped from behind the screen.

"My lord, could you–"

My tongue stumbled to a halt at the sight of Irvaine.

The hue of his dark blue tunic almost matched my gown. The soft wool fit the width of his shoulders like it had been tailored for them. The only decoration, a simple silver pattern accenting the neckline, drew the eye to his face. He looked less exhausted clean-shaven as long as I didn't look into his eyes. Weary and worn, they betrayed his anxiety about the evening ahead. However, the worry melted as he focused on me.

My cheeks flamed beneath his approval.

"The color suits you." His gaze traveled my length before he stepped closer.

"It still needs some adjustments." I offered him my back. "Could you tighten the laces?

He set to work fitting the waist of the gown. "Is there anything you need to know about tonight?"

"My mother taught me how to behave at public events."

"Even an Earl's table?"

"A duke and three earls courted her before she married my father."

He stopped tugging. "Your parents were a love match then?" Lifting my hair from my hand, he spread it about my shoulders. The still damp curls were tightening. I didn't have time to comb them out. I hoped he didn't mind my mane in all of its wild glory.

He turned me so we faced each other. Bracketing my face with his hands, he tilted it back so he could see the whole at once. Dark eyes studied my features. A shiver flicked my spine. I shuddered as his attention fell upon my mouth.

"I am not sure how to shorten the skirt." By sheer will I kept my voice steady.

"Recent fashion calls for overlong skirts." His eyes

continued to examine my face. "Remember our agreement about affection in public."

"Yes." I willed my gaze to meet his steadily. Warmth filled my belly despite its hunger pains. "Should I initiate occasionally?"

The heat in his half smile made my heart rate accelerate. He opened his mouth to speak, but a tap at the door interrupted him.

"Come." He stepped back, suddenly aloof again.

Jarvin opened the door and leaned inside. "They are awaiting your arrival, my lord."

"We are coming." He strode over to the table where the abandoned bowl and pitcher lay. Picking up the dagger lying next to them, he placed it in its sheath before turning back to me. For the first time, I realized his sword hung from his belt.

"My lady?" He offered his left arm to me.

I slipped my hand around his elbow for a secure hold. He pressed his arm against his side, gently squeezing my arm against his ribs.

The great hall had transformed in our hour above stairs. Trestle tables between backless benches marched the length leaving a great space in the center of the room. The table on the dais remained in the same position, but now a tablecloth covered it and evergreens decorated it. The lit candles did nothing to soften the clawed holders high above us, but they illumined the faces that turned our way.

"Tomas Nirren Dyrease, Earl of Irvaine and Wisenvale." The crier's voice overwhelmed even the rustle of cloth as everyone turned to stare. "His lady wife, Brielle of the house of Solarius and daughter of Evenetta of Marienedale."

All eyes moved from Irvaine to me. I struggled to keep the veil of indifference over my features. My mother, before her marriage, gained renown for her beauty and grace. I took after my father. Strong features, solid build, and red hair. As proud as I was that Evenetta was my mother, I wanted to flinch at the comparison because I fell so short.

Irvaine led me down through the midst of the crowded hall. Try as I might, I couldn't lift my eyes to meet the gazes of those we passed. They were not my people.

Then reality struck me so hard I stumbled. Irvaine paused long enough for me to catch my step. We continued our procession. I raised my head and looked into the faces of the people as we passed.

These were Irvaine's people. They lay claim on him. He carried a duty to provide for them and protect them. Already, he worked to do just that. I, as his wife, also bore obligations to them. They were my responsibility now too. I tried to memorize features and read personalities in the faces turned our way.

Finally we reached the dais. Lord Rathenridge and a woman awaited us there. Lord Rathenridge greeted Irvaine with a bow and then turned to the woman behind him. "This is my wife, Moriah."

Almost matching her husband in height, Moriah's angular features softened into a warm smile as she dipped a curtsey.

Irvaine bowed to Moriah before drawing me forward. "My wife, Brielle."

"Welcome to Kyrenton, Lady Irvaine. I hope you enjoy your time among us." Moriah's soft voice soothed the ear. Still, her words rubbed at the sore place I was trying to ignore. Irvaine was leaving me behind. My smile wobbled. I could not find the voice to answer.

"About time you two got here. Newlyweds will tend to run late, as we know well." Rathenridge winked at his wife. "But I was preparing to send out a search party."

Irvaine gestured to the empty table. "I don't see the food, Aiden. We are hardly holding you up."

"You are their lord and master now. They delayed until you appeared. Even now I see the page leaving for the kitchens to alert them all is ready."

Irvaine ushered me to the seat at his right hand. To my surprise, Rathenridge and his wife took seats to my right, leaving the left side of the table empty.

A lad in green livery poured the wine.

"May we join you?" The query brought everyone's attention to the left. Sir Landry loomed, a dark shadow in all black attire. With his beard and wild hair, his resemblance to a great bear grew hard to ignore. Rolendis Briaren appeared tiny as she lingered a few steps behind him.

"Of course."

Irvaine and Rathenridge stood almost in unison.

Landry bowed. "I found the lady lingering in the passage to the kitchens. She tells me she fears she is not welcome here."

Keeping her attention on the wooden platform beneath her feet, Rolendis said, "I am not certain of my place now that..." She looked up into Irvaine's eyes.

Sitting, I could not judge the message she emoted at Irvaine. I could only read the infinitesimal tightening of his shoulders. He stepped back and rested a hand on the back of my chair.

"You are welcome at our table. As my wife promised your father, we will be certain you and your child are safe."

"Thank you, my lord." She dipped a deep curtsey, chest thrust outward and artful curls grazing the front of her low cut dress.

My sympathy for her precarious position warred with my anger at her obvious maneuvers toward my husband.

Irvaine retook his place, leaning over to claim my hand as he spoke to Rathenridge across me. Preoccupied with the strength of my reaction to Rolendis, I didn't pay any attention to their words.

Landry assisted Rolendis into the seat to Irvaine's left before taking the place on her other side. I observed the tightening of the fabric across her middle as she moved. The obvious swell of her abdomen supported her father's claim of pregnancy.

Anxiety pressed against my breastbone. Duty demanded that I be with child soon as well. The people of my village would expect it. My duty to the residents of Kyrenton demanded it. Even Irvaine planned for it. Children were part of our vows. What if I took after my mother in the very area I didn't wish to? My stomach twisted. I needed to tell Irvaine about the possibility. *Kurios, please have mercy. Make me fruitful when the time comes.*

*When the time comes...it might be tonight.* I closed my eyes. Flutters of anxiety gathered beneath my ribs.

"Are you well, my lady?" Rathenridge's voice cut through my worries. I glanced at Irvaine to discover Rolendis had captured his attention, though not his hand. His fingers still covered mine on the table between us. I turned back to my other dinner companion.

"Yes, Sir Rathenridge, I am well."

His blue eyes examined my face with more care than I wished at that moment. "If you fear the widow will steal your husband, you need not."

"I know Irvaine will not stray."

"Oh?" He raised his eyebrows in obviously mock surprise. "Then what has your lovely brow all in wrinkles?"

I struggled with an answer. I couldn't tell him the truth, but I didn't want to lie either. Lowering my gaze, I attempted to hide.

"Something you would rather not share. I understand. My wife tells me frequently that I am too curious for my own good. Wouldn't you agree, Tomas?"

Irvaine leaned over so that his chin hovered above my shoulder. "Your tongue ought to be leashed, Aiden. What stories have you been telling my wife?"

"What did Rolendis want?" I asked before I lost my nerve.

"Nothing of any weight. She wished to speak with me tonight."

"Alone?"

"That might have been her intent, but that is not mine. Rest assured if you aren't there someone else will be."

"That widow intends to snare you, Tomas." Rathenridge lowered his voice. "I don't know whether it was her or her father's doing, but her wedding to Kolbent happened abruptly and without any pomp. One week she was just the steward's daughter and the next she was Kolbent's wife. Even his sons thought something was amiss."

"Good to know."

Irvaine stroked the inside of my wrist with his thumb. Awareness radiated up my arm. I glanced at Irvaine's face, but his attention focused inward. He was apparently not aware of his hand's actions or its effect on my senses.

"I will be extra vigilant." He gazed into my eyes. Anyone watching us would think he was desperately in love with me. If only it were true.

"Don't worry," he whispered.

"When do you want the men assembled tomorrow?" Rathenridge asked. His facial expression lightened as though discussing war were less taxing than guarding against infidelity.

"Have them gather at dawn. We will march out as soon as we are properly assembled."

"Moriah and I will be there." Rathenridge smiled at me. "Moriah insists on seeing me off at the beginning of every campaign. What about you, Lady Irvaine? Are you going to rise early to wish your husband well as he rides into battle?"

I opened my mouth to protest that I would be riding by his side, but Irvaine spoke first.

"Of course she will."

The parade of food began. Pages bearing meat and vegetables doused in sauces passed before us. Irvaine saw to it the most succulent morsels found their way onto my trencher. However, I found my appetite fled with the thought of being left behind.

Irvaine was my anchor in this new world. If he left, I would have to face it all alone. Despite my knowledge of how to sit at table and the basic social graces, I knew nothing of running a household of this size. Horacian would certainly not need my input on crop rotations, hunting, sustaining a herd, slaughtering pigs, plowing a field, maintaining records or keeping a village from starving.

Another course paraded past. More food appeared before me. I swallowed a few bites of mutton and a hunk of bread. Even those threatened to reappear.

"Is something wrong or did your mother tell you that ladies only eat sparingly at the table?" Irvaine's voice edged my thoughts aside. He moved so close that his breath caressed my ear and the scents of soap and leather filled my nose.

"I have lost my appetite."

He frowned. "You were hungry before we came down. What disrupted your interest in food?" His dark eyes studied my face with more care than I wished. Still, my parents taught me that honesty was always best, especially between friends.

"I don't wish to stay behind. I belong by your side. I am useless to you here."

He seemed to weigh my words. "I disagree." He paused. "In part." He played with the curl lying against my cheek. "You do belong with me, usually, but when I am riding off to war, you aren't safe at my side. I need you here, safe and secure. I need someone to look out for my son when he arrives. Also, I need your eyes. I don't trust Horacian or his daughter. They will be more likely to try something while my back is turned."

"What could they try?"

"I don't know. If we watch and wait, they will reveal their true colors eventually."

I processed the new situation slowly. Irvaine and his

men would ride out tomorrow morning. After meeting the remainder of his men, they would confront the joint forces of Orwin, a nameless foreign baron, and possibly Jorndar's missing men. Meanwhile, I would have to adjust to my new role of faithful wife awaiting her husband's return.

"And your son. You aren't planning on him joining you either, are you?"

He shook his head. "When we encounter the caravan, I will be sending Darnay and Elise on to you."

"Elise?"

"Quaren's daughter."

He expected me to protect two children as well as navigate the maze of my new duties as lady of the vargar. Panic clutched at my throat. I lifted a hand to rub against the pressure growing in my chest.

He reached back to claim his goblet and offer it to a passing servant. As the boy filled it, my mind raced with possibilities. Once the goblet returned to his hand, he sipped, but didn't swallow. He set the cup on the table and turned back to me. As he eased in to study my features again, I met his clear-eyed scrutiny.

He smiled at my frown of concentration. "People want a lord who drinks. It is a sign of a man willing to relax."

He brushed my hair back from my shoulder, fingering the curls a moment before releasing them. "I will not leave you alone, Brielle. Jarvin will remain. Kuylan and at least seven others cannot join us due to their injuries. Twelve able-bodied men claim injury as well, under my orders, and they will obey your commands. Six of Rathenridge's men guard Jorndar. They will also be loyal to you. Landry appears

101

honorable but he might be under the influence of Rolendis' charm." He glanced down the table. I followed his gaze. Rolendis leaned over Landry's arm speaking earnestly, "His true allegiance will show soon enough."

Guilt edged my conscience. Were we judging Horacian and his daughter unfairly? "What if Rolendis and her father are innocent?"

He stroked my cheek, sending shivers down my spine. I closed my eyes. I didn't want him to see the yearnings his touch brought forth. I welcomed them and feared them. Until I understood the feelings better, I didn't want to confess them to him.

"If our suspicions are wrong, then there is no harm done." He kissed my temple. My cheeks burned. "Eat, love. You will need it. We have a full evening ahead and breakfast is a long way off."

# Chapter Twelve

After the fealty swearing ceremony, I wanted to sleep. The exhaustion of earlier pulled at my limbs, reminding me of the abuse of the past days. Yet, the troubadour continued to sing of a woman with flame-touched hair. The hero of the tale set off on a foolish quest to win her love by bringing her water from the fountain of youth. I held a small smile on my lips despite the vanity of the lady and the foolishness of her swain. Irvaine was wise enough to know that love cannot be bought with gifts.

"Your smile is slipping." Irvaine's hand closed over mine as it lay on the table. "Are you ready to retire?"

I nodded. "I am not accustomed to sleeping on the ground."

"No ground for you tonight, my love. Tonight there will be a well-stuffed mattress, soft bedding, and me to keep you warm."

I looked up in surprise to spot Rolendis walking behind him. She passed close enough to hear his words. Irvaine's free hand brushed beneath my chin, setting my skin on fire as it tilted my face. His thumb grazed the corner of my mouth

"I wanted to do this all evening."

His mouth caught mine gently, exploring and savoring. My senses whirled. Catching his forearm, I tried to anchor myself to reality. Instead, the movement of his lips and the delicate pressure of his fingertips against my cheek pulled me into a world of his creating. I fell beneath their spell.

Only when he withdrew a hand's breadth to study my face did reality gradually reassert itself.

"I should have tried that sooner." His dark eyes studied my face, lingering on my mouth before returning to gaze deep into my eyes. That was when I realized the murmur of conversations around us had died down. I glanced out at the hall. The troubadour finally finished his song. Most of the crowd's attention focused on us. I didn't dare look Rolendis' way.

With a scrape of wood against stone, Rathenridge rose to his feet and raised his goblet. "Hail Lord Irvaine and his lady, the beautiful Brielle of Wisenvale! May their marriage bring bounty and security!"

Irvaine smiled down at me. Over his shoulder, Rolendis avoided my gaze as she lowered her cup unsipped.

"Come, it is time we retired." Irvaine rose and offered me a hand.

Amid calls of encouragement from men tipsy with too much wine, we descended from the dais and walked once again through their midst. I took comfort in the upturned faces that looked upon Irvaine with hope.

A vargar without a master meant uncertainty for the inhabitants. They would wish him to stay as long as he brought security, full bellies, and warm shelter. But would their hope fade when he left so soon after his arrival? Most of the men and women pressed around us didn't know of the greater threat coming from the east. Suddenly their high expectations fell over my shoulders like a damp cloak, snuffing out the lingering embers of Irvaine's public affections.

I shivered as we stepped into the corridor. Irvaine led me toward our chamber at a swift pace. We reached the top of the stair, and our door waited only a dozen steps beyond.

"My lord?" Rolendis' voice echoed in the stairwell behind us. She paused in climbing the last turn of the steps. One hand on the wall for balance, one clutching her skirts to keep from tripping, she looked up at Irvaine with bright eyes and parted lips. The neck of her gown slipped over her shoulder, offering a hint at what was beneath the cloth. The torch light added a subtle glow to her bared skin. "You promised me an audience tonight."

Despite Irvaine's mildly distracted expression as he examined the mortar of the wall to her right, the arm beneath my hand tightened like a bow string.

"I did? What do you wish to say?" He turned partially away from her, maneuvering me between them.

"In private, my lord? It is a personal matter."

Irvaine covered my hand with his, pressing it in place. "There are only the three of us here. Surely my wife's presence cannot be objectionable no matter how personal the matter. Now please speak or hold your tongue until my return. I have things to do before I sleep."

Her surprise at his curt reply quickly melted into pretty tears. "I just wanted to ask for a special dispensation. My sleep has been restless of late. I have taken to walking the halls at night to try to wear myself out. The wise woman says I need to rest for the child's sake." She caressed her abdomen. "She gave me some herbs, but insisted they be taken before bed with mulled wine. My father denied my request for the additional wine. He directed me to you."

"If that is all, then tell him to allow it. One extra ration of wine should be adequate, unless you require more to forget your husband?"

She had the sense to blush and tug her dress back into place. Still, anger flared in her eyes. "How dare you mock my grief? My husband has been in his grave barely two months. Why shouldn't I lose sleep over how I shall survive without him? He was my future, our child's future. Now my son shall grow up without his father, without a title, or land." She sniffed and tossed her head, jabbing her sharp chin into the air in injured defiance. "Why do I even try explaining? No one understands. It isn't like you have ever lost a spouse."

Irvaine stiffened. "You have your additional wine. Good eve."

Then without waiting for a response, he propelled me down the hall and through our chamber door.

He closed it solidly behind us. Leaning back against the wood, he closed his eyes and pressed the heels of his hands against them. The glow from the fire and a single lantern near the door cast his features into stark relief.

My anger at Rolendis' obvious advances warred with my shock at Irvaine's comment about her husband.

He groaned. "I owe her an apology. I went too far." He pushed off from the door and launched himself into the center of the room. Casting off his belt and sword as he went, he paced toward the far wall.

"She was practically offering herself to you before me, your wife." The anger won. "I don't think you owe her anything."

He laid his weapon and belt on the table beneath the single window, now shuttered against the night and covered by heavy curtains. "Losing a spouse, even one who does not claim the usual emotional attachment, is not something to be mocked." He shoved his hands through his hair. "No matter what the circumstances, I should have been kinder."

Tension gathered between his shoulders.

As I watched him, I realized that five years since his first wife's death wasn't a long time. The three years since my father's death seemed an eternity of hardship and toil. When I lingered on the strength of my longing to see him again, his death felt like it happened only yesterday. Losing a spouse could hardly have been less traumatic, especially if she left a living reminder of their union, Darnay.

"Did you love her?"

"Love who?" He turned to search my face in confusion.

"Your wife."

"Elenawyn?" He considered the question with confusion. "Ours wasn't a matching of love. From her perspective, I served a purpose. I felt affection for her. We rubbed well together, but not closely."

"Then how did you end up married to her? Was it another royal decree?"

He shook his head as he sat on the edge of the bed to work at removing his boots. "Quaren asked me, she needed me, and I was the only one who could help at the time." He dropped the first boot onto the floor with a thud. "Do you mind if we don't discuss this now. I hoped for something very different tonight." The second boot came free and fell. He plucked them from the floor and crossed to set them beneath the table. Turning back to face me, he raised an eyebrow. "You are planning on sleeping, right?"

"Yes." My head ached with all the new information. I couldn't figure out how Quaren could have possibly figured into Irvaine's marriage with his first wife. The fact she needed him did make sense. Irvaine would assist a woman in need. "Was she Quaren's sister?"

"By marriage, not by birth."

My thoughts stuttered and my mind went blank.

A feather-light brush of a finger against my jaw startled me. Irvaine stood before me. His hand lifted my chin so his dark eyes could roam my face. Their unspoken query pulled at my gaze, capturing them in a web of fascination. "It is not a hard thing to explain. He was married to her sister."

"You and Quaren are brothers-in-law?"

"We were. Now rest your mind. Your thoughts are pulling at your brows and tightening your mouth. What is it that worries you so? It is that I was married before? Do you compare yourself to her?" He dropped his attention to my mouth. "Don't, Brielle. Elenawyn was like ice, cold and painful. Incapable of love, she treated every kindness with suspicion. You are not her."

His hand released my chin so that his thumb could

brush my bottom lip. "Warm, vibrant, and alive, you are capable of far more than affection. Give me a chance, Brielle. Keep your heart open. Give me a chance."

His mouth lingered a breath from mine. Not touching, barely breathing, he waited. My whole being cried out for him to bridge the small span between us, but he ignored my silent scream. A heartbeat passed... seven...twelve in quick succession. Finally I couldn't stand it anymore. I stepped forward, pushed up on my toes, and met his challenge.

The slight pressure of lips and his gentle response brought an unexpectedly intense reaction. Acute awareness of him flooded me. He radiated warmth and the heady scents of soap and pine. My fingers entangled in his tunic in an effort to balance against the onslaught of my senses. He followed my movement, mouth never leaving mine. Liquid heat sluiced through my veins, comforting and entreating. Slightly frightened by the strength of my desire for more, I stepped back.

His hands spanned my ribs and stopped me from moving away more than a few inches. "Why are you retreating?"

"I am afraid."

"What do you fear?"

"Doing something wrong."

"Do you trust me?"

Flashes of memory from our wedding night teased. He had asked me exactly that question then. It seemed much more distant than a few nights ago. So much had happened in such a short span of time.

"Yes."

"Then trust me to take care of you."

I did.

# Chapter Thirteen

Morning came too soon. I woke to Tomas' absence. When I ventured a hand out from beneath the covers to look for him, the bedding was cool to the touch. The soft shuffles of someone moving about in the predawn darkness brought my attention to the only light source in the room. The recently revived fire outlined Tomas easing his under-tunic over his head. Chainmail lay in a heap at his feet. His breastplate and other armor leaned up against the wall.

Memories of last night urged me from the warm cocoon of covers. Frigid air greeted me as I climbed out of bed to join him. My bare feet against the icy wooden boards brought my breath hissing in through my teeth.

"What are you doing?" he asked.

"Getting dressed." I pulled the top blanket off the bed with me to wrap around my chemise as I searched for my clothing.

He crossed to catch my arm. "I don't leave for hours."

"Time I don't want to waste." I looked up into his face. The now familiar planes of his cheeks, the firm line of his mouth, the inky depths of his eyes, even the riot of his dark curls called to my fingers. I wanted to spend more time exploring them. They were mine to memorize; just as the rest of him was mine to explore. If only he didn't have to leave. "I know you will come back, but I don't want to lose a moment..." *in case you don't return.* I closed my eyes. I couldn't speak the words. They caught on the lump of fear at the back of my throat. *Kurios, please be merciful. Bring him back to me.*

"I am only going to train. I will come back for you so we can break our fast together."

"Let me come."

The surprise in his eyes made me laugh.

"I would love to watch you spar. I might learn something."

He smiled and released my arm to brush the side of my face. His fingers radiated tempting warmth against my cold skin. "I forgot how many noses you have broken. Dress warmly, the water in the wash basin iced over last night."

I nodded and looked around for my gear. After finding it beneath a chair in the corner, I chose my practical brown woolen leggings, a rust red tunic that fell below the knee, and a forest green surcoat slit at the sides for ease of movement. The red accented my hair, or at least that was what Loren claimed when she dyed it last spring. Once I belted my weapons about my waist, I set to combing my hair. I separated the strands for a braid.

"Leave it."

"What?" I turned to find him watching me intensely. Now dressed in padded jerkin and most of his armor, he lacked only his mail, breastplate, and helmet to be completely ready for battle. He gestured to where my fingers were entangled.

"Leave it loose for now. I like it wild and down around your shoulders." His gaze skimmed me from head to foot. A half smile pulled at his mouth as his focus settled on my face. "In fact, I think I like you just as much in leggings as I do in a skirt."

Dropping the mail in his hands to the floor with a thump, he crossed the space between us in two strides. Catching my face between his hands, he pressed his mouth to mine. Visions of the night before flooded my head as my senses honed in on the sweet pleasure of his kiss and the delightful possession of his fingers in my hair. My arms encircled his neck, pulling the rest of me up to meet him. For the first time in my life I was thankful for my height.

After what seemed like forever and only a few seconds, he withdrew with a ragged groan. "This is madness. I don't want to leave you." He cradled my face with his right hand, caressing my bottom lip with his thumb. The desire in his eyes almost prompted me to plead for him to heed the impulse. Instead, I closed my eyes.

I forced myself to say the words. "I don't want you to leave, but we both know you must. For Rhynan and for our future, you must do this."

The depth of his sigh made my chest ache. He kissed me once more, deeply, and then stepped away.

He returned to where his mail lay and claimed it from the floor. With his back still turned away, he said, "Perhaps you shouldn't come to watch me train."

The sadness in his voice brought my head and attention around to focus on him. He avoided my gaze by concentrating on adjusting his mail. Disquiet undermined my confidence. What had I said to bring

113

on this change?

"Why ever not?"

Something about the way he held his shoulders as he reached for his breastplate dropped a thought into my head. Had he interpreted my reminder of his responsibilities as rejection? Before I lost my nerve I blurted out, "I am not Elenawyn."

"What?" He stared at me.

"I wasn't pushing you away. I care about you and don't want you to die. I..." the words stuck in my throat. My heartbeat thundered in my ears. "If only your title and lands were at stake, I would beg you to stay." I couldn't look at him for fear he would laugh at me.

"Thank you, Brielle." He took a deep breath. "If Darnay and Elise didn't need someone to care for them here, I would take you with me. I want you near me."

Pleasure at his words flooded my cheeks with heat. I hid it by concentrating on donning my heavy cloak. "Could you show me how to improve my skills? After you finish your own training, that is."

He smiled. The brief lifting of worry from his face made my stomach flutter. *Kurios, please bring him home safe and whole.*

He offered me his hand. "Come. Show me what you know. I will help how I can." I claimed his helmet from the table and took his hand.

We navigated the quiet corridors and stairs to the bailey in silence. Only the sounds of the kitchen workers beginning their day followed us out the door into the gray light of pre-dawn.

"You two are up early." Rathenridge fell into step next to Tomas. His easy lope contrasted with Tomas' purposeful stride. I lengthened my normal stride to keep up with the two of them. They matched each other's steps without apparent thought.

"Moriah not up yet? She used to join you for your morning training."

"Not since the birth of our first child, she hasn't. The children tire her out these days. Enjoy your time alone, my lady, while you have it. Once the children come, you will wish you savored it more."

"I intend to." I glanced Rathenridge's way only to encounter Tomas' gaze. The intense attention of his regard warmed my face.

"Weapon preference?" Rathenridge asked as we passed beneath the open arch into the practice yard. A handful of men already spread across the area.

"Broad sword," Tomas replied. "You should watch from a distance, Brielle."

"Over there would be safe." Rathenridge pointed toward a crude wooden bench in the shadow of the curtain wall.

I started across the center of the yard toward the seat only to wish I had chosen a different route. The men stopped their practice to greet me. I was bowed to and asked if I required anything. One of them claimed my hand and offered to escort me the rest of the way.

I looked up into his boyish features and wondered if he truly thought I was incapable of walking across a field without help. I opened my mouth to ask him just that when Tomas appeared at my shoulder.

"I will retain that privilege for myself, soldier."

"Very well, my lord." The soldier bowed over my hand. "I am always at your service, my lady." Finally releasing my hand, he returned to his sparring partner without even a backward glance.

Tomas glowered at his back. "You have my permission to break his nose if he ever handles you in such a high-handed manner again. Better yet, I will speak to him myself." He claimed his helmet.

Rathenridge joined us, blunted broadswords in his hands. "Don't be hasty, Tomas. Rolendis and her ladies sopped up flowery drivel and grand gestures. Kolbent encouraged it, fancied himself a hero of high romance. Rolendis and her ladies bestowed smiles and small favors on the men who fawned the most. You can't blame the men who haven't noticed the new Lady Irvaine is more discerning. Their confusion is understandable considering she puts Rolendis' beauty to shame."

I almost choked.

"Beware, Aiden. I doubt Moriah takes kindly to you complimenting other men's wives."

Rathenridge laughed. "I can't help speaking the truth. Besides, Moriah outshines every woman in every way. She need not fear me noticing your lady, Tomas. My wife is the only woman for me. Come, show me how soft you have become."

"Soft? I am not the one who has been sitting by the fire in a great hall, enjoying my wife, begetting children and growing flabby."

Rathenridge's lean frame could not be called flabby by any stretch of a troubadour's tongue. Tomas' physique was the opposite of soft. Both men confused me even more by grinning at each other.

"Are you going to hand me a weapon and allow me to defend myself?" Tomas asked, stepping away from me.

Rathenridge threw him the sword in his right hand, retaining the weapon in his left. Before I reached the bench, the two descended into playful jibes and jeers as they exchanged blows. I watched, admiring both of their skill.

Tomas moved with surprising agility considering his size. Rathenridge's movements took on more of a fluid quality. However, he did seem to rely heavily on his occasionally random strikes in odd spots in attempting to keep Tomas off-balance. They moved across the practice area, weaving back and forth between the other trainers. Neither man gained the upper hand for more than a few strikes.

Finally, Rathenridge began to show signs of fatigue. His blocks grew sloppy. He stopped attacking with his words. After a few more minutes, he made a relatively minor error of lunging the wrong direction when Tomas feinted left, exposing his right side. Tomas pressed his advantage, scoring a resounding whack to Rathenridge's breastplate. The two of them fell back, breathing hard and circling.

"I wouldn't recommend another match, my lord." Antano's voice at my shoulder made me jump. I hadn't noticed his arrival thanks to my concentration on the bout before me. "Breakfast awaits you in the great hall. Your men are preparing for departure soon after dawn."

Tomas glanced at the brightening in the eastern sky. "Well met, Aiden. I am afraid we will have to rematch another day."

Too winded for words, Rathenridge saluted with his sword.

Tomas crossed the field to me. Despite the stink of sweat, I couldn't resist answering his smile with one of

117

my own.

"Feel more confident that I will return?"

Just the possibility that he wouldn't knotted my stomach. Some of the anxiety must have reached my face because he sobered instantly.

"I am sorry. I have lived with the constant reality of death for so long I have lost the sensitivity of those who haven't."

"Don't die," I pleaded. I was all too aware that he possessed no control over when he would die. Only Kurios held that power.

He dropped his sword in the dirt, caught my head between his hands, and took my mouth in a heated kiss. For several thundering heartbeats, I was aware of nothing beyond him. Finally releasing me, his black gaze burned into mine.

"If there is breath in my body, Brielle, I will return to you. I promise." He pressed a gentle kiss to my forehead. "Come, wife, let us eat."

The following hour passed more quickly than I anticipated it would.

I ate little.

Once Tomas finished working his way through his repast, he escorted me back to our room to gather his gear. Jarvin took the saddlebags and disappeared in the direction of the stairs to the stables. Tomas waited until he was out of sight before claiming my hands. His tan fingers traced the length of mine.

"I expect we will encounter the caravan on our way to Wisenvale. We will send them on almost immediately. I will speak with Darnay and tell him to seek you out."

"How will I know him?"

"He and Elise will be the only two children in the caravan. You will know him."

Tomas kissed the back of my fingers. His mouth lingered on the one that held the simple gold band symbolizing our relationship.

"I instructed Horacian to give you the tour of the castle workings in my stead." He lowered our joined hands while still stroking my ring finger. "You are my heir. Should something happen to me, and I..." He looked into my face, tracing my features with his gaze. "Before I came to fetch you, I secured a promise from King Mendal. He will allow you the right to remarry who you wish and still retain your widow's portion, half my property."

"But Darnay–" His finger pressed against my lips.

"Darnay will be well provided for. Mendal will designate a guardian for him and you will be free to do as you wish."

I didn't want to be free. The reality struck me hard. Memories of the village men leaving and never returning twisted my stomach. Freedom was not worth Tomas' life. Before I could tell him, Antano appeared on the stairs to the hall.

"My lord, the men await you."

"We are coming."

He waited until Antano turned before kissing me once more. "We won't have much opportunity in the yard."

He claimed my left hand by intertwining his fingers in mine. Then he picked up his helmet and led me down the stairs. The great hall echoed as we strode across it. No one lingered in the passage, but the massive doors to the inner bailey stood open. Beyond

119

them, a crowd gathered. Our appearance caused a sensation. The people parted, clearing a path from the keep doors to the entrance of the outer bailey where the soldiers waited.

"Ready?" Tomas asked.

"No, but I will manage."

"The pageantry will all be over soon enough."

I opened my mouth to explain that was not what I dreaded, but a trumpet blast from the outer bailey put an end to conversation. We stepped forward.

People pressed and jostled each other to see us. Their faces expressed curiosity or boredom. I tried to smile out at them. It felt like such a farce. They didn't know us. We didn't know them. I barely knew the man at my side. Yet, we all played our parts. They sent off their lord and champion in grand style and I acted the role of a dutiful wife left to tend the castle in my husband's place.

My chest ached with fear. Tomas might not come back. Men fell in battle all the time. He could return to find my management skills lacking. Darnay could hate me.

I shook away the thoughts. No. I couldn't think that way. I glanced around at the faces watching us. The Kurios placed me here for a reason. I needed to trust him and obey.

We stepped beyond the wall separating the baileys. I gasped at the sight. Easily three hundred men and a hundred horses crowded the space. Voices rebounded from the stone walls, intermingled with the neighs and whinnies of the mounts. Early morning sun glinted off polished shields and weaponry among the array of colored livery: green, gold, red, brown, midnight blue and yellow. Our arrival elicited a general cheer followed by a scramble to mount. The volume rose to such a level I would have had to yell to be heard.

Antano led Tomas' mount forward.

After squeezing my fingers a final time, Tomas dropped my hand to don his helmet. Within moments, he was mounted and out of my reach. My thoughts rushed forward, filling my head with questions I wanted answered and things I wanted him to know before he left.

But, it was too late.

The herald blew the signal to ride.

Tomas, a now familiar figure in plain armor among the many others of the same, turned his horse toward the gate. He might have looked back once. I thought he did, but he might have been checking one of his fellow rider's distance from him. Regardless, I raised my hand in farewell.

*Kurios, spare him. Place a hedge of protection around him. Please bring him back to me.*

Feminine laughter broke through my prayer.

"Don't worry, child, he will return. Either dead or alive, he will return."

I turned to find Rolendis and three strange women standing in the shadow of the gate. Their bright silk and satin skirts peeked out from beneath fur-lined cloaks. The widow's cloak draped about her shoulders, unfastened, displaying the front of her elaborately embroidered bodice.

"Hope that he is dead when he does. For if he isn't, you will wish you were."

"Ignore them." Moriah slid an arm through mine. "Rolendis does not mourn her husband as we would mourn ours. Would you walk with me, my lady?"

I nodded, uncertain my tongue could form words without something foolish bursting forth.

She drew me back toward the keep, but instead of walking up to the main doors, she led me along the wall to the right.

"There are some things you need to know." She dropped my arm to open a gray door. It blended into the wall so that the eye passed it over if one wasn't looking for it. "We will have more privacy in the gardens."

I had not realized how I missed greenery until the moment I set eyes on the paradise beyond the door. Barren climbing rose vines, plants of every shape and size, trellises of grape vines, fruit trees, and an herb garden patterned out in a wheel greeted me. I could feel the tension in my shoulders easing even as I took a deep breath of the familiar scents of earth and life. Slipping into the slumber of winter, it wasn't as fragrant as full bloom. Still, if the sounds of hooves on stone and the voices didn't drift over the wall, I could close my eyes and half believe I stood in my mother's garden while she still lived.

"My lady, you are in danger."

My eyes popped open. "What?"

"You are in danger here." Moriah's eyes searched my face urgently. "Rolendis is bent on revenge. Kolbent's death robbed her of power, rank, fortune, everything she sold her body to gain. She intends to regain what she lost. The fastest way to do that is through your husband."

"Are you saying she will try to kill me?" Rolendis didn't seem cold enough for that. Bitter, jealous, and manipulative perhaps, but I couldn't see her as a murderess.

"No, she will not wield the knife. However, she would willingly hand you over to someone who wants to get rid of you for other reasons."

I peered into her face. "Who would want that?"

"I don't know who she will enlist, with Jorndar restrained and watched. But, she will be seeking a way."

I studied Moriah. She was the wife of one of my husband's friends. At least I thought they were friends. Mulling over Sir Rathenridge and Tomas' exchanges, they certainly acted like friends. But, I hadn't heard Tomas mention Moriah beyond the single message of greetings she sent through her husband. Was she a friend of Tomas' or another woman bent on stirring up trouble?

Her face seemed honest enough. If only I could see through to the character beneath.

"What do you think I should do about it?"

"Come home with me." She smiled warmly. "We can leave word for Irvaine and escape this place. I would love the company. The children enjoy visitors. You will be safe, and we can look for our husbands' return far from Rolendis and her poisonous tongue."

"I have to wait for the caravan to arrive. Irvaine's son and another child are counting on my protection when they arrive."

"Then you must wait. When will the caravan arrive?"

"I don't know. It could be any time in the next few days."

Genuine concern pulled at her brow. "I can linger no longer than a day. My children expect my return by a

123

set date. If I don't appear when I said, they will grow distraught. You can always follow after."

"Even if the caravan arrives in time, I need to stay here. Irvaine requested I watch over the running of the vargar for him. He does not trust Horacian."

Moriah's eyebrows drew together. "Horacian is harmless."

"Perhaps, but I need to stay."

She studied my face. "Irvaine expects a lot of you, doesn't he?"

I considered his requests for a moment. "No more than I would expect of myself. I have experience with crops and managing, but caring for the children frightens me a bit. Although I have been around younger children, I have never been the sole caregiver for one, let alone two."

Moriah's face softened. "Feed them, provide security, consistency, and above all else love them. Oh, and don't be afraid to say no." She squeezed my hand gently. "You will do well."

I wanted to ask her how she could know that, but before I could, a servant approached from the keep. The girl bobbed in and out of a curtsey with a wobble. She met my gaze with the unashamed attitude of one much younger than her covered hair and long skirt indicated.

"My lady, Steward Horacian is seeking you. He wishes to escort you on a tour of the fields at your earliest convenience."

"Thank you." I smiled at her. The corners of her mouth lifted in reply. "Please notify him I shall meet him in the outer bailey."

Forgetting to acknowledge my instruction, she turned and bounded off the way she had come.

"Beware of insolence among the servants. Rolendis plays favorites."

I watched the girl-child's retreat. "I will keep that in mind."

Rolendis might have played favorites, but I doubted she favored a maid as innocent-mannered as that one.

"Farewell, Lady Irvaine." Moriah took my hands. "Should you need shelter or support, you send word my way."

"I shall."

After a final squeeze, she dropped my hands, curtseyed, and left in the direction of the keep.

I lingered a bit longer in the garden to pick apart the mess of emotions roiling in my gut. Seeking a few moments of prayer and quiet seemed the best way to hush the chaos.

# Chapter Fourteen

Touring the fields brought my village's past into stark clarity. I witnessed well-tended fields, maintained equipment, efficient workers, and the bounty that came with hard work, good ground, and the seasonable weather of the past few years. Wisenvale's land was just as arable. If my cousin had only left us to ourselves, we would have made it with food to spare. His yearly tax of the harvest had cost us more than he realized.

I paused at the thought. No. He had known. I had told him repeatedly.

"Then there is the seed that we purchased from Lord Wisten last year." Horacian pointed to an entry in the ledger before me. I shifted the book so I could see it more clearly in the afternoon sunlight pouring in the great hall's window. A sum completely out of proportion to the amount of grain received jumped out from the page. The handwriting of the entry was obviously different from the normal recorder's.

"Who kept the accounts then?"

"I did, my lady. Why do you ask?"

"You didn't make this entry."

"That is true. The late Lord Irvaine handled that transaction himself."

"And you didn't question the obvious overpayment?" I studied Horacian's face. He blushed.

"It wasn't my place, my lady. I noticed the disproportion, but no one questioned my late master and kept his position."

"Did this happen every year?"

"Now that you mention it, it did. I also noticed that Lord Wisten left with most of the grain he brought with him."

"Bribery?" I wondered aloud, not really expecting Horacian to answer.

"Possibly, my lady. The late Lord Irvaine's dealings with King Trentham were not easy. Trentham kept demanding more than my master wanted to give. He was even reluctant to defend when the call for arms came. He dallied with the idea of joining the rebels. Marrying my Rolendis changed his mind. He threw his lot in with the King."

I frowned. My cousin sided with King Trentham then. Trentham demanded complete loyalty. Even unsubstantiated rumors of wavering could lead to the stripping of title and lands. If Orwin learned the late Lord Irvaine seriously considered joining the rebels, he would have leverage. Armed with proof, he would have drained the coffers dry. Considering the prosperity I witnessed since my arrival, Orwin didn't have proof.

"When was the last inventory of your winter stores?"

"A month ago. Last harvest brought in far more than we needed."

"You have no idea how happy I am to hear that. I need to know how much Kyrenton can spare."

Horacian's expression spoke eloquently of his disbelief. "My lady?"

"Wisenvale is now under Lord Irvaine's protection. Lord Wisten left us inadequate stores to last the winter. Lord Irvaine wishes to know how much Kyrenton can spare without hardship. We are not asking for your seed grain, just the excess of your winter stores."

"I will see what I can do, my lady."

"Thank you, Horacian."

The following day passed swiftly. I barely gathered two moments together during the daylight hours to realize I missed my new husband.

At night I fell into the bed we shared for a single night and found myself wishing he rested there too. It was strange how I longed for his support and company. In our brief time together he had become a friend.

The third day dawned in cold light and muted silence. I rolled over to resume sleeping when the sound of raised voices in the inner bailey jarred me awake again. Men and horses raised a racket below. It was still too early for that much activity in the inner bailey.

Grabbing the fur-lined cloak next to the bed, I lunged toward the window. I thrust aside the heavy curtain which promptly fell closed again behind me. Then, I threw open the shutters and stuck my head out. The window opening overlooked the outer bailey, offering a view of the gate into the town beyond. Even in the gray dawning light, I could spot a wagon easing through the gapping gate.

The caravan was here.

Abandoning the window, I flung the curtains aside again and dove for my clothing. I dressed quickly. My fingers shook with cold so that I fumbled tying my second boot, but I managed at last. Taking the stairs two steps at a time, I almost plowed into Horacian on his way up. I hit the stairwell wall a bit hard with my shoulder instead.

"Pardon, but the caravan is here, my lady." He took in my rumpled gown, twisted surcote, and unbound hair with widened eyes. "I see you already know."

"I heard the noise." I tugged at the surcote in a futile effort to straighten it.

"I shall plan on you not being available until the afternoon then. You will want to settle Master Darnay before we resume our tour of southern borders."

"Whom do I speak with about quarters?" We hadn't reached that aspect of the estate management.

"Sarena Farwyn oversees the room assignments."

I straightened my shoulders and pushed from my mind the fact I looked more like a wayward child than a lady of the manor. "Have her attend me and Master Darnay in my quarters in a half-hour. Also, see that a proper fire is built in the hearth there. Master Darnay will need warmth to fend off the cold of his journey."

Horacian smiled, a slight lift to the corners of his mouth.

I blinked in astonishment. It was the first positive expression I had seen on his face since his obvious relief at Tomas not punishing him for handing the account books to Sir Jorndar.

"I shall see to it myself, my lady." He bowed and continued up the stairs.

Instead of pelting down the rest of the steps, I took a moment to right myself. I finally reached the great hall a few minutes later with my surcote straight and rumpled gown covered. I could do nothing about my hair, having left my leather ties in my room, but I figured I was within the acceptable range of propriety.

Crossing the empty hall at a trot, I reached the outer doors as the last of the wagons halted beyond them. Men jumped down, women scurried about, and a handful of soldiers moved among them. I saw no children.

Then the first wagon rolled off toward the stables. Beyond, I spotted two small figures, unnaturally still among the chaos of movement.

"Darnay?" The name fell from my mouth in my surprise.

They both turned my way. Two pairs of almost identical dark eyes sought my face while a sharp breeze stirred the dark curls framing the girl's features. The boy regarded me impassively as I approached, but the girl stepped closer to her cousin. Darnay clutched at the wooden sword in his hand.

"Darnay? Elise?"

Darnay studied my face with intensity so like his father my stomach tightened in a sudden desire to see Tomas' face. "Grandma?"

A woman detached herself from the group carrying three bags stuffed so tight the leather strained at the seams. "What is the problem?"

"I am Brielle." I met the woman's curiosity with a smile. Darnay stepped back into her skirts, and Elise crowded behind him. "I am Lord Irvaine's new wife."

"Her hair is red." The girl's eyes locked on my wild hair.

"Hush, Elise, don't be rude." The woman settled a lithe hand on the mop of dark curls on the child's head.

"But it is."

"I know." She smiled down at her charge. Then she

131

turned her gaze to my face. "Tomas asked that I give you this." She pulled a piece of thrice folded parchment from her belt. She handed it to me with a warm smile.

I smoothed it flat.

*Beloved, she is my mother. Make her welcome for me. Tomas.*

"He sends his love."

I looked up to discover the woman watching me. I returned the regard. She obviously wasn't a woman to fuss about appearances with her thick, gray-laced hair pulled back into a sensible plait. I could see why when I really looked. Buried beneath the laughter wrinkles and the usual ravages of time was the fine bone structure of a natural beauty. Her bright eyes and warm smile gave her an appearance of a woman much younger even now.

"I am sorry." I averted my eyes. "I didn't mean to be rude."

"He didn't warn you, did he? A great man for the important decisions, but he forgets to share all the extra bits."

"He said that Darnay and Elise would come with the supply caravan."

"But he didn't mention me." She laughed. "Yes, that is typical of him. He has grown too accustomed to working with soldiers. I am Anise Dyrease." She offered a handclasp in greeting, which I accepted. "When did he tell you about Darnay?"

"I guessed, sort of."

She nodded knowingly. "He isn't hiding things. He just doesn't remember to share."

A wrench of longing for Tomas caught me unawares. I swallowed at the sudden tightness in my throat. "I know." Straightening my shoulders, I lifted my head to smile at my mother-in-law only to find her watching me with keen eyes.

Instead of commenting, she nodded.

"Are we going to sleep on a real bed tonight?" Darnay asked her.

"If you wish," I answered.

He frowned at me in confusion.

"Darnay, say hello to your new mother." Anise propelled him forward with a gentle push between his shoulders.

He obediently bowed and offered me a hand in friendship, the one not clutching the toy sword. His dark eyes clearly communicated his unease.

I clasped his hand firmly. "I am pleased to meet you, Master Darnay."

Darnay squared his shoulders and lifted his chin. "Father said I am to call you mother, but–" He lost his nerve.

"You can call me Brielle."

Profound relief passed behind the boy's eyes, but like his father, little emotion appeared in his features. I found the boy's reserve disquieting in many ways. It hinted at the difficulty of his young life. To grow up without a mother and rarely see one's father appeared to have aged him beyond his seasons. I wanted to hug him. I wondered if he looked like his father when he laughed. Most pressing of all was the desire to show him all the love my parents gave me.

"Have you eaten this morning?" I took care to address the question to the two children.

"Not yet. We traveled all night," Elise offered without emerging from the safety of the woman's

133

skirts.

"You didn't sleep?"

"We slept in the wagon." Darnay grimaced.

I attempted the same thing a few years ago and did not sleep a bit.

Elise tugged at my mother-in-law's sleeve. "I'm hungry."

"I am too. Come, I will find us all some food." I smiled at Elise and offered my hand. "There were some lovely smells coming from the kitchen when I passed it."

Elise regarded my outstretched hand with suspicion. I immediately regretted offering it. Doing so had pressed an intimacy she obviously was not comfortable with. Yet, I didn't feel it was wise to retreat now.

"She won't hurt you."

Elise looked up at Anise. "How do you know?"

Anise and I shared a smile. Darnay observed the exchange with a frown. Then he studied me as though measuring my character. My stomach tightened as I recognized Tomas' habit of weighing people. "I like her face."

Elise turned identically colored eyes on my face.

"I don't like her hair."

"I like it. I like red. It is my favorite color."

I supressed my laughter. Elise stepped forward and placed her tiny hand in mine. "I like porridge."

"I am certain I can find you some."

"If you can't?"

"I will make you some myself." I led her toward the keep.

"You cook?" Darnay's surprise broke through his reserve. "Grandma says my mother never cooked.

Father did." He frowned. "He said he wanted his next wife to be able to cook so he didn't have to."

"Then he got his wish." So Tomas cooked. I would have to ask him to prepare something for me after he returned.

We entered the keep via the door to the kitchens. A few of the servants paused to stare, but generally, we passed unnoticed until we reached the passage outside the great hall.

"My lady, madame." Jarvin bowed deeply. "Master Darnay, little Elise, it is a pleasure to see you both again."

"Jarvin!" Dropping my hand, Elise launched herself at the man.

"We didn't expect you to be here, sir."

I glanced at Darnay with a frown. The miniature Tomas expression and attitude were back. Jarvin and Anise exchanged concerned looks over the children's heads. Obviously this odd behavior was new to both of them.

Addressing Jarvin, I said, "Elise has declared she would like some porridge for breakfast. Is there any chance we could have food brought up to my room? I believe it will be warmer there than in the hall."

"I will see to it personally, my lady." Jarvin set Elise down, bowed to each of us, tousled Elise's hair, and then left.

"Why is he here and not with my father?" Darnay asked as I herded them toward the stairwell.

"Your father wanted me to have a friend among all the strangers."

Thankfully he accepted the explanation without additional questions. I didn't want to burden him with greater detail. Anise would be a different matter. I would have to find a way to catch her alone and explain the situation. I glanced back, but she was studying the tapestry we were passing.

A fire roared in my fireplace by the time we arrived. Anise and I helped the children out of their layers. Darnay refused to give up his play sword. I dragged the top fur from the bed and spread it on the floor a safe distance from the fire before bidding the children to sit. Anise dropped the bags in the corner and began hanging the wraps on the hook behind the door.

Elise flopped down as though she had just climbed a mountain and lay back with a sigh of exhaustion. "Why are there so many steps?"

"We are high up in the keep," Darnay replied seriously. He scanned the room. "Where are we going to sleep?"

"We will find that out soon enough." Anise settled on the fur. "Now sit down."

Elise lay down and curled up. "Come, Darnay. It is so warm and soft. Ever so much more comfortable than the ground." She rubbed her cheek along the fur. "I am so glad we are going to be sleeping inside tonight."

I smiled. "I know what you mean, Elise." I settled on the rug next to her. "The bed is especially soft and warm. The first night I slept so deeply that I didn't want to move until spring."

As I hoped, once he was the only one standing, Darnay sat down. However, he didn't relax. His narrow shoulders remained squared and he rested his sword across his knees. He was ready to defend himself. I feared he considered me the enemy.

*Please help me, Kurios.*

A knock on the door signaled Jarvin's arrival with four bowls of porridge, a carafe of cream, a pitcher of milk, and a bowl of sliced apples. The hunger in both children's eyes prompted me to immediately pass the bowls of cereal around. Both of them began eating as soon as their hands closed over their spoons. Even Darnay relaxed enough to gobble his first mouthfuls. Thankfully the food cooled adequately in the journey from the kitchen. I poured out milk for both of them and Anise before claiming my own porridge.

"How long have you been on the road?"

Elise spoke around her food. "Months."

"Three weeks and four days," Anise clarified.

Darnay frowned. "Not even a month."

Rolling her eyes at him, Elise made a face.

"My lady?"

I looked up to find Jarvin's concerned expression.

"I spoke to Farwyn when I met her in the kitchens. She informed me that nurseries are currently unavailable. The former lady ordered preparations for her child. The work halted upon Lord Irvaine and your arrival. The children will have to bed down with the servants in the great hall."

Elise looked as though she would cry. Darnay's features tightened to hold back his disappointment. Anise remained silent, her attention focused fully on the food in her hands.

"They will stay here with me. This room will be far warmer, and they will be safer here too. Are there spare mattresses somewhere to use on the floor? If not, they can have the bed. I will sleep on the floor."

"Nay, my lady," Jarvin protested. "I am confident I can find mattresses." He bowed and left.

"I will take the floor." Darnay straightened his shoulders. "You ladies should have the best."

I smiled. "Thank you, Darnay, but I don't think that will be necessary."

He frowned. "Father says men should take care of their women."

"That sounds like something your father would say. But I am sure he wouldn't make you sleep on the floor."

His brow lowered and his jaw tightened with a slight stubborn lift. "You don't know my father."

Praying for wisdom, I scrambled for an answer. "It is true that I don't know him well, but I look forward to getting to know him better. Perhaps you can help me."

Dark eyes so like Tomas' weighed my worth.

*Kurios, please soften his heart. Help me to say the right thing.*

I smiled warmly at him before glancing at Elise. She had fallen asleep. Head resting on her crossed arms, she breathed evenly. Her bowl, scraped clean, lay abandoned at her elbow. I caught Anise's slight nod of encouragement before I turned back to Darnay. He yawned so wide my jaw ached in sympathy. Anise and I gathered the breakfast leavings without comment, collecting his bowl last. We took our time arranging everything on the tray. When I finally turned back to the children, Darnay had joined Elise. He cradled his wooden sword to his chest. Even in sleep he looked like a miniature of his father.

I collected two blankets from the bed to cover them. Once confident they were warm and as comfortable as I could make them without moving them, I crept to the door. Anise followed me out, the tray in her arms.

138

# Chapter Fifteen

"Are the little dears asleep?" Rolendis' voice at my shoulder made me jump. I spun around faster than was wise and almost collided with Anise and the tray of breakfast leavings.

Rolendis eyed Anise for a moment before focusing on me once again. Her expression oozed concern and sweetness. I resisted the urge to cringe.

"They are sleeping." My instinct nagged at me that she was up to something.

"Are you going to leave them? I can sit with them if you wish." Her smile widened into a forced grimace.

"No, thank you."

"I am going to stay with them," Anise said before I could come up with a better reason for declining.

Rolendis sniffed at Anise, nose in the air, and looked her up and down. "And you are?"

Tomas' mother answered in completely reasonable terms. "I am the children's nurse. We simply stepped outside to speak without waking the children."

Rolendis apparently didn't know what to do with the discontinuity of a servant who spoke as an equal.

While she struggled to find the right response, Anise handed the tray to me. "I will remain, my lady."

Without waiting for my reply, she ducked back into the room, closed the door, and locked it.

"Is there anything else you need?" I asked.

Rolendis still stared at the closed door. "Did she bring news?"

"Of what?"

"Irvaine." She glared at me as though I was being purposefully obtuse. I wasn't.

There were so many things that we were waiting to hear about: Loren, Wisenvale, Quaren, the battle. I was as eager for news of Tomas' safety as I was for Loren's, but there was none.

"He sent none."

"Not even in the note?"

My head snapped about as I pinned her with a glare. "You were watching me?"

"You were a bit hard to miss standing in the middle of the bailey humbling yourself before children and an old servant woman. From the way you treat her, one would think she was an equal."

I bit my tongue. Anise told Rolendis she was the children's nurse, truth, but not the whole. There was no point to giving Rolendis any more than that. The only reason she talked with me now was because she hoped I would give her something she could use. I aimed to disappoint her.

"I must go." I propped the tray against my left hip and lifted my skirt with my right. "Excuse me." I pressed past her and down the passage toward the stairs to the kitchens and undercroft.

"Mind you watch that nurse," she called after me. "The insolent ones poison your children's minds against you."

I didn't look back. But the click of her trying the lock on the door echoed after me as I descended the stairs. She was up to something. Moriah's warning tugged at me. My eating knife suddenly seemed inadequate protection.

After leaving the tray in the frantically busy kitchen without anyone giving me more than a nod, I headed to the practice yard. About halfway across the inner bailey, I realized that it seemed unusually quiet for the time of day.

Other days at this time, horses and men passed through regularly. Women lingered to gossip, and children ran underfoot. Now, only a single cart full of empty barrels rolled through the gates, lumbering off toward the village. The guards waved it through with barely a glance. A stray cat wandered across the courtyard to sun on the edge of the well in the center.

I slipped through the arch to the practice yard, preoccupied with the change. The yard also lay abandoned. However, I expected it. The guards drilled in a meadow outside the town walls. Only some of Rathenridge's men and the few Tomas left behind could possibly be about. Most of them preferred to train in the early morning hours. The shadow on the sundial in the bailey had marked it at least midmorning.

I crossed to the armory at a trot, pulling the key ring Horacian gave me from my pocket as I approached the door. But, I didn't need it. I stumbled to a halt. The door stood ajar. Surely this wasn't normal.

"Hello, my lady."

I turned sharply to the right and blinked at the shadows there. He didn't move, but I could make out his position by the deepening of the shadows from my

141

position in the full sunlight. Beyond that I had to guess.

"Why is the armory door unlocked? Shouldn't it be locked when no one is around?"

"I am here."

He moved along the wall toward the door and closer to me. The hair on my arms prickled.

"I was under the impression it was kept locked."

I couldn't see his eyes, but the outline of his head seemed to indicate he was looking at me. If the feeling in my gut was accurate, he undressed me with his eyes.

"Excuse me, would you mind stepping into the light. I can't see your face and wish to know to whom I am speaking."

"A pleasure, my lady."

He threw something to the ground and stepped forward. Ash blonde hair caught the glare of the sun. Bold blue eyes assessed my appearance from beneath red-tinged blond eyebrows. A young beard of dark red hair covered his neck and cheeks. He hadn't bothered to shape and trim it. In contrast to his insolent expression, he wore the garb of a house guard, one of the men I would have expected to patrol the inner corridors of the vargar.

"Are you of Lord Irvaine's household?"

"Aye, Lady Irvaine. I served the late noble on the fields of battle, and now I serve the man who claims the title after him. Should you need something your new husband can't provide, I would be happy to serve you as well."

My eyes focused on his face again. I wasn't sure I heard him correctly.

"No, thank you."

Thinking better of entering a room with him as

company, I turned back toward the bailey.

"Surely you haven't found what you sought, my lady. Might I aid you in locating it?"

I wanted a knife, something to defend myself from the likes of him. Now that I faced exactly what I feared, I wished for a sword. If I walked away now, I wouldn't have another chance to come again for a while. I looked back over my shoulder.

"Are you the usual armory master?"

"Yes. I am here every day from daybreak to sunset. Do you wish for a weapon?"

"My eating knife grows dull. Lord Irvaine said I might have one of the knives from the armory." I hated the lie, but I didn't trust the man enough to give him the truth.

"Then let me select one for you. Wait here."

He ducked through the doorway and returned in a moment. "Here you are, my lady."

A jeweled hilt glinted in the sunlight and gilt swirled along the length of the sheath. Gaudy and pretentious, it would have been my last choice, but appearance wasn't its primary purpose. I lifted it from his hand just fast enough to escape his other hand's attempt to catch my fingers.

I drew the blade. The edge was sharp enough. For all its affectations, it balanced perfectly. It fit my hand well enough. A bit of leather wrapped around the hilt would improve the grip and hide the sparkles. I examined the sheath. I could hide the gilt as well.

"It will do. Thank you." With a perfunctory bow that left no room for comment, I strode across the practice yard toward the bailey. Head held high, shoulders straight, I tried to add a confident glide into my quick steps. Once I turned the corner into the bailey and was out of his sight, I hitched up my skirts and broke into a run toward the door to the undercroft.

The idea of seeking out Jarvin pressed at me urgently. I needed to be reassured that the rest of the men Tomas left behind were not like the armory keeper. Surely there were some I could trust to defend the women of the vargar, not take advantage of them.

I stepped into the dimness of the undercroft with relief.

"Oh, Vorter."

A cascade of feminine laughter set my teeth on edge. Rolendis was somewhere just out of sight around the corner at the bottom of the stairs. She giggled.

I turned to leave the way I came, but the sound of my name stopped me.

"Don't worry about the pretender. Brielle will be getting what she deserves before the night is through."

"So soon?" The male sounded distracted. I didn't recognize his voice, but I could guess Rolendis was the reason for his lack of focus. By the sounds of it, they were locked in a very inappropriate embrace.

"You said it would take a fortnight to make your plans."

"Jorndar's capture pressed us to move more quickly. His men lie in wait for King Mendal even now. If we just free Jorndar and deal with the new Irvaine's allies here, they will all be neatly trapped."

"And at our mercy."

"Rhynan will be ours." She laughed. Noisy sighs followed, ending with a low chuckle from Rolendis. "Now, now, Vor. You and I both know that is not allowed."

144

"If I can't have you, at least let me be first in line for her. Our new Lady Irvaine is an appealing dish. I want to have my go at her before her spirit is broken."

"How can you say that? Her hair alone..." Rolendis' genuine horror hurt despite my efforts to ignore it.

"Jealous?"

"Of her? Never. She is a stuttering simpleton with a face to match."

"But her figure..." The man made an inappropriate sound.

I gagged. The taste of acid burned my throat. I slipped back out into the bailey. My lungs filled with the icy air and the scent of horse leavings. Carefully closing the door behind me so it wouldn't betray my retreat, I tried to reel in my floundering thoughts.

Harkening to the urgent need to escape, I walked swiftly around to the front entrance, panic growing with each step. Now the words of the man in the practice yard took on greater significance. He had said he served the man who claimed the title. If he had meant Tomas, why not say so? He must be loyal to Jorndar, the man who laid claim to the title before Tomas. My stomach twisted.

*Oh, Kurios, what do I do?* I knew what I wanted to do. Run. But that wasn't an option.

Turning sharply to the left upon entering the double doors, I headed toward a stairwell I had never tread before. Horacian pointed it out the first morning on the beginning of the tour of the vargar. Narrow and dark, blocked off at the head and foot by doubly thick doors, it led down to where the only men I could count on were keeping Jorndar locked up. Letting myself in the top door, I locked it behind me. Musty darkness closed

145

in around me. I climbed down the uneven stairs with only the dim light creeping around the upper door for guidance. Then I pounded on the door at the bottom.

A muffled male voice responded. "Who is it?"

"Lady Irvaine. I need to speak with Kuylan."

Silence.

My heart thundered in my chest despite my deliberately slow breathing. Finally the lock turned and clunked, each sound echoing in the space around me. The door opened few inches, and the half familiar features of Kuylan peered at me through the crack.

"It is she," he informed someone behind him. Stepping back, he made room for me to enter. The moment I was through, he closed the door again and a second man locked it.

I swallowed back the panic that gripped my gut. One door in and out. The one locked door to which I did not hold the key. I forced myself to focus on assessing my surroundings.

Long and low, the room offered little to cheer its occupants. The dirt floor was swept clean. Three pallets leaned against the far wall and the fourth lay next to them, made up as a bed and recently slept in. Considering Kuylan's rumpled appearance, I surmised he had been resting. Four lanterns and a roaring fire in the fireplace lit the whole room in a golden glow.

A scarred table crowded the center of the space. Two of the four chairs around the table were occupied by young men, neither familiar. A fourth man, the one with the key, stood—no, stooped since he was unusually tall and lean. The ceiling barely cleared Kuylan's head and he hunched slightly cradling the thick bandage about his middle.

146

"Stand to attention men," the tall, lean one barked, "Lady Irvaine is here. Captain Parrian at your service, my lady." He bowed gracefully.

The other two scrambled to their feet and saluted as best they could considering the conditions.

"Woral and Isankin," Parrian introduced the two. Isankin looked like he was barely old enough to leave home, and Woral's smile warmed my heart with its sincerity. All of them were a refreshing change from the stranger guarding the armory.

"Parrian, I have reason to believe that an escape is being planned. Are you the commander of the remnant of men my husband left behind?"

"I am, my lady. What kind of escape? How do they plan on getting him out?" He nodded toward one of the doors lining the far wall. "It isn't as though they would get far. We post four on duty in constant rotation. No one has keys to both locks, not even yourself, my lady."

"I don't know their plans, but I do know they plan an attempt tonight."

Parrian frowned. I could see him debating whether or not to request my source.

"I overheard two of the conspirators, the former Lady Irvaine and an unknown man." I pushed back against the shame, but I couldn't hide the heat rushing to my face. "They were discussing me as an incentive, should he cooperate."

Genuine sympathy warmed Parrian's eyes. "I am sorry, my lady, but I am not sure what I can do to prepare beyond extra vigilance and giving you a personal guard."

I could see they were already doing all they could to ensure Jorndar stayed right where Tomas had put him.

147

"I will consider it. For now, be wary of Rolendis and anything connected with her."

"I assure you we shall, my lady. Thank you for informing us." A chorus of thank yous from the other three supported his gratitude.

Realizing there was nothing more I could do, I turned back toward the locked door. Parrian unlocked it for me. When he eased it open to let me pass, he spoke again. "Pardon my forwardness, my lady, but is there more?"

Looking up into his honest, friendly face, I wanted to spill the whole story of the scene at the armory, including the plot against Mendal. But then he would feel obligated to confront the man. Dealing with that man would not deal with the root problem, and I knew Parrian had very few loyal men at his disposal.

"Thank you, Captain, but I intend to handle it myself."

He frowned slightly, but nodded. "I understand, my lady, but should you need anything, ever, please let me know. Lord Irvaine made it explicit that you were to be protected at all costs."

I shifted my attention to climbing the stairs as though he had not mentioned Tomas. But, in the depths of my heart, I was pleased Tomas took the time to see that I would be defended should I need it. Pausing on the first step, I turned to meet the Captain's watchful gaze. "Thank you, Captain, you have eased my fears already."

I climbed to the outer door by the light of the open lower one. The key came to my hand readily. The moment I set the teeth into the lock, Parrian closed the door at the foot of the stair and secured it. I stepped out into the suddenly expansive corridor and turned my face to the sunlight pouring through the casements high above.

I needed a better solution. Waiting for the conspirators to move seemed more foolish by the moment. If they wanted me, they would have to find me. I was going to go and do what I could to stop another civil war.

I strode to the entrance to the great hall. The doors were spread wide. As I hoped, women moved about preparing to serve the coming meal. I spotted the young serving girl from the garden among them. Approaching her, I was once again struck by her youth.

She didn't notice me until I stood practically at her side. She dropped the jug of ale in her surprise. I caught it, barely.

"My lady?" Her face drained of color. "I am sorry, my lady, I didn't see you there. Here, let me take that for you." She reached for the jug.

I pulled it closer to my chest and stepped back out of her reach. "Not until you tell me your name."

Her confusion swiftly melted into suspicion. "I am Tatin."

"I am pleased to meet you, Tatin." I extended the jug to her. "May I ask a favor?"

"You are the lady, my lady." A sullen curl pulled at her bottom lip.

I tilted my head as I studied her expression for a moment. "No, this truly is a favor, Tatin. You may tell me nay."

"Without punishment?"

"None."

"Then no." She took the jug and settled it on her hip.

I was disappointed and didn't bother to hide it. "Very well, thank you for your honesty." I glanced around to find all the other servants had fled. I would have to find another person to help me.

"My lady?" The hesitancy in Tatin's voice gave me hope.

"Yes, Tatin?"

"What was it that you wanted me to do for you?"

"I need a personal maid, someone I can trust to run errands and not speak of what she sees or is asked to do."

"Then why me?"

I smiled warmly to balance the possible sting of my words. "You don't seem to be fitting well into your role as a server. You might be better suited for a different role. I need someone willing to stand alone and apart without friends among the lower servants. My position at this time demands a certain tenacity of character in my personal servant."

She peered into my face. "You are in earnest? You aren't making me into a fool for the amusement of the others?"

"I promise to never purposefully make fun of you."

Her eyes widened. "In that case, may I change my answer, my lady?"

"You wish to accept?"

"Yes."

"Then, take the jug back to the kitchen and tell your immediate superior—"

"The cook," she supplied.

I nodded. "Tell the cook that you are now my personal servant, accountable directly and only to me."

"She won't believe me."

"If she doesn't, bring her with you when you complete your first task. I need you to find my husband's personal servant, Master Jarvin."

She nodded enthusiastically. "I know who he is."

"Good. Ask him courteously to attend me in my chamber. I wish to speak to him. Then report to me in my chamber. I will have many more tasks for you to accomplish before the evening."

"Are you going to be eating in the great hall, you and the children?"

"Now that you mention it, I don't think we shall."

"Then I shall order trays brought up." She turned and bounded a few steps, but then stopped and spun to face me again. "If that is what you wish."

The mixture of excitement and barely maintained humility on her face made me want to laugh, but that would have been cruel. I smiled instead.

"Yes, that would be perfect, Tatin."

She curtseyed quickly before leaping into a run in the direction of the kitchen.

# Chapter Sixteen

My chamber door was still locked when I reached it. I knocked. Anise readily unlocked it after she verified my identity. Her brow creased at the sight of my face.

"What is wrong?"

"We must leave at twilight." I crossed to the chest where I stashed my travel gear, but she beat me there and stopped my hand from raising the lid.

"I am not about to drag my grandson on the road again without good reason."

I closed my eyes and drew a deep breath. "I would not ask you to do it without reason. However, someone wishes to take him from you. Rolendis, that woman in the passage, is the former Lord Irvaine's widow. She carries his child and is involved in a plot to claim the title for her child instead of your son."

"How?"

"Sir Jorndar promised her the title in exchange for freeing him."

Anise turned pale. I had thought nothing would shake her.

"Sir Jorndar is here?"

I nodded and opened my mouth to ask what hold he

had on her but was stalled by a sharp knock on the door. The sound disturbed the children. Elise woke with a cry of fear. Darnay rolled to his feet, shedding his covering as he drew his wooden sword.

Anise moved to quiet the children and I answered the door.

Three surprised faces greeted me on the other side.

"You wished to speak with me?" Jarvin's features regained his usual impassive expression as though I summoned him every day, but his eyes questioned me. I couldn't read the particulars in his gaze, though.

"Yes, I do, Jarvin. Please step inside. I will be with you momentarily."

As he stepped past me into the room, the cook finally recovered her shock that I had personally opened the door.

"My lady, Tatin here has informed me that your ladyship has promoted her to personal attendant to your person."

I hadn't heard it called that before, but it sounded about right for the position I intended her to fill.

"That is true."

"She has a reputation below stairs, my lady, for being insolent."

"I have seen the evidence myself."

"She tends to forget the niceties I strive to drill into her."

"I know."

The woman peered at me. Her eyes narrowed in her wide face. "We have many more qualified girls who would be happy to serve you, my lady. I can provide someone much more suitable immediately. I am not saying she isn't a good lass, just rough. In a few years, perhaps, she might be ready, but—"

I cut her off with a slight raise of my hand.

"As I explained to Tatin before she accepted the position, she has some qualities that I value more than respectfulness, humility, or knowing her place. I will teach her the niceties she should know, but for now I will take her with her rough edges."

The cook's ruddy face broke into a wide smile. "Oh good, my lady."

"This pleases you?"

"Oh, yes, Tatin is my baby sister's youngest, my lady. She is a good one at heart, but many can't get past that prideful streak in her to see it." She nodded toward Tatin, who stood silently by turning red as a pickled beet. "I just wanted to make sure you wanted her, tongue and all."

"I do."

Tatin met my gaze with relief, and I smiled at her.

Cook curtseyed and made to return to her kitchen, but I stopped her. "Cook, if you need a replacement set of hands, please speak to Horacian. Tell him I said you can replace Tatin with a girl of your choice."

"Thank you, my lady." The woman's smile lifted her cheeks into balls. She strode off down the passage obviously intent on returning to her domain and overseeing the pending meal.

Tatin slipped past me with a murmured appreciation, her behavior far different than the bold child of before. I knew her brashness would return soon.

"What are you about, Lady Brielle?" Jarvin asked the moment the door closed.

I locked it before answering him.

"Rolendis is plotting to release Jorndar tonight. I

155

have been—" I halted when I encountered Darnay's wide gaze. I tried again. "A certain prize..." I lay my hand on my chest. "...was offered as incentive for the men of the vargar guard to assist."

"Surely not our men!" Jarvin's horror blanched his face.

"No. I warned Captain Parrian that a prison break was planned for tonight, but there is little he can do beyond what he is already doing. I certainly don't expect him to arrange a personal guard for me, Anise, and the children." A single glance at the two youngsters listening earnestly to my words made it clear that I couldn't speak of the plot against King Mendal yet. Such a secret was too grave to trust to such young ones.

"What do you intend do? How can I help?" Jarvin asked.

"If Anise is willing, I propose we all leave tonight at twilight as quietly and secretly as possible."

"I can arrange for horses to be ready, but where?"

"Is there a postern gate somewhere?"

"I haven't discovered one yet," Jarvin admitted.

Tatin waved her hand at me. "I know where you could get out. The gate is in the garden, from when the gardens served as the kennel. There is a tunnel that you can crawl through. Though I don't think you could fit through, Master Jarvin, with your limp and all."

"Don't you mind me." He frowned. "I can get out just fine on my own." He turned to me. "But what about supplies and gear? I can't go gathering up food and such without drawing some attention."

"That is where I hoped Tatin would come in handy."

The girl nearly glowed with pleasure. "I can get you food stuffs, right enough. Breads, cheeses, wine, ale, you name it, I will get it."

"I will make a list."

"No." Anise laid a hand on my arm. "I will make a list. I suspect I know more about such things than you."

"Then you will come?"

Her dark eyes scanned my face. "Aye, we will come. If Jorndar gains control of the vargar, the children and I are in just as much danger as you."

"Rolendis doesn't know you are Tomas' mother."

"But Jorndar does and he will be ruthless in his revenge."

*What did Tomas do to spark such hate?* The question burned on my tongue, but Jarvin's voice made it impossible to ask, yet.

"Will you need a wagon for the children? I am not sure I can manage one, but if necessary, we might be able to procure one on the way."

"No." Anise rested a hand on Elise's head. The thoughts behind her eyes clearly did not concentrate entirely on the current crisis. "The children can ride with the adults, Darnay with me and Elise with Lady Irvaine."

"Brielle," I said.

She looked at me and focused for the first time since I spoke of Rolendis' plans for me.

"My name is Brielle. I would be honored if you would call me by it." I waited with tense hope.

"Of course." She smiled warmly. "I will pack the children. We don't need everything we brought. Can you write?" she asked Tatin.

The girl shook her head.

"Read?"

"Some."

"Good. Jarvin?" Anise turned to Tomas' man expectantly.

"I can write the list for you."

"But I can't read well." Tatin glanced from Anise to Jarvin in confusion.

"You can memorize it; the list is to keep us organized." Anise patted Tatin's hand.

"I will teach you to read, Tatin," I assured her, "when all of this is over." Another thought gripped me. "Do you have family or a place you can go far from here, someplace safe?"

She shook her head. "Do you think he will come after me?"

"I think if he believes he can get to us through you, Jorndar will do what is necessary to get the information from you."

My mind scrambled to find an option. I didn't know many people this far from the village. The cost of growing up isolated was everyone I knew well lived in my village. Then I remembered Moriah. "You can go to Rathenridge's estate. Moriah offered me shelter. She will shelter you in my name until we return."

"You are going to return?"

"I doubt Lord Irvaine is going to let Jorndar claim Kyrenton. Without the food in the vargar's storage barns, my village, or what is left of it, will starve." I swallowed back the sob that suddenly pressed at my throat. So much changed so swiftly. *Kurios, I want to go home.*

Anise's hand squeezed my shoulder gently. "Tomas will return, Tatin. My son never forgets his responsibilities. He will do his duty and fight for the people of Kyrenton."

Taking solace in Anise's faith in Tomas, I turned my focus to packing amid the frenzy around me. Within an hour, we made our plans, packed, and ate. Anise, the children, and I all caught what sleep we could. Tatin promised to wake us in time to slip out to meet Jarvin on the other side of the garden wall.

Leaving the vargar proved disconcertingly easy. The passages were empty and the shadows thick.

Tatin led us into the garden and pointed out the hole. The top of the entrance lay four inches below the topsoil and behind a barren rosebush. I dug with my hands while Anise helped the children into their heaviest clothing to protect them on our journey. Finally, I unearthed a wooden cover. The gap beneath dropped roughly four feet down and spanned only three feet from the wall before disappearing underneath. The wooden square easily shifted when I shoved at it. It would be adequate for us to crawl through one at a time. There was no way to know whether or not the other side was clear or buried as this one had been.

I consulted Anise.

"It is there. We can each fit, but I cannot see the other end. It could be buried like this one."

"Let me try it." Darnay scrambled forward and, before I could stop him, disappeared inside the tunnel. Within moments, he emerged. Black mud caked his knees and hands. "It is clear."

Anise handed him the three packs of supplies before lifting Elise down to join him. The children moved farther into the tunnel as she climbed down to join them. She paused at the opening, waiting for me. I motioned her on before turning to Tatin.

"You are clear on what you need to do?" The covered lantern offered very little light, but I caught her nod.

"I will hide the tunnel opening and depart before your absence is discovered."

"You have the directions Master Jarvin gave you?"

She tapped her temple. "I will be fine, my lady."

I envied her confidence. Perhaps I had watched too many harvests fail, argued in vain with my cousin too many times, only to listen to village children cry themselves to sleep with hunger gnawing at their bellies. Too often I could only rage at my own inability to change the situation for the better.

*Kurios is just.* I reminded myself. *He has a purpose. Orwin will receive his due.* Although I clung to the truth, I could not muster even a small share of optimism to match Tatin's innocent buoyancy.

"I will send for you when I return."

"Thank you, my lady."

"For what?"

"For trusting me."

She waited until I crawled a few feet into the tunnel before replacing the cover. The fall of the dirt against the grating made my heart race. I hated enclosed spaces. Ever since the night I spent in the root cellar, locked in by Orwin, I avoided any place remotely resembling it. The musty stench of earth and moisture smothered me. I shuffled forward, feeling along the damp stone away from the sound of shifting dirt.

"My lady?" Anise's whispered query echoed.

"Coming."

# Chapter Seventeen

The snow appeared a few hours after the last sign of Kyrenton melted into the inky darkness behind us. Lacey flakes the size of one of my fingertips drifted through the trees. The children enjoyed the sight. Elise, who rode with me, reveled in watching them dance as they fell. She caught them on her mittens and laughed as they dusted her sleeves and the blanket wrapped about her legs.

The flakes came sporadically at first, appearing when we passed through breaks in the trees. Then the snow fell heavy, wet, and fast. Limbs above the trail began to creak beneath the burden. The occasional crack of a branch giving way in the distance disrupted the muted stillness of the waiting forest.

The tense silence broken by falling boughs kept us all on edge. But Kurios was gracious and none fell on us or in our path.

I congratulated Jarvin on his choice of mounts for our journey. The horses barely flicked an ear at the abrupt noises and the tension of their riders.

"Captain Parrian chose them for us. Retired warhorses are accustomed to the chaos of battle, this is nothing to them."

"Then, I must thank Captain Parrian and recommend him to Lord Irvaine for promotion," I commented.

"He deserves it, if his efforts succeed."

"What efforts?"

"He is organizing counter measures against whoever is going to attempt releasing Jorndar." Jarvin's mouth curled up on one side. It was the most sinister expression I had ever seen on his weathered, mild features. "He will not give in easily."

"Then we can hope that Rolendis' plot to free Jorndar will fail?"

"Hope and more, perhaps."

Elise shifted against me, adjusting her head against my shoulder. The abused muscles in my back complained.

"How long do you think we should keep moving before seeking shelter?"

Jarvin glanced back along the trail. The horses left long troughs of overturned snow through the midst of the smooth white behind us. "The snow will cover our tracks at this rate, but I doubt they will have to guess at where we are headed. The question is whether or not they will bother to follow us."

It was a question I couldn't answer. None of us could.

"I know of a hovel near here, if you wish to stop." Anise's calm voice startled me. She had not spoken since we left Kyrenton behind.

"How close?" Jarvin asked.

"How do you know of it?" I tugged at my horse's reins and waited for her to catch up. Jarvin circled back to join us.

Anise met my scrutiny in the glow of the lantern Jarvin carried. "I spent my girlhood and young adult

162

years in this forest. I know its ways very well." She pointed off into the dense brush. "The shack lies about a mile south. The turning is a bit farther along between a gnarled oak and a birch. It used to be a hermit's hovel. A one-room shack with a fireplace will be better than camping out in the open in this snow."

"They won't expect us to stop or to leave the main trail."

"I say we should rest there." I jutted my chin toward the children. "I don't like the idea of these little ones sleeping in the open."

A tree branch cracked close by. Muffled crashing preceded the heavy thud of it hitting the ground. Jarvin's horse tossed his head, and mine edged sideways a bit. Only Anise's mount placidly chewed its bit.

Jarvin frowned in the direction of the sound. "It isn't safe to stop under the trees."

"Then we are agreed." Anise nudged her horse into motion.

Jarvin and the lantern took the lead. Anise's and my mounts settled into step together.

I glanced at my mother-in-law. Her hands held the reins firmly. She sat on the horse like she and the animal were one flesh. Darnay rode behind her, head resting between her shoulders, yet she showed no sign of the pain that prodded the muscles of my back. She looked younger and acted spryer than my mother ever did. Even in my earliest memories, Mother was sick and always moved with graceful caution.

"What are you wondering, my lady?" Anise asked.

I turned my head to find her dark eyes watching me.

"Have you been raising Darnay for Tomas?"

She laughed. "Hardly. Tomas insists on doing

everything himself. He has demanded it from the beginning." She focused off into the distance. "Elanawyn was a fay creature, my lady. Wild and slightly mad, she refused to be confined, hated being married, and fought Tomas every moment of their marriage."

"Then why did he marry her?" I bit my lip. "I am sorry. I shouldn't have asked."

"I asked him that." She frowned.

"And?"

"'Because no one else will,' he said. 'Her father used me to destroy her chances of a future. He means to abandon her and I can't.'"

"I asked him if he loved her," I confessed.

"He didn't." Anise voice was barely audible.

I glanced to where Darnay's head rested against her back. His dark eyelashes feathered against the paleness of his cheeks.

"He sleeps," she assured me. "I wouldn't have said it otherwise."

We rode in silence for a ways. My back protested every step.

"You fit Tomas better."

I laughed. I couldn't help it. "You haven't even seen us together."

"I don't need to. Tomas needs a partner, an equal. When he rides off to fulfill his duty, he can count on you to take care of what he leaves behind. You are what he needs."

*But am I what he wants?* The thought annoyed me more than it should have. I knew from the beginning our marriage wasn't a love match, but still...

"What did he tell you about me?"

"Only what he thought I needed to know and nothing I didn't already know. I remember you."

I swung to face her in my surprise, startling Elise into half-wakefulness. It took me a few moments to settle her again.

"I traveled through your village a decade back. I came back to the area because my brother died and left me a small legacy, some land, a house, and a pittance of a savings. It was small, but I needed all I could get. Tomas had just entered the service of Lord Firorian then, and I didn't want to bother him for funds.

"I passed through Kyrenton after my brief encounter with Jorndar and his sire over the money. Your father left word that any healer passing through who could heal his wife would be generously compensated. So, I went to Wisenvale and attended your mother. She suffered from a barren womb and unnatural bleeding, if I recall correctly."

I nodded. Vague memories of a wiry woman with black hair, kind eyes, and a sharp tongue drifted into focus. "You recommended an herbal draft and no more attempts at pregnancy."

Anise nodded. "I suspected tumors and guessed she would last a few months. How long did she linger?"

My chest grew heavy with the memory of those months. "She lasted two years. No one told me that she was dying."

"I had hoped that the herbs helped. I am glad to hear she lasted longer than I predicted. I told your father my diagnosis. Your mother knew before I examined her."

"Then why did my father keep seeking healers?"

"Hope and love. It keeps us seeking answers after all chances have been exhausted. He didn't want her to

165

leave him."

"She didn't want to leave him." Mother wasted away before our eyes over those last few months. The fire of her personality kept her breathing the last week. Her bright eyes were the only sign of life in a body surrendering to death.

"She didn't want to leave either of you. The whole time I examined her, she spoke of you. 'My flame-haired beauty' she called you. When I told her I didn't think any more children were in her future, she feared you would pay the greatest cost."

I blinked back tears. "She and Father already knew what a louse Orwin was becoming. They brought him into our home a week after you left. In retrospect, I suspect Father was attempting to redeem him from the bad habits instilled by my aunt over the years."

"It was a commendable goal, though futile in this instance."

I agreed despite the horrible memories formed in those years. Orwin's introduction into my family forced me to grow up, face the future, and realize that my idyllic childhood would not last forever. Seeking to reform Orwin's character was the only remaining thing my father could have done to improve the future of his people. It made sense in hindsight, but had been horrible to endure.

My one comfort after Mother's passing was Loren. The memory of her laughing features after I proved once again my inability to dance made my chest ache. Would she be able to laugh after this ordeal? Would she survive? Orwin possessed a great capacity for cruelty. Loren scorned him in the past and he tended to repay offenses, real or imagined, tenfold. A sob pressed against the back of my throat.

"Is this the turning?" Jarvin waited beside a great gnarled oak. A birch grew a few feet beyond. Between them, a snow-softened gully ran south. Only visible when viewed from one angle, the path disappeared with only a slight variation in either direction.

Anise glanced at the trees. "Yes, that is it. The trail grows less clear farther along. Do you want me to take the lead?"

Jarvin handed the lantern to her. I followed and he brought up the rear.

The rest of our journey was filled with silence. I turned my attention to the forest around us seeking distraction. An owl snared a rabbit. Occasional movement hinted at life beyond our party, but nothing engaging enough to keep my thoughts from Loren. In an effort to not dwell on the dismal possibilities of her fate, I pushed my thoughts to Tomas.

He had turned out very different than I expected. After meeting Anise, I could see where he gained his strength, calm, and uncanny ability to read people. And after a childhood of having to prove his worth despite the circumstances of his birth, I understood why he worked so hard. Of course, hard work alone hadn't kept him alive on the battlefield.

Anise forged ahead, her bobbing lantern a lonely bright spot in the darkness. She was competent and capable, but I saw no indication of the unusual coordination necessary in a great warrior. Heart, yes, but balance and dexterity, no. He must have gained those from his father.

What if he died? My chest constricted involuntarily. Men died on the battlefield every day. *But not Tomas,* my heart cried. My thoughts tumbled onward despite the plea, following through on the original thought.

What would happen to me? What would happen to my village? The people of Kyrenton would fare well, perhaps, regardless of who their master was, but Wisenvale wouldn't. What would I do if Jorndar succeeded in becoming our master?

I shuddered.

What if the king died? Jorndar's plot to kill the king could plunge the whole country into another civil war. I held no illusions that Jorndar possessed the intelligence to hold the reins of power. He did not command the respect necessary for a leader. Schemes and bribery went only so far. He could not bribe a man into dying for him, let alone an army. Men needed something to believe in before they would pick up arms and fight.

Should the plot succeed, chaos would tear Rhynan apart.

No. I couldn't think that way. I hoped Kurios would not test me in that way. I lapsed into prayer, pleading for all of our sakes that Tomas would live and Jorndar would not succeed in his coup.

Just as I was pulling my mind free from its worries, the cabin appeared. Split logs, thatched roof, and chimney, it promised exactly what Anise predicted. We woke the children and handed them down to Jarvin. The movements of dismounting made me ache in ways I hadn't thought possible. I didn't realize I had groaned until Anise appeared at my side and placed a firm hand on my back.

"Relax, ease back slowly."

I obeyed as she applied pressure to my lower back.

"I have a salve that will help those muscles relax and ease the pain a bit. Tomorrow, Jarvin and I will ride with the children. Your back needs time to strengthen."

I reached for the saddlebags, but she stopped me. "Let Jarvin get them. We need to settle the children."

By the time we entered, Jarvin had a blaze going in the fireplace.

"Someone keeps this place well stocked. There was dry firewood under the back eaves. Do you visit here often, Anise?"

"I used to pass through once a year. Now more time passes between visits. I always replace the firewood I use before I leave."

Jarvin nodded before tramping back out into the snow to tend to the horses.

I silently agreed with Jarvin. The heat from the fire warmed the small room quickly. Jarvin returned with the saddlebags and we passed around blankets. There was barely room enough for all of us to lie on the dirt floor, but we managed. The children fell asleep almost the moment they lay down. Anise grew still and Jarvin began snoring. I adjusted my head on the saddlebag I used as a pillow and prayed for sleep to come swiftly. When it did, it wasn't restful.

# Chapter Eighteen

My dreams tormented me. I watched in growing horror as Tomas died time after time. By sword, crossbow, and knife, the methods grew ever more grotesque. Each time, I watched helplessly as the life flickered and died in his inky, black eyes. My heart screamed silently. I clung to his hand as it grew cold and limp. Then only the shell of his body was left. His spirit, soul, all that I truly liked about him slipped away. I was alone again.

Each dream ended the same way, with me kneeling over Tomas. I was alone and dry-eyed, unable to cry in the midst of a corpse-strewn battlefield, while Orwin's disembodied voice demanded to know how it felt to watch him die. "Does it hurt?"

I woke to the sensation of drowning. I scrambled into the sitting position, gasping for air. My heart raced. Unshed tears burned my eyes and a hard lump blocked the back of my throat. Nerves raw with the grief, I gained my feet and stumbled for the door, narrowly missing Darnay's out-flung hand on the floor above his head. In my efforts to keep my balance, I tumbled outside. The door swung closed behind me as I landed on my back in the snow.

Cold sluiced through the fabric of my tunic as the snow soaked to my skin. Yet, I couldn't bring myself to move. My breath came out in a rushing sob.

*Oh, Kurios, have mercy!*

My tears fell hot and fast, sobs ripping through me with frightening force.

Suddenly someone was there. Strong hands pulled me from the ground and arms pulled me close.

"Hush!" I recognized Jarvin's voice.

Unable to fight to be free, I let him hold me. My heart wanted Tomas. Just to touch him. Reassure myself that he was still alive.

"Let it out. It helps at times."

"No." I fought for control. "No. I know the dream is wrong."

"Dream?" He drew back, finding my face among my wild half-damp hair. "Whatever did you dream about?"

"Tomas." My breath caught. I closed my eyes against the images, but it only made them return. I opened my eyes again. "Repeatedly dying on the battlefield."

"They were only dreams." Jarvin's steady blue eyes studied mine as he held my shoulders between his palms.

"I know. But..."

"They were so real." Understanding softened his stare. He dropped his hands and stepped back. "At times I dream of the battle when I gained this." He smacked his damaged thigh. "The agony flares up so I swear the wound is ripped open and raw once again. But then dawn comes and the pain goes away." He smiled wanly. "Give it time."

I tried. Still the sense something terrible was going to happen and might have already occurred continued to

172

press me. It urged my steps and hurried every movement. By noon, my impatience with our progress annoyed even Anise.

"Do you intend to burn our meal?" She pulled the spit from my hand. "You have it too close to the fire. Burned food will not get us there any quicker." She propped the stick-speared rabbits a short distance from the fire and began rotating them slowly. "Now what is bothering you so?"

Darnay and Elise chased each other around the clearing. I watched them play, wishing for some of their innocence. Jarvin was hunting for supper.

"If I don't hurry, something terrible is going to happen to Tomas. I dreamed about him dying on the battlefield all night last night, variations on the same theme. I couldn't see the face of the man who kills him, and I couldn't stop the act. The whole time, a horrible certainty I could have prevented it all strangled me. If I'd only arrived a few moments earlier I could have prevented it all."

Beyond Anise, Darnay danced away from Elise, just beyond her grasping fingers. His taunting laughter echoed around the clearing.

"I want to get to Tomas as fast as possible."

Anise turned the spit.

"I give up!" Elise stomped over and threw herself down on the ground, showering Anise with snow. The bits that fell in the fire spit and hissed.

"Don't give up." I nudged her boot.

"He runs too fast." She pouted prettily. Her mother must have been a beauty. One glance at her features and one could see the potential in her wide eyes, narrow chin, and elegant cheekbones.

"Who says?"

"I do. I can never catch him."

"Then wait and catch him unawares."

"Win by waiting?" She screwed up her face in confusion.

I couldn't help smiling at her. "Yes. He will grow bored when you don't chase him and resort to acting foolishly to enliven the game. Another thing you could do is don't chase him as hard. Then when he slows down to taunt you, catch him."

She considered my suggestions. "I think I'll try that. Later, though. I am tired now."

Darnay tramped over and squatted on the other side of Anise. "What's to eat, grandma?"

"Rabbit."

"I thought it was Brielle's turn to cook."

"It was," I admitted before Anise explained. "Your grandma offered to help me for a bit. I can take it back now."

We transferred the spit without incident. Anise rose to her feet and brushed her skirt clean. "I will speak to Jarvin when he returns about your concerns about..." She glanced down at the children and then jutted her chin to the east.

"No, let me. I have other things I need to discuss with him." I had never mentioned the plot against the king's life. "Things I couldn't speak of before..." I nodded toward where Darnay sat. "We have many reasons to press on more quickly."

Anise lifted her eyebrows. "You will share the same with me when you get a chance."

I promised I would.

"I suspect Jarvin will agree to us pushing harder."

Anise ruffled her grandson's hair. "It will be hardest on the children, but I think we can manage it."

"What are you talking about?" Darnay demanded. His sharp eyes darted back and forth between us. "Is something wrong with Father?"

"No, Darnay." Anise smiled at him with more assurance than I would have been able to muster. "I am sure your father is just fine. Brielle is just worried about him."

"Why? She isn't his daughter."

"But she is his wife. She loves him."

"She can't." Darnay frowned. "I love him."

"We can both love him," I tried to explain.

"No." His eyes filled with tears. "He is my father, not yours."

"Calm down." Anise rubbed his arm. "All of us love your father, Darnay, just in different ways. You have to learn to share him. He is my son, Elise's uncle, and your father, but he is also Brielle's husband. She loves him too."

I was so thankful Anise explained it for me. I wasn't sure I could bring myself to say the words. I cared for Tomas. He touched me in ways that none other did, but up until now I had only applied the word love to three people in my life: Mother, Father, and Loren. Only one of them lived. I still grieved the other two.

"I don't want her to love him."

Anise lowered herself until she was face-to-face with Darnay. "She wants to love you too."

"She can't." He folded his arms. "Father and I are a family." He turned away and ran for the trees.

Anise straightened slowly as though her back hurt. "Give him time. He needs to get used to the idea."

I nodded and prayed for the right words to say when the time came.

"Best rotate that spit or the rabbit will burn and Darnay will not believe you know how to cook." Her warm smile soothed the fear that rose at the thought. "He is a child, Brielle. He will adjust."

Suddenly remembering Elise, I looked around only to find she had wandered over toward the horses. She tramped in circles, making paths in the few remaining smooth expanses of snow in the clearing.

Within minutes Darnay joined her. Together they laughed. Apparently, my intrusion into Darnay's ordered world was forgotten for now.

"Now would be a good time to tell me of those other reasons we must hurry." Anise settled at my side and adjusted her skirt.

I told her of Jorndar's men lying in wait for King Mendal.

# Chapter Nineteen

We doubled our pace, traveling farther into the evenings and waking earlier in the mornings. It still took another day's travel for the scenery to grow familiar. Since we didn't follow the main trail, we almost missed the village completely. I noted it in time and we corrected our course and pressed onward.

Mid-morning the third day, we broke through the tree line southwest of Wisenvale.

To the south spread a sea of tents. I recognized the low-lying shelters of Tomas' men among Rathenridge and Landry's regular-sized pavilions. The triple standards of Irvaine, Rathenridge, and Landry whipped in the wind.

Identical colors flew above the army arrayed along the slight rise between us and Wisenvale. I was encouraged by the restless mass of men and horses blocking our view of the village.

Without thought to my traveling companions, I heeled my horse into motion. Only as I approached the hindmost ranks did I become aware of another rider joining me. I glanced over expecting Jarvin. It was Anise. She rode alone.

"Jarvin is taking the children to the camp."

"Willingly?"

"Of course not."

We were spotted. A small stir among the ranks resulted in two mounted warriors breaking off to ride to meet us.

I slowed my mount as they approached. Anise fell back behind my left side into a place of subservience.

"This is a battlefield, not a place for women." The senior warrior's bushy dark brows gave his frown a menacing edge that didn't match the tone of his gravelly voice. He wore Rathenridge's colors of red and brown.

"Where is Lord Irvaine?"

His brows lowered even more. "Who asks?"

"Lady Irvaine and his mother, Anise Dyrease."

Sharp blue eyes scanned my face, evaluating my honesty. "You don't look like a lady, my lady."

After three days of hard travel and little time to attend to my appearance, I probably didn't. "We fled Kyrenton and the journey has been rough. Is Lord Irvaine with the army?"

"No. He meets with Lord Wisten and Baron Areyuthian in an attempt to negotiate peace. King Mendal hasn't appeared, and we are outnumbered."

Anise sucked air in through her teeth. "Areyuthian?"

"Aye."

"You know him?" I asked.

Anise avoided my gaze. "You might say that." She addressed the warrior. "Is this the first meeting between the men?"

"Aye." His puzzled frown didn't clear up anything.

I pressed again. "Where are they meeting?"

"Over there." He gestured northwest. "We have orders…"

I didn't wait for him to finish. Heeling my mount forward, I urged him toward the battle line.

"My lady!" The warrior's yelled consternation rang in my ears, but I ignored it. I had to see Irvaine. Just a glimpse to see that he lived would be enough, or at least that was what I told myself. I dispelled the lie from my thoughts as I came abreast of the forward-most ranks. Gaining horrified and annoyed glances from the men on either side, I craned my neck to gaze out over the fields.

Arrayed across the opposite rise just outside the village a host of gleaming shields caught the sunlight. Bouncing light and the glare of the snow made it difficult to estimate the number of opposing soldiers, but I guessed at least five hundred men stood at attention beneath orange and gray banners. Beyond them, I spotted the roof of Nariahna's cottage marking the edge of my home.

A wide gully of perhaps a quarter mile lay between the armies.

"My lady." The older warrior on his mount pushed abreast of the line on my left. "You should not be here."

"On the contrary, I need to be here. Where is Irvaine?"

"There, my lady." The soldier on my right pointed off to the west. A cluster of men stood beneath the shade of Whorl's Oak and beyond the last ranks of both armies. Even at this distance, I recognized Tomas' helmet and the set of his shoulders. The urgency in my chest eased slightly. He lived.

But as I calmed and turned my attention to the

others in the group, one man raised his hand and made a flippant gesture that brought dread rushing back. Orwin stood behind Tomas.

A glint of sun on a blade was the only warning of the deadly intent of Orwin's downward thrust.

A cry ripped from my throat as Tomas crumpled. My heart screamed and my vision swam as I gasped for breath.

For a single heartbeat silence reigned. Then as one, the sea of men around me heaved forward with a great roar. Horses plunged past me. Glimpses of swords raised in challenge and rage-contorted faces amid wild cries of revenge flooded by. They broke around Anise and me as though we were a boulder amidst a sea. The army rushed down into the gully only to be met halfway up the other side by the slower moving wall of Baron Areyuthian's army.

Despite the roar of battle, the rush of blood through my head, and the unreal touch of shock chilling my limbs, a small thought nagged at me. *He isn't dead.* I refused to believe what my eyes had seen, what my dreams forewarned, and what my heart feared to be true. Despite the overwhelming evidence against the possibility, I clutched at the frail hope. *Please, Kurios, let it be true.*

I tightened my grip on my horse's reins and kicked the poor beast's flank. He lunged forward, half wild. I clung to his back and fixated on reaching Tomas. Nothing else mattered. Whether I would arrive to discover him alive, dead, or dying, I belonged at his side.

The wind howled in my ears, but I could hear someone calling my name. The steady rhythm of another rider kept pace. I dared not glance back. I urged my horse even faster.

Over the horse's pumping head, I could see the group of men. Orwin now stood over Tomas. He said something to the man I assumed was Baron Areyuthian. The Baron didn't respond. His gaze fixed on the battle.

I thundered straight in among them. The hurtling body of my mount drove Orwin scrambling for safety.

Not waiting for the horse to stop, I dropped to the ground a few feet from Tomas' body. As I fell, I smacked the horse's flank to irritate it more. The gelding pounded the ground and reared, scattering soldiers before his flailing hooves. In the chaos, I ran to Tomas' side and slid to my knees in the dirt at his side.

"Tomas." The sound of his name tore at my raw throat. A sob threatened to break free, but I held it back.

His helmet covered his face. I fumbled for the strap, encountering warm skin. The heat strengthened my hope. My fingers couldn't move fast enough. An eternity passed before the leather band finally fell free. I eased the helmet off his head.

Dark hair fell free. His head lolled to the side, face toward me. He breathed. The slight stir of air moved past his lips.

He lived.

I found his left hand, pulled off the glove and sought a heartbeat in his wrist. A steady throb pulsed against my fingers. A sob of relief burst forth from my chest. I blinked back tears. No, I couldn't cry yet.

He bled, a pool of red collecting under his left shoulder. Before I could investigate further, my gaze fell on the mark darkening the left half of his face.

Someone had kicked his head after he fell. Rage at my cousin brought my head up just in time to see Anise ride up.

Regal and white with anger to match the wrath burning in my chest, she dismounted with elegant flare. She marched past the scattered men trying to calm my horse and Orwin spouting orders.

"Alonzian Areyuthian, I demand to know why you allowed this…" Anise hurled a slur at Orwin "…to lay hands on your son in such an insidious and dishonorable way."

I expected the baron to retaliate. Instead he stared at Anise, face slack with shock.

"Anise, what are you doing here?"

"What you should be doing." Anise spat in the dirt at his feet before turning to me. "Does he live?"

My overtaxed brain began to process her words. *Son?* Areyuthian was Tomas' father? But how?

"Brielle, is Tomas alive?" Anise's voice finally broke through my stuttering thoughts.

I blinked. "Yes. Yes, he lives."

Clutching the limp fingers of Tomas' hand, I stared up at the Baron.

"What do you mean 'my son'? How could he be my son?"

Ignoring Areyuthian, Anise knelt by Tomas' other side. "Has he spoken?"

"Forget the horse, fools, seize that woman." Orwin strode past the baron to jab a finger at me. "She will ruin everything."

An expression of great longsuffering passed over Baron Areyuthian's face. "No more than you have already done on your own, Lord Wisten. Please cease your yelling."

"She is a harlot and a meddling witch. She will–"

Areyuthian turned on Orwin. "Hold your tongue or I shall make you hold it."

Owin's lip curled. "You answer to me, Areyuthian, not the other way around."

Areyuthian rested his right hand on the hilt of his sword and lifted an eyebrow.

"Your king shall hear of this." Orwin finally closed his mouth with a mutinous glare.

Areyuthian turned back to us. "Now, let us begin at the beginning. Anise, how can this man be my son?"

"I doubt I need to explain the details, Alonzian. You were there for his conception." She gestured to Tomas. "He was born in the spring twenty-eight years past."

When Areyuthian turned his gaze to Tomas' face, I reached for my knife hanging from my belt. The feel of the hilt in my palm reassured me. The blade was small. It wouldn't be much of a threat to a swordsman. But still, it was something.

"Why didn't you contact me? I would have–"

"Taken him from me." Anise cut him off with eerie calm. "You were newly married. I saw your wife. She was a sweet thing. I wasn't about to drag your indiscretion out into the open and flaunt it. It would have broken her heart."

Shame and regret tugged at the baron's shoulders. He watched Anise with a strange mixture of admiration, sorrow, and genuine affection. "I could have at least given you some support. Though, from the looks of it, you did well by him on your own."

"For now, I would be content if you sent for a healer before he bleeds out."

Areyuthian signaled one of his men to approach.

"Fetch my healer."

Despite the confusion on the soldier's face, he saluted and complied.

Orwin's pudgy features turned florid with indignation. "I must protest! He is a prisoner of war! Just because this tramp claims he is your son–"

Areyuthian drew his dagger so quickly Orwin didn't even have time to slow his tongue before the tip pressed against the underside of his jaw.

"Do not speak of what you do not understand." The baron did not raise his voice, but the threat resonated all the more through his cold control. This was a man used to killing. His dark brown eyes sparked with anger.

Orwin swallowed with great care. "Should you harm me, your king will see you hanged."

"That I doubt. King Farian only agreed to this venture because he thought there was nothing to lose and everything to gain. He is not here and my men will say what I tell them to say. Who will be alive to tell your lies then?"

"I have friends in influential places."

Areyuthian laughed mirthlessly. "That I doubt. Blackmailed or manipulated fools caught in your web of lies and half-truths more like."

"Baron Storkage."

Areyuthian flinched infinitesimally. "A fool." He lowered his weapon. "Keep silent."

I turned my attention back to Tomas. He still breathed. Movement beneath his eyelids offered hope that he might wake soon. I stroked the back of his hand where it lay in mine and prayed for his recovery. It felt strange for everyone to be discussing him without his awareness. I suspected he would have words to say to his father.

Tomas' fingers tightened around mine.

The tremors of approaching horses shook the ground.

"Messenger coming, my lord," one of the soldiers cried.

"And a healer?" Areyuthian strode to see.

The soldier's reply was lost in the distant roar of the battle.

Tomas stirred with a groan. Moving his head, he winced at what must be a great throbbing pain. I remembered the sensation well from the first time I was thrown from a horse. Within moments, he was blinking up at me.

"Brielle?" He squinted up at me and then closed his eyes as though not believing what he saw. His grip on my fingers tightened painfully, yet I couldn't find my voice to tell him. All the words in my head rushed forward at once and none of them made it past my lips.

A kit bag struck the grass at my side startling me from my struggle.

"Let us see how he is." The healer's muddy boots nudged the worn satchel aside. "It looks to be on this side. Would you mind moving?"

Extracting my fingers from Tomas' grasp, I scooted out of the way despite Tomas' protest.

"Pain?"

Tomas responded promptly. "Shoulder and head. Brielle?"

"Right here." I moved to his other side and he reclaimed my hand while the healer worked at the breastplate's straps. The metal and leather came away to reveal red-stained chainmail beneath. I visually searched for a break in the links.

"It must be behind his shoulder." The healer shoved his kit out of the way. "Can you sit up, my lord?"

Tomas nodded and then cringed. "If my head allows me."

Suddenly intent, the healer prodded the deepening bruise covering half of Tomas' face. "Dizziness? Double vision? Nausea?"

"Pain enough to cause all of the above." Tomas opened his eyes only to close them again with another groan. "No double vision. My stomach has nothing to give up should I vomit, though with this head I desperately hope I don't."

"Clear speech is a good sign." The healer caught Tomas' head again. "Open your eyes. Look at me and then we will get you up. I want to look at that shoulder. How long was he out?"

"I don't know."

"He could be fine. His eye looks only swollen. Only time will tell. Okay, let us get you sitting up. Grab a hand, woman, we are going to have to pull him to sitting."

I scrambled to my feet, gripped Tomas' forearm and hauled. He came up with a grunt of pain. His face paled even more. The healer moved around behind and I knelt before Tomas. Dark eyes a bit glassy from pain scanned my features. With his face tight with pain, I couldn't guess if he was happy to see me or not.

"Where is Darnay?"

"Safe. We left him at the camp. Jarvin is seeing to him and Elise."

"We? Who else is with you? Mother?" He groaned

and tensed as the healer prodded at his shoulder.

"Can you move your arm?" the healer asked.

"Yes."

"Then I need this mail off."

We hauled the mail shirt over his head. He didn't make a sound through the whole procedure, but one glance at his ashen face afterwards made me wonder if the decision had been wise. The wound had opened up more. The healer instructed me to apply pressure. So, I was leaning into Tomas' back when Areyuthian stepped away from a conversation with an officer to confront Tomas.

"Lord Wisten has fled."

Tomas' shoulders tensed beneath my hands. "Did he take anyone with him?"

"No."

"Then I suggest finding him." Tomas lowered his head cautiously as though it might fall between his knees to the ground.

"Already done. I have three of my personal guard searching. That is all I can spare until my order to sound a retreat takes effect."

"Retreat?" Tomas stared up at Areyuthian.

"I am not about to sacrifice more lives to Lord Wisten's foolish schemes."

"Tired of him tugging your strings?"

Areyuthian's dark eyes narrowed. "My strings lay in more honorable hands than Wisten's muddy paws."

"You could have fooled me."

I jabbed Tomas in the ribs. It wouldn't do to antagonize Areyuthian. Tomas' father or not, the baron was still the enemy. All of our lives depended on his sense of honor and value of family ties. One word from him and Tomas, Anise, and I would be dead. The fate of the army beyond and the country would be inconsequential then.

"Where are the women?" I rejoiced that my voice held steady.

"Under guard in the lord's hall." Areyuthian's dark gaze turned to me. Studying my face for a few moments as though struggling to remember something just out of his grasp, a frown deepened the corners of the baron's mouth.

"Who are you?"

Just then, the healer gestured for me to move aside so he could begin stitching the gap in Tomas' shoulder.

I stood. It felt better to be on my feet when facing an uncertain situation. Still, Areyuthian towered over me, his whole body tightening as he waited for my answer.

I lifted my chin and met his suspicion with my only viable weapon, truth. "I am Brielle Solarius, daughter of Tyranen Solarius, late Lord of Wisten."

"My wife," Tomas added without lifting his head.

"And Orwin–Lord Wisten's cousin."

"Fire!" A distant cry of alarm and a blast of a horn sounding the ordered retreat cut through the remaining chaos of battle.

Still, Areyuthian's gaze didn't waver from my face. I dare not drop mine. Instead, I watched as the depths of Orwin's deception dawned on the baron's face. The realization became rage.

He cursed Orwin, the situation, his deity, and a great many other things.

Once he regained control, he began acting. He summoned his men with a wave of one hand before ordering his forces to move out.

I looked east. Smoke billowed black into the clear blue of the cloudless afternoon sky. The village was on fire. I could easily guess who had set it. Orwin. In childish revenge he sought to destroy what he could not possess. My heart grieved despite my mind's resignation. Moisture leaked down my cheeks.

"Urarge!"

The healer jumped. "My lord?"

"Get to the battlefield. Pluck the wounded from the mud. I want no man left behind: alive or dead. No reason to return. We shall shake this country's soil from our feet. Ryhnan is a cursed place. I'll show King Farian the cost of his grasping foolishness—pointless death."

# Chapter Twenty

The healer handed me the linen for a fresh bandage later. "Keep the area clean and he should heal just fine. No using the arm, mind."

Tomas nodded, but didn't otherwise acknowledge the healer's words.

"Good luck." Then he plucked his kit from the ground and mounted his horse. Within a few moments, he was galloping off toward the battlefield.

"Help me up."

Tomas offered me his good arm, which I grabbed and hauled. He gained his feet with a half yell, and clamped his good arm to his ribs.

"Should I call the healer back?" I checked the bandage on his shoulder beneath the shredded remains of his tunic.

"Nothing he can do for a cracked rib."

A wave of anger at Orwin washed over me. Only he would be dishonorable enough to beat an unarmed, fallen foe. If he hadn't been out of my reach, I would have shown him exactly what I thought of his low behavior.

"My lord!" Rathenridge approached with a company of ten mounted soldiers. They careened to a halt in a spray of slush and mud. "The enemy is retreating, should we pursue them?"

Rathenridge's eyes widened when he spotted me. He lifted an eyebrow, but otherwise didn't acknowledge my presence. The soldiers with him were less discreet. One of them even leaned over to speak with the man next to him.

"No." Tomas tried to square his shoulders with authority, but only managed to straighten up. "See to putting out the fire and tending the wounded. Areyuthian no longer has a quarrel with us. Also form a search party. Lord Orwin is loose and I wish to have him found before Areyuthian finds him."

"Yes, my lord." Rathenridge nodded to three of the men with him. They immediately broke off and rode back in the direction of the battlefield.

"Where is my mother?"

"In the middle of an argument with Landry last I saw her." Rathenridge signaled the soldiers. They disbursed, forming a perimeter around us. "Do you need your horse?"

Tomas grimaced. "I doubt that would be wise at the moment. Orwin worked me over pretty well." He reached for his helmet, but I intercepted his awkward movement by picking it up myself. "How did my mother get down there so quickly?"

"Grabbed a horse from someone and rode. She tore into our group and demanded Landry take men up to meet you. He took exception to her orders. They were still yelling things at each other when I left." Rathenridge dismounted.

Tomas moved forward, placing each step with care. I gave him space. I didn't want to insult his pride by offering to help.

"Orwin is the one I would prefer to yell at right now." Rathenridge commented as he fell into step with me. "For a while there, we all thought he had killed Tomas."

"A bit more force and accuracy and he would have." I was never so thankful for my cousin's incompetence.

Tomas stopped and turned to face us. "What are you two talking about?"

"Your recent scrape with death. What else would we have to discuss? You shouldn't have trusted Orwin."

Tomas' features tightened even more. His eyes glinted in anger. "I didn't. It was more a matter of trusting Areyuthian to be honorable. We were close to reaching an agreement. Baron Areyuthian extended his hand. Orwin attacked when I reached for Areyuthian's hand. He caught me by surprise. I still don't know how he got the knife beneath the mail, but once he did he twisted it, driving me down. Once I was there, he started beating me. Next thing I know, I am looking up into my wife's face." He frowned at me. "How did you get here? I left you in Kyrenton."

"Rolendis, with the help of some of her husband's men-at-arms, was plotting to breakout Jorndar. I discovered their plot by accident the afternoon before they put it in motion. I spoke to Captain Parrian but there wasn't much more he could do than what he already was doing. Or at least that was what he said. But Jarvin mentioned plans after he spoke with him later." My stomach twisted in a renewed wave of dread. Now that I was reiterating it all, it sounded as though I panicked and ran when it wasn't necessary.

"You brought Darnay and Elise with you, right?"

I nodded. "They are in the camp with Jarvin."

"And mother?"

"I had to convince her before she would allow me to move Darnay again."

Tomas stepped closer. I could feel his gaze on my face but I couldn't bear to meet it.

"She only came because if Jorndar escaped none of them would be safe."

"Brielle."

The sound of his voice so close resonated through me. I wanted to look up into his face, but I feared what I would see. So, I stumbled on with my telling.

"Rolendis promised me as incentive to some of the conspirators. I panicked."

"It doesn't sound like it." His hand touched my hair.

"No, I did. I decided that I wasn't going to sit around and wait for them to use me that way. After speaking with Parrian, I knew I couldn't fight them. So, I ran."

"So, Kyrenton might be under Jorndar's control."

I nodded in shame. "And his men, the ones we have been wondering about, are lying in wait for King Mendal."

Rathenridge tensed beside me. "Why didn't you say so earlier?"

His words so mimicked the ones in my head, I cringed.

"Hush, Aiden." A weary note underlined Tomas' voice. "Go and gather the men. We will ride south as soon as the fire is under control."

Rathenridge swung onto his horse.

"Bring back a horse for me. It looks like I am going to be riding after all."

Rathenridge acknowledged the request with a curt

nod. Then he set heels to his horse's flanks and they sprang off at a gallop. We watched him go together.

"He means well." Tomas turned and caught my shoulder. Pulling me around to face him, he caught my gaze with his. "Now what have you not told me?" Half-stranger and half-friend, he studied my face, reading my emotions and giving nothing in return.

"Have you found Loren?"

"No, and I am not letting you change the subject. What pushed you to recklessly barge through a battlefield to find me? An action I forbid you from ever repeating. One stray arrow, a wild swing, and I could have lost you." His eyes darkened even more.

"I feared if I didn't reach you, you would die. I know it is irrational. But I couldn't banish the thought after dreaming about it two nights past."

His hand lifted to touch my cheek. "Promise me you will send someone else next time. I have lost one wife. I don't wish to lose another."

I nodded my agreement.

"Thank you." He kissed me. Quick but powerful, it left me wanting much more. But I had to be satisfied with the mirrored regret in his eyes. The distant sound of approaching horses signaled the end of our time together.

"I'll return. When I do, we'll deal with the issue of Jorndar. We will leave a remnant to organize things here." He swung up into the saddle of the offered horse with a great groan.

"After stopping in the camp for supplies, I'll speak to Darnay. I plan on being gone before you return from the village."

The seven horsemen who had been guarding us

moved to follow him, but he stopped them. "No, guard Lady Irvaine. I lay her safety at your feet. I hold you each personally responsible for her wellbeing. Understood?"

"Yes, my lord," they replied.

He turned his horse toward the south and the camp. Then as though by a signal I couldn't see, the whole company moved forward at once, falling into ranks without fanfare of any kind. Before I knew it, I and my personal guard were left alone in a field of mud and slush beneath the afternoon sun.

My stomach growled. My formerly gray skirt was now brown with mud and heavy as I turned to meet my new companions.

"Which of you is the man in command?" I asked.

They exchanged glances. Not one of them more than five summers older than me, they looked impressive sitting tall and high on their elegant horses.

"Captain Eirianware at your command, my lady." He bowed slightly.

"Captain, I need to get to the village immediately and I seem to have misplaced my horse."

"You may ride behind me, my lady, if that isn't too…"

I waved his objection away. "I hope you don't mind my dirty boots, Captain."

"If you would give me your hand, my lady."

Within moments I was astride his horse, clinging to his waist, and riding swiftly toward the ominous cloud hanging over Wisenvale.

"Where would you like us to stop, my lady?" he asked as we approached the first cottage.

"The Lord's hall."

We slowed to a walk. I wished we could've passed the devastation more quickly. Broken doors, forced in from the outside, and shutters hanging by single hinges spoke clearly about the events of the past week. I tensed for the worst as we entered the village square.

Only a short time before, Tomas and I had exchanged our vows here. Now broken furniture, bedding, and broken barrels from my father's wine cellar were piled in obvious preparation for a bonfire.

"Brielle!" Loren's voice pulled my attention across the square. There, with the still smoking remains of the lord's hall looming behind them, was a sea of familiar faces.

I swung down to the ground before my escort had come to a complete halt. Hurtling an overturned bench and circumventing a broken chair, I raced the distance to her.

Soot stained and sweat streaked, she began to cry, smiling through her tears. We clung to each other. The crowd of women encircled us in a dancing, laughing throng, giddy in their relief. I hugged Loren and wept, finally releasing all the pent up emotion of the past few days. Tomas lived, Baron Areyuthian retreated, and Loren could still smile. *Thank you, Kurios.*

"Did Orwin touch you?" I pulled back to scan her tear-streaked face.

"No. The baron locked us in the lord's hall and ordered none of the men to touch us on pain of death. He and Orwin had a dreadful row about it right in front of us. Orwin wouldn't accept the terms until the baron leveled a crossbow at his head and ordered him to back down."

"So you are safe?"

"Safe and hungry." Loren smiled wanly. "The baron's chivalry didn't extend to feeding us more than starving rations. Not that we weren't already used to that."

"We were well treated, my lady." One of oldest women, Granny Toren, edged closer. "As I was telling the young ones, they should praise the Kurios. The border raids during the last coup left multiple women pregnant, many of them young things without means of support. This time we were blessed in our oppressor. Compared to them, Baron Areyuthian was a gentleman. They were no more than drunk ruffians then."

I bit back my sudden thought that Areyuthian probably participated in those border raids. My husband might count his life from one of them.

"My lady." I turned at the male voice. It sounded partially familiar. A stillness fell over the crowd and the women parted to reveal a man kneeling in their midst. He hid his face and offered his hands in the classic position of supplication. "Have mercy."

"Rise."

Captain Eirianware pressed through the subdued women to join me. He made a comfortingly solid presence at my back. I was grateful for his support when I recognized the man.

"Brevand."

"Aye, my lady."

Despite his contrite appearance, anger rose as I remembered exactly what he was asking forgiveness for.

"I was told you betrayed my village, escorting the enemy into the heart of my home. Is the claim true?"

He lowered his head, hiding his face again so that I couldn't see his eyes. I suppressed a frown.

"Yes." His tone was clear and even, but it bothered me that he wouldn't look up.

"And now you have the gall to request mercy?"

Loren touched my arm. "He let us out before the fire killed us, Brielle."

A murmuring of assent passed through the crowd. I glanced around at their faces. Yarni with her daughter pressing against her side nodded. Durana watched Brevand with good will, a rare event. She usually regarded any man other than her late husband with wariness. Finally, I turned to Loren.

She pled for leniency. "Despite his part in our capture, he has been kind to us, offering what help he could in the circumstances."

I suspected he had played both sides of the fence until it was clear which side would win, but I couldn't point that out to Loren. Her eyes begged for me to show mercy.

"His betrayal of Lord Irvaine is a far greater offense than his treachery against us." I turned back to Brevand to find he had finally lifted his head. He eyed me dispassionately from behind a contrite expression. My stomach turned. I prayed he wouldn't be able to fool Tomas with the mask. "Lord Irvaine can hear his case when he returns."

"What do you wish done with him until then, my lady?" Captain Eirianware asked.

"See he gets a taste of the women's captivity until then."

I caught the captain's signal to his men out of the corner of my eye. The six converged on Brevand with surprising speed. Within a few movements, he was bound and gagged.

I selected one of the women. "Yarni, would you be kind enough to point out the best place to store this man? We will set about making sure he can't run until Lord Irvaine gets here."

Yarni nodded and led two of the men off in the direction of the nearest cottage. They dragged Brevand between them.

I strode toward the lord's hall, Loren in tow. Many of the women came with us. A few left to see to their children or set their homes to rights now that the invaders were gone.

The smoke still rose from my childhood home, eroding my hope of recovering even a small measure of my family's heirlooms. My mother's chest full of her prized gowns, linens, and jewelry weighed the most heavily on my mind.

The lord's hall stood, barely. Stone walls stripped of all wooden adornment supported a blackened skeleton of beams, half broken, against a sky still marred by smoke. It wouldn't be safe to walk through the ruins yet, but I could see that hope for recovery was slim.

I stood as close to the doorway as I could, the heat of the recent flames still radiating from the stone, and tried to grasp the finality of the ended chapter. My favorite tangible connections to my past were gone. The special scent of my mother's rose and lilac perfume mixing with the smell of sun-warmed linen were now only a memory consumed in the stench of scorched stone and charred wood. I could no longer bring out her perfume bottle and revel in reminiscences of her laughter, her bright eyes, or the feel of her arms around me. Only time would reveal if her jewelry escaped the blaze, but the memories entangled with the cold metal and stone were not as precious as those stolen golden moments of just Mother and me. Orwin, in his typical way, burned away the most precious of my possessions, leaving the less valuable.

I stepped back away from the wreckage, struggling to control the mixture of anger and grief tearing through me.

"At least the barns survived." Loren's out-flung hand indicated the low structures just visible through the smoke.

I was not in the mood for counting our blessings. Still, I nodded. "Come, let us assess the rest of the damage." I led the way off toward the nearest cottage.

Following my lead, the women set to work, picking up debris.

# Chapter Twenty-One

I threw my anger into my work. In a few days we cleared out five cottages, lugging out broken furniture, sweeping floors, and cleaning hearths. The women and I labored tirelessly to reclaim a small measure of the life the invaders stole. Red-gold sunlight cast a long patch of light through the western facing door of my current project when I heard someone say my name. The shadow of a woman's head fell across the moisture-slick stones beneath my brush.

"Brielle?"

I pushed up onto my knees and squinted into the light. It was Anise.

"What are you doing?"

"Cleaning."

I couldn't see her frown, but I could sense it in the tilt of her head.

"Why?"

"I cannot hunt down my cousin and hurt him the way he has hurt me and those I love. Durana cares for four children. One is just learning to crawl. She needs a clean floor. So, I am scrubbing it for her."

"I saw the lord's hall."

"Then you know that nothing survived."

"Not completely true. Some of the men pulled out some furniture from the bedchamber. The linens didn't escape, but some jewelry and an ornamental sword were spared."

I locked my jaw so my chin wouldn't tremble. "At least it is something." My voice quavered.

"I am sorry."

Her kindness was too much. A sob escaped. Like a breached dam, the flood followed. Before I could gasp for breath, Anise was there. Strong arms and the scent of lemon surrounded me. I stopped fighting the tears and let them flow. She offered no platitudes and no excuses, just the warm assurance I wasn't alone.

My tears dried up at last. She offered me a clean, dry rag and moved back to give me space to use it. "We received word Tomas is on his way back." She picked up my scrub brush and the bucket of dirty water. "He met up with King Mendal. Apparently Jorndar's men were discovered before they could attack. Lord Dentin extracted the truth from them and they are all coming to deal with Jorndar."

"When will they get here?"

"Tomorrow. Mendal travels slowly these days."

I puzzled over her reply, but she continued before I could ask for more details.

"Tomas sent word that Mendal and Dentin want to meet you. I wouldn't be surprised if Tomas has been speaking of you."

I would've been astounded if he had. If so, what had he said? I ran at the first testing of my strength and courage. Tomas wouldn't have run.

"We will need to find you better clothing."

I surveyed the ruined mess of cloth that was once a

tunic, surcoat, and leggings. The formerly heather gray wool hung stiff with mud and grime and heavy with water. It was salvageable, possibly, but not in time for me to wear the next morning.

"I have worn everything I brought. The other clothes are not as dirty as this one, but still none are fancy enough to wear before a king. I packed for the road not a court event." I did not mention that I didn't own anything fine enough even if I carried my whole wardrobe with me. "My wedding dress and all of my mother's clothing burned." Moisture flooded my eyes, but I refused to cry again. They were only things. I would learn to live without them.

"Surely some of the villagers still have some finery. We shall see if we can find some for you to borrow."

I didn't share her optimism, but I felt obligated to try for Tomas' sake. I didn't want to let him down again.

Much to my surprise, the women had some treasures to share. Loren produced a dress she intended for my birthing day. Deep green wool trimmed at the neck and wrists in dark plum-colored purple, it was elegant in its simplicity. Only the hem remained unfinished, a task easily completed in the time allowed. Granny Toren produced combs for my hair, remnants from her wedding well over half a century past. Yarni offered a girdle of green wool so dark it was almost black. She had been trying for a spring green and mixed the dye wrong. We agreed that we could hide my sturdy shoes beneath the skirt of the dress.

By the time we gathered the selection, the sun hung low in the sky and it was time for the evening meal. The village women spread a lean table, but they made sure there was some for everyone. Anise had Jarvin bring the children from the camp. Darnay avoided me, but Elise offered me a warm hug before running off to play with the girls gathering around the stacks of broken furniture. As far as I could see, they were rearranging it into pretend houses for play.

Despite my protests that sleeping would bring my hair's wild side out again, Anise and Loren insisted I bathe right before bed. They predicted I would sleep late and not have time for much beyond eating and dressing before meeting the king the next morning.

"Now to see to those hands." Anise rummaged through the satchel she brought from the camp.

I surveyed my hands in dismay. Chapped and red from work, one of my knuckles was bleeding.

Anise handed me a salve.

"When you emerge from the bath, slather it on and then don't touch anything."

She led me into the smallest of the newly cleaned cottages. After the scalding bath and vigorous scrub down from Anise, Loren combed the gobs of knots from my hair. I fell asleep before the fire while she twisted my damp curls into tight braids in an effort to keep them tame for the morning.

My anxiety followed me into sleep. I dreamed of meeting the king all night. Rather, I dreamed of preparing for the meeting with the king. First my hair fell out, then my teeth. My dress ripped. I tripped walking across the battlefield to meet them. When I finally arrived, Mendal was an ugly hag, Dentin leered like the guard outside the armory, and Tomas was nowhere to be seen. When I asked about him, Mendal waved away a fly and said, "I had him executed for treason. Now we can marry you off again." I screamed.

He laughed, and Dentin reached for his sword to run me through.

I awoke cold and tense. Loren was shoving my shoulder.

"You were screaming in your sleep." She peered into my face. "Are you well?"

My neck felt like a bowstring and my shoulders ached as though I was lifting a boulder instead of my hand. Forcing myself to my feet, I began working out the stiffness.

"I dreamed badly. I will be fine."

"Good." She smiled encouragement. "We need to get you into your dress and start on your hair. We only have a few hours before your honor guard returns for you."

"So soon?" I checked the window. Overcast skies blocked the sun.

"King Mendal arrived early. His camp is growing larger than Irvaine's. Every time we think they have raised the last tent, the crew lugs out a new bundle of canvas and starts driving stakes into the ground. At this rate we will have no untouched land to plant next spring. We will have to prepare all the fields from scratch."

"At least you will be planting in Ryhnan in relative freedom and not under a western baron's oppressive eye." I couldn't turn my head to the left without shooting pain. I quit trying.

"True." She dragged a bench into the middle of the room and arranged my dress across it along with a clean chemise and the girdle.

"Have you seen Irvaine?" I rose, taking the blanket with me, but it couldn't shield my stocking-covered feet from the winter chill of the hearth stones. It cut through to my skin almost immediately.

"No word from anyone about anything beyond the presentation."

I didn't know enough to guess if this was normal or abnormal for wives being presented to the king for the first time. Or, it might have simply been a matter of ability. Tomas might be overwhelmed with other responsibilities. My duty was to stand alone if necessary. And stand I would.

I dressed quickly. Loren assisted with the buttons and seeing to the fall of the girdle and skirt.

"Lovely," Anise proclaimed when she bustled in as we finished putting on my heavy shoes without wrinkling the skirt. "Let me see to that hair and we will make Tomas proud."

As I predicted, curls escaped the braids in all directions. Thankfully Anise didn't have an elaborate style in mind. She combed and then twisted it all into a loose braid that fell to my waist like a long red cord and tied the end with a leather thong. Then she brought out my belt with my knife still attached. When she moved to put it about my hips, I stopped her.

"Won't it hurt the appearance we are seeking?"

"No, quite the opposite." She pulled the leather through the buckle, caught it on the tongue and tucked the excess into the belt so it didn't hang down awkwardly. "You are a warrior woman from a village of strong women. You are not seeking the king's protection as a maiden to be bargained with and sold as a political pawn. You come to the king as one who will swear an oath and stand at your husband's side. He needs to see you can do your part to support his reign."

"But to carry a blade into the king's presence?" I searched her face. To me, it seemed as though to do so would be asking to be cut down.

"The men carry much more dangerous weapons and skills with them." Seeing that my concern did not lessen, she offered a compromise. "Glance around, if the men are all unarmed, offer your knife as a show of fealty. The king should accept such a gesture."

A thump on the door ended the conversation.

"It is time." Anise hugged me briefly. "You will do well."

I didn't share her confidence, but I smiled my thanks all the same.

Loren's hug lasted longer. She pulled my cloak around my shoulders. As the heavy layers settled, I was reminded of the first time Tomas threw it about me.

I stepped out into the cold.

"My lady." Captain Eirianware greeted me with a bow. His six men were still with him. They all appeared well rested despite the rotating shifts they must have taken outside my door.

"Have you spoken to Lord Irvaine?"

Although puzzled at the question, Eirianware answered glibly enough. "Not since you have, my lady. I have heard that he arrived with the king, but other than that, I have heard nothing."

I nodded. It was well known where I slept. I sent word to Jarvin the first night. Anise had been back and forth from the camp to the village since Tomas' departure. If he sought me, he would have found me.

"So, which way are we walking?"

Eirianware led me to the southern edge of the village. The battlefield, still a mess of mud and frozen slush, spread across the gully between the village and the southern-most fields, which were occupied by Irvaine's camp. The banners of Rathenridge and Landry flapped in the wind beneath Irvaine's emblem of a golden hart on a field of green.

The king's camp lay sprawled across the eastern-most fields. A great flag on a pole twice the height of a man marked the edge of the camp. A hawk, wings unfurled and claws spread, shown red on a field of caramel brown. Gilt highlighted the bird's claws and crazed eyes. The sight of the banner was enough to slow my steps.

"Where am I to present myself?" I asked Eirianware.

"Outside the king's pavilion. I was told we would be met at the edge of camp."

As he spoke, I spotted a group of men lingering beneath the crimson bird. As we approached, they fell into formation, a tall but unassuming man at their head. He was the man who stepped forward to greet us.

"Lady Irvaine, I presume." He bowed with the practiced air of a man who performed the movement often. As he straightened, we locked eyes.

"Lord Dentin, I presume."

"Why do you assume I am he?"

"You have the look of a man more accustomed to the background than the focus of attention. Also, you wear the colors of Dentin's household."

His eyebrows rose in what I hoped was appreciation. "Tomas said you were bright, but he didn't mention observant."

A burst of warmth flooded my chest. Still, I remained outwardly reserved. Tomas indicated Lord Dentin could be a valuable ally or a dangerous friend.

Considering the complicated depths of my husband, I expected the same of his friends.

"I don't know whether to be afraid or flattered."

"Why?" He smiled, but his eyes narrowed.

"The king sent the man responsible for the security of the realm to escort me to my presentation. Does he think I intend to assassinate him?"

"You are armed." His eyebrows rose and his eyes challenged me, but the corners of his mouth lifted slightly.

"It is intended to be for show. You may take it." I offered the knife, but Dentin made no move to accept it.

"Keep it. Tomas sent me."

I returned the dagger to its sheath. "Is he afraid I will assassinate the king?"

Dentin laughed. "Hardly. He thought you would need support, a conclusion I do not share."

"So you are here as a friend?"

"In part." He offered his left arm to me.

"The other part?" I laid my hand upon his forearm.

"Parts, my lady. First and foremost, I am a loyal subject of the king." He led the way through the tent city. Our men fell into formation behind us like the train of a regal gown.

"I am as well."

"So, treason does not run in the family?"

I tensed. "I am not my cousin, my lord. We are nothing alike."

He turned to scan my face with a care. I met his scrutiny with a steady regard. His brown eyes were pleasantly shaped. He had even features, a strong jaw, well-proportioned nose, and a pleasing smile hidden

211

behind the tension of the moment. I returned my gaze to his eyes. I had nothing to hide from this man.

"The king sent you, didn't he?"

He focused straight ahead. "No, he didn't, but I wouldn't be much of a defender of the realm if I didn't take advantage of the opportunity allotted me."

"So, you are searching for an assassin?"

"Always."

"How do you live in constant vigilance?"

"Are you suggesting I shouldn't?" He turned his head and regarded me for an instant out of the corner of his eye. "I haven't decided whether or not to trust you yet."

"Why would I want to kill him?"

"He accepted you as part of your cousin's loyalty demonstration."

"My cousin sold me to save his life. I have much more reason to hate Orwin than the king."

"He gave you to Tomas."

The awarding of my life into Tomas' hands as though I was a possession still irritated my pride, but I had to admit the truth. "Tomas has been a kind and dutiful husband, better than any I would find on my own."

"I think it is much more than duty that drives Tomas' actions. He is always the dutiful man, sometimes to a fault."

Thinking of Rolendis and Jorndar, I had to agree. "His best attribute and his worst."

"Not his best. Once he loves, he loves for life."

Before I could ask him what he meant, we stepped into an open space among the tents and the opportunity for speaking passed. A great space spread before us. Contrasting the mud and slush underfoot, all the men awaiting us stood about in court dress.

Gold, scarlet, and brown were the basis of every man's clothing except for three. Tomas, Rathenridge, and Landry stood out in their house colors. It took me a moment to locate the king in the similarly dressed men. Then I realized only one man sat.

# Chapter Twenty-Two

Reclining on a wooden chair against multiple cushions, King Mendal's chin rose infinitesimally as my gaze fell upon him. His attitude clearly indicated I should react, but I was at a loss as to how. His clothing, though perhaps slightly more trimmed, didn't stand out as unusually lovely or horrible. In my opinion, his features inspired neither admiration nor disgust. Then my gaze fell to the cane leaning against his chair. Was he sensitive about a limp? *Help me*, I prayed desperately as Dentin led me forward .

The king waved at Dentin.

"Your majesty." Dentin turned to me and stepped back. "I am honored to present Brielle Dyrease, Lady of Irvaine and Wisenvale." I didn't get a chance to glance at Dentin's face, but judging by his voice, anyone would be convinced he was deeply honored. I wished I knew for sure. Dentin struck me as a man I would like to impress.

Stepping forward, I dropped into one of my best curtseys. My mother would have been proud.

The king motioned for me to rise. "So, Lady Irvaine, what do you have to say in defense of your cousin?"

Fear constricted my chest. Despite the urge to look to Tomas for support, I couldn't implicate him in whatever the king considered me guilty of doing. "I am not my cousin, your majesty. There is no love lost between us to urge my tongue on his behalf."

"And why would that be? Does not similar blood flow through both of your veins?"

"We share a grandsire not values, your majesty. I am a loyal citizen of Rhynan, as was my father before me."

Mendal's frown deepened. "Yet, your father fostered Lord Wisten, taking him into his home and protection."

"It was an effort to curb his rebellious spirit, your majesty."

Mendal scoffed. "He failed."

"Not for lack of effort, sire. No one can change another's heart through determination. My father worked to touch my cousin's heart until the day he died."

"I have difficulty believing that."

"Your Majesty, if I may ask, why am I being judged by my cousin's actions and not by my own?"

The men around the king tensed and the king's frown deepened. Panic set in as I realized what I had done. Questioning the king tended to lead to a quick and messy end. By shear will I kept my head up and my gaze steady. No matter how strongly I wished to glance toward Tomas, I didn't. Instead, I kept my gaze on the king's face.

Then support came.

"She has a point," Lord Dentin said loudly.

"Be still," the king muttered.

"My lord–" The welcome sound of Tomas' voice cut off at the abrupt gesture of the king's hand.

"I told you to be silent, Irvaine. I will not let you harbor a viper in your nest even if you have sworn to protect her."

"Even you cannot undo the wedding vows, my king." Dentin passed behind me to stand at my left shoulder. "You demanded the oath of him. He swore it and carried it out...to the letter."

"Are you saying I will have to accept her?" Mendal grabbed the cane and struggled to his feet. "Are you saying that I, the sovereign of Rhynan, will have to settle with her being bound by her husband's oath?"

"If you fear her husband's oath will not bind her, sire, demand she swear the oath herself."

I wanted to blurt out my willingness to take the oath, but Dentin gripped the back of my arm. Out of the corner of my eye, I saw Tomas shake his head. I clamped my lips closed.

Dentin dropped his hand and resumed speaking. "Then, should the traitor's words be proven true and she be found guilty, you can condemn her to a traitor's death as a warning for other women who would fall back on their gender for mercy."

"Very well." The king sat again. "Bring in the officiate to record her oath taking."

Movement to the left drew everyone's focus including the king. I took advantage of the distraction to look at Tomas. He stood to the king's right, a place of honor despite the accusations against me. He met my gaze for a moment and nodded his approval before turning to observe the appearance of the officiate.

A familiar figure shuffled into the meeting space. His balding head had manifested no more hair than the last time I had seen him. A few long wisps of hair contorted

217

in the wind that cracked the banners overhead.

Dentin led me forward to the edge of the rug beneath the king's chair. Using his hand for support, I knelt.

The officiate grunted. "Lady Irvaine, offer your hands palms upward to his majesty."

I complied. King Mendal leaned forward in his chair, pulled off his gloves, and gripped the insides of my wrists with cold fingers. I looked up into his eyes. Intensely blue, they searched my gaze as though hoping to read my unfaithfulness in the depths of my eyes.

"I accept your homage." Then he released my hands as though I was dirty and eased back into his chair. Twitches of pain crossed his face as he moved. I wondered at the nature and root of his infirmity.

"Now place your hands on the holy book and repeat after me," the officiate prompted.

"I promise on soul I will be faithful to Mendal Advicatius Firorian, King of Rhynan, never cause him harm, and observe my homage to him completely above all other persons in good faith and without deceit."

Once I said the words, Dentin helped me to my feet and guided me back to my place.

A man to the king's left rose and after bowing to the king, took a position between the king and myself. He struck a pose meant to inspire admiration. With his pot belly and straining, gilded tunic, he fell short.

"Bring in the prisoner."

I looked expecting to see Orwin. Instead Tyront was dragged through the muck and thrown to the ground at my feet.

He came up spitting and swearing. I backed away, instinctively reaching for my knife only to find it gone.

"Thought you wouldn't get caught, witch?"

"Be silent before your sovereign."

"I am no subject of yours." Tyront laughed. A slightly crazed light glinted in his eye. "I no longer serve you, Jester." He shuffled his feet in a mad dance. "Neither does she." He pointed to me. "We are puppets on Master Orwin's strings. Simply puppets doing our master's bidding. Bow to the king, missy, he is about to have a hissy." He bowed to the king with great fanfare and beckoned for me to do likewise. "Bow to his chief monkey." He dipped to Lord Dentin.

"Cease your shenanigans, fool." One of the other men stepped forward as though to suppress Tyront.

"Why? I am condemned if I do and condemned if I don't." He pulled a face at the king. "At least I shall enjoy the trip to the gallows."

"What of your master?" The new speaker asked.

"Orwin, pardon, Lord Wisten, left me to take the fall for him. Always the plotter our Orwin, eh, Bri?"

"I am not Bri." I responded with instinct born of habit. "My friends call me Brielle."

"And your family call you Bri," Tyront supplied in a stage whisper.

"They do not." There was no way to prove it.

"Enough of this farce." The king struck his cane against the leg of his chair. The crack brought even Tyront up short. "I grow tired of this man's blathering. Remove him."

The two who brought him in, dragged him out again.

"How long until we locate Lord Wisten?" The king addressed the heavyset man to his left.

"Four to five days at most, sire. He has few places to hide in this part of the country."

"Double your efforts. In the meantime, Irvaine?"

Tomas stepped forward and bowed deeply.

"Rise. I entrust Lady Irvaine into your care."

"I accept." Tomas bowed again, but the king waved him away.

"You are all dismissed." Grabbing his cane, he pushed himself to his feet. With great effort, he hobbled into the tent immediately behind his chair.

The moment the last of his attendants passed between the canvas flaps, the court flew into action. Men walked every which way. Two of them intercepted Tomas on his way to where I stood. I would have met him halfway, but Dentin's grip on my elbow stopped me.

"It is wiser to wait, my lady."

So, I waited.

When the last man released Tomas, he crossed to us, meeting Dentin's gaze first. "Meet you in a quarter hour in my tent."

Dentin nodded and, after a truncated bow to me, strode off to the left with purpose.

I opened my mouth to ask Tomas what was going on, but he stalled my request with a kiss. One hand dove into my hair and supported the nape of my neck while his other arm pulled me against him. My senses flooded. I fell under the twofold spell of his touch and the smell of him. I could barely stand when he finally released me. Thankfully, he didn't retreat very far. Resting his forehead against the top of my head, he sucked in a deep shuddering breath.

"Don't speak here." He smoothed a curl back behind my ear. The dark depths of his eyes were troubled. "I have missed you."

A stranger wearing the king's livery brought Tomas' horse. Tomas mounted without comment and pulled me up behind him. He kneed the horse into motion immediately. I had to clutch at him to avoid falling off.

The journey from the king's camp to Tomas' was long enough for the euphoria of his kiss to dissipate. I began to wonder if he had truly meant what he said about missing me or if the whole wasn't just a pretense to warn me not to speak.

As we slowed to pass among the tents, I noted activity. It seemed a heightened level for the afternoon. Then one of the tents came down as we approached and men began packing it up.

"We are moving out?"

Tomas gripped and squeezed my hand gently but didn't respond. I interpreted it as a signal to stop talking and obeyed.

Finally he pulled us to a halt outside one of the larger tents. Antano appeared from within and greeted me with a grave nod. Taking the leads of the horse, he held it still while we dismounted.

"When Lord Dentin arrives, send him in." Tomas strode into the tent, holding the flap for me. I was surprised to see a smaller tent within the larger canvas one. The inner tent was constructed from a heavier cloth. It looked like wool, but I couldn't be certain since Tomas held that flap up for me too. As I stepped inside, I realized the inner tent wasn't a tent at all, but heavy curtains. The roof above us remained canvas and filtered the sunlight down from above.

Tomas closed the flap and crossed to throw his gloves on the wide cot on the far side of the space.

"We don't have much time." He pulled a camp chair

from its place by the curtain and set it next to the table. "Please sit. We will be leaving soon, but we can't talk on the road. Mendal is going to see to it we are watched every moment we are not within these walls."

"What is going on? Why am I suspected of treason?"

"Your cousin's informant—"

"Tyront," I clarified.

"Yes, him. He has been doing his best to implicate you in your cousin's plots against the king."

"How long has he been playing the madman?"

Tomas pinned me with one of his masked looks where I couldn't read his features, just his body language. His shoulders were tight and his movements quick and deliberate. "You don't buy it?"

"Not for a moment. He used to put on a similar act when we were children to entertain Orwin and his gang of thugs. I am surprised he is doing it now. Doesn't he know I would give away the game?"

"Perhaps that is why he is so determined to take you with him. By handing you over, he might think he will gain leniency, though he goes about it shoddily."

Tomas rotated his shoulder with a wince. My own muscles twinged in sympathy. "How is it healing?"

"Well enough. Mother and Jarvin tend to fuss, but I have survived much worse."

Thinking of his scarred back, I nodded. "I know."

Lord Dentin burst through the inner curtains. "What do you know?" He threw his gloves and my knife on the table. Then he grabbed the only other chair and planted it directly across the table from me. "You, my lady, are not just a pretty face. I am not sure if your intelligence is an asset or a detriment in this case."

"Lay off her, Dent."

"I can't. Mendal isn't convinced she isn't our mole. Until he is, I am going to be spending a lot of time with the two of you."

"What does he want?"

"A full confession or Lord Wisten." Dentin folded his arms across his chest and leaned forward until they rested on the table between us. "Do you know where your cousin is, my lady?"

I met his intense scrutiny with intensity of my own. "I don't. Until a few days ago, I last saw Orwin when he was riding away with Wisenvale's food for the winter."

Dentin grunted, but didn't look away. He examined my face, but not in the same way Tomas had. Tomas weighed value. Dentin's regard was blatantly assessing my honesty.

"You can't expect her to be keeping track of his every move." Tomas came to stand behind me, resting a hand on my shoulder.

"I don't, but the sooner we find Lord Wisten, the sooner she can prove her innocence."

"Stop dodging and weaving, Dent. Do you believe she is innocent?"

"Yes. I am convinced as I can ever be of such things."

"Which means not completely."

A flash of exasperation passed across Dentin's face. "Tomas, you know me. You know my skepticism makes me good at my job."

"That is my point. You know me. Do you suspect me of treason?"

"Of course not. It isn't in your nature. You are a man obsessed with loyalty and duty."

"Do you trust my judgment of character?"

"Better than my own at times." Dentin's eyes flicked

to the side as though he hated admitting that weakness in his skills.

"Then trust me Brielle is not a traitor. She loves her people, she does her duty, and she is loyal beyond reason. She has been with me practically every moment until about a week ago. Between the time I left her and now she kept constant companionship with Jarvin or my mother. She was the one who brought the news of Jorndar's treachery. Her efforts sent me riding to the king's rescue. If she wanted Mendal dead why would she send me to aid him?"

"Good point." Dentin offered open palms in defeat. "From now on I will work from the premise that she is innocent."

Tomas seemed to accept this. He sat on the cot and deflated. I watched, wishing I could go to him. It didn't feel right, though.

Dentin glanced between us. "I hope you two aren't going to be like some of those overly affectionate couples."

Tomas rubbed his forehead as though it ached. "We will try to keep it to a minimum for your sake, right Brielle?" He lifted his head to wink at me. I stared at him in confusion. My head was just wrapping itself around the idea that Dentin was a trusted ally and not a possible foe.

"We have confused her speechless." Dentin smiled.

I blinked. The simple act of smiling transformed him from forbidding to approachable.

"You just made it worse, Dent. Get out of here. I want a few moments with my wife before they pack up this tent too."

Dentin chuckled. "Fine, but I will expect restraint

beyond these walls." He gathered his gloves from the table. "Remember we leave in an hour." Then he exited.

We sat for a few moments in silence. I was afraid to look at Tomas. Being alone with him felt both familiar and strange. Part of me longed for the companionship we established in Kyrenton, but that last night together seemed so long ago.

"Thank you." He sounded tired.

I chanced a glance. He watched me through inky black eyes dark and inviting, waiting. Caught in their pull, my glance became a stare. "For what?"

"Protecting Darnay, running instead of staying to fight a losing battle, keeping your head instead of panicking—I could list more."

My cheeks burned. "I didn't do it alone."

"I know, but my mother said you were the reason they escaped."

"Was Jorndar successful?"

He closed his eyes, cutting me off. "The vargar fell, but Captain Parrian was able to get most of his men out alive."

"Did the captain bring the news?"

"He was taken prisoner."

I remembered his sympathetic concern and feared he would not find the same in the hands of Jorndar. "Will Jorndar kill him?"

"Not as long as Jorndar believes Parrian is withholding something of value."

I suddenly felt like screaming. We kept trading lives for lives. Loren and the other women were free, but now Captain Parrian suffered. I could only hope that Tatin escaped in time. I ached in ways I couldn't relieve with movement or warmth.

"This time Jorndar will pay for his greed with his life. The king signed his warrant of death already. Mendal is set on peace one way or another. If he cannot gain it by fealty oaths, he means to remove the cancer of rebellion by force."

"You do not appear to support his tactics."

He laughed without mirth. "I see the wisdom. I tire of being the tool used to cut out the tumor. When he handed me the title of Earl at the end of the war, I hoped that I could settle down in peace, raise a family, and learn to live without needing my sword." Running his hands through his hair, he stood it on end. Dirt ringed his eyes like it had the morning we first met. A similar exhaustion marred his face. "Instead I am continuing as I did before. Killing, marching, politicking, and the same drudgery I endured for the past decade. I need a rest, Brielle. I am weary."

His face was lax with exhaustion and lined with the scars of tension. I knew there were laugh lines somewhere among the fatigue, but I couldn't spot them.

Without thought, I rose. He welcomed my approach with open arms, resting his face against my middle. I threaded my fingers through his curls, massaging his scalp. He relaxed against me, a pleasant weight I could easily bear.

"It will get better," I assured him.

He didn't reply except to pull me down into his lap and kiss me thoroughly. The strength of his hold on my waist and the pressure of his palm on my back, pulling me closer, told me he still needed reassurance. I willingly returned his caresses, offering assurances that no matter what the future held, we would face it together.

# Chapter
# Twenty-Three

Anise intended to stay behind in Wisenvale with the children and help with the recovery process. Before we left, she brought Darnay to say goodbye.

"Father!" Breaking free of his grandmother's hand, Darnay ran to Tomas.

Catching his son in a crushing hug, Tomas swung him around once before setting him on his feet again.

"I missed you." Tomas mussed the boy's already rebellious hair.

Curls fell into Darnay's eyes. He pushed them away impatiently to frown up at his father. "Grandmother says you are going away again and I have to stay with her and the women." He glanced at me with the last word.

"There is nothing wrong with staying with the women. They need someone to protect them while we are gone."

"Why can't you stay?"

Tomas took a slow breath. "A man has taken something that isn't his."

"You are going to make him give it back, right?"

"That is the idea."

"But why can't Uncle Quaren take the men and do it

for you? I want you to stay."

"Quaren isn't the Earl, Darnay. I am. I promised the king I would take care of what the man took. It is my duty to make the man give it back."

Darnay threw back his shoulders and stuck out his chest. "A man doesn't go back on his promises."

Tomas smiled. "That is right."

Darnay nodded, but then his gazed strayed to me. "What about Brielle?"

"What about her?" Tomas turned so he could smile at me.

"Do you want me to protect her also?"

"I will take over that duty for a bit. She is coming with me."

Darnay's brow lowered and his bottom lip came out slightly. "Why does she get to go with you when I can't? She is a girl."

I tensed for the coming storm, but Tomas didn't even pause.

"She is my wife now Darnay. She stays with me all the time. I explained this before. Brielle is special to me now."

"More special than me?" He avoided his father's gaze.

"No." Tomas caught his son's head between his hands and tilted it so they were almost nose to nose. "No one will replace my Darnay. You are special to me in a way completely different than Brielle. You are my son and she is my wife. I know it doesn't feel like it now, but we are a family."

"My lord?" Quaren spoke from behind my shoulder, making me jump. I hadn't heard him approach.

Tomas didn't look away from Darnay's face, but he answered. "Coming." Stopping an escaped tear in its tracks with his thumb, he gazed deep into his son's eyes. "I love you, son. You are one of the greatest gifts I have been given."

"More important than Brielle?"

"You are my only Darnay. Irreplaceable. I love you."

The boy's narrow shoulders suddenly sagged. "I love you, Father." He threw his arms around Tomas' neck and cried. Between sniffles he pled, "Please come back."

"As soon as I can."

"To stay?" Darnay pulled back to pin his father with his gaze.

"To stay."

The boy's bottom lip trembled. "I guess Brielle can stay too." He still didn't seem thrilled at the prospect.

Tomas kissed his son's forehead and then offered his rough cheek for Darnay to kiss.

"Don't forget to rub it in for later," Darnay prompted. They both massaged the kisses into their skin.

Rising, Tomas turned to offer me his hand.

I took it with that acute awareness that Darnay watched our every move.

Tomas knew it too. He pulled me close with a possessive arm around my waist and pressed his lips to my cheek. The kiss was chaste compared to the ones we shared only moments before in his tent, but it warmed me more because of what it symbolized. I was his wife and he meant for everyone to see it, even his son.

He lifted me onto my horse before mounting his. We both waved to Darnay.

Anise had already drawn the boy closer with a hand on his shoulder. He leaned into her skirts, all dark eyes and determination not to cry. His chin betrayed him.

"He looks so much like his mother."

I studied Tomas in surprise as we turned our horses to the west. "I keep seeing a smaller version of you."

"Oh, I hope not."

"I disagree. There isn't a better man he could emulate."

Tomas avoided my gaze. "I could think of many better men, Aiden for one, or Quaren."

Lord Dentin rode past us absorbed in a conversation with one of his underlings.

"Not Dentin?" I asked.

"Oh, no, I wouldn't wish Dentin's past on any man."

"I spoke not of your past. I referred to your character. You are kind, generous, loyal, honorable–"

"–Base-born, stubborn, strong-willed, myopic, exacting, and harsh," he added. "My reputation as a demanding commander is painfully accurate I am told."

"Yet, I suspect, you demand no more than you give yourself."

He fell silent. The murmur of conversations before and behind us filled the quiet. Even the horses contributed, with snuffing and snorts.

"I shouldn't have left you in Kyrenton."

For a moment I wasn't sure I heard him. His focus fixated on an object far ahead on the trail. He didn't even glance my way. Yet, I had heard him.

"You couldn't have known what Jorndar and Rolendis were plotting."

"I should have investigated his missing men."

"And abandoned Wisenvale?"

"No," he shook his head. "I would have handled Areyuthian with fewer men."

"You didn't know it was Areyuthian then. You didn't know it was your father. I suspect even if you had, you didn't know how he would take the news that he was your father."

His jaw tightened, but no other movement betrayed that he heard me.

I played over the scene in my head. "If your mother hadn't spoken, you would've never told him."

"I don't want to discuss it."

I pressed forward. "I need to know."

"Why?" The flare of anger in the blackness of his eyes as he turned to confront me induced hesitation, but not enough to still my tongue.

"I am your wife and his daughter by law. I have a right to know."

The stubborn will he'd confessed only moments before tightened his jaw and hardened his eyes. He opened his mouth to deliver a harsh set down, but I spoke first.

"Our children are going to want to know who their grandfather is, especially since he is their only living one. What do you want me to tell them? What have you told Darnay?"

"Nothing. He hasn't asked."

"He will."

Releasing a grunt of frustration, Tomas turned his face away from me.

"At least tell me what you want me to tell him."

"If you must know, I didn't plan on even telling Areyuthian. It would have complicated matters, not improved them. I was attempting to work out a better solution. Areyuthian cooperated with me until your cousin attacked me."

"Orwin didn't want a better solution. He wanted a war," I pointed out.

"And I stood in his way yet again." My puzzled frown prompted Tomas to explain further. "He tried manipulating Mendal into war with the barons before. I pointed out the holes in his fancy arguments."

"He probably sold his loyalty to them for land if the invasion was successful."

Tomas nodded. "He counted on carnage and victory to cover up the fact he was playing both sides against each other."

"It almost worked." I would never forget the collective gasp of the army around me, nor the force of rage they summoned before charging toward Lord Areyuthian's army set on avenging their fallen leader. "Now that Areyuthian knows..."

"There will be no further contact between us, Brielle. He is a high ranking noble under his king. He is trusted. He will be forgiven for fathering a son on one of many border raids in his wild days of youth. However, his king cannot forgive fraternization with the enemy. Family or not, I am still Areyuthian's enemy. I shall serve my king, and he shall serve his. I will continue to pray we will never meet in the heat of battle." Pain, deep rooted and aged, etched his features as he finally met my gaze.

I nodded. "I will tell Darnay both of his grandfathers were noble and honorable men like his father."

Tomas opened his mouth to protest, but I reached across the gap between our horses and grabbed his forearm.

"Even if you don't believe it of yourself, let Darnay believe it of you. It is important for a son to think well of his father."

Finally he nodded. "I can see the wisdom in that.

234

Don't lie to him, though. I am not a perfect man."

"I know." Despite the knowledge, a warmth glowed within me like the embers of a fire.

"My Lord Irvaine?" One of the many familiar men, who I had yet to learn to name, rode back to us from farther up the trail. "Antano wishes to speak to you about our speed. It appears the king finds our pace too quick."

Tomas stifled a groan so that the young man could not hear it. "Dentin?" he called back to where Lord Dentin was still arguing with his underling.

"Tomas?" Dentin dismissed his man with a wave of his hand.

"There is a disagreement about our traveling pace that I need to see to. Could you escort Brielle?"

"With pleasure," Dentin replied with no indication that he enjoyed the prospect more than any other. As he guided his horse to fall into step with mine, Tomas nodded to me and rode off toward the back of our company.

"Your first marital spat?" Dentin inquired with mock innocence.

"Hardly. Are you a married man, Lord Dentin?" I fluttered my eyelashes at him.

He shot me a confused look. "I haven't found a woman willing to put up with my history."

"Then you know that it couldn't be our first. Besides, it was hardly a spat."

"Anyone listening would think you counted many years as a couple."

"I think it is safe to say we have established a friendship at least at this point."

He nodded. "Many marriages cannot even boast

235

that."

We fell into silence for a half mile. Content in my own thoughts, I prayed for Tatin and Captain Parrian. I wondered how I could prove to the king I was not in collusion with my cousin. Orwin wronged me more times than I could recall. My late childhood memories crowded forward. Fight upon fight came to mind. We scarred each other in so many ways, some physical and some mental.

I rubbed the scar behind my ear from the time he cut my saddle cinch. Father whipped him for that one. The only time I had ever seen my father lift a hand against any of his fostered boys.

"Headache?" Dentin asked.

I shook my head. "Old scar from the first time Orwin tried to kill me."

"Kill you?"

"I was thirteen. Orwin had lived with us over a year at that point. Mother was dying, and Father realized Orwin refused to be reformed. Father petitioned King Trentham to issue a special decree and allow me to be his heir instead of Orwin."

"I didn't know that was possible."

"I am not sure there was a precedent, but my father grew desperate. Orwin made no attempt to hide his scorn of my father and hatred of me."

"What did Orwin do?"

"He wasn't supposed to find out, but somehow he did, probably through Tyront or one of his other friends. They all took great joy in spying on the rest of us and reporting back interesting tidbits of information. Once Orwin heard, he notched the cinch on my horse's saddle so it would break if stressed enough. He knew I loved to jump my horse. The groom missed the cut. I jumped a hillock, the leather broke, and I fell. My head struck a rock. I lost my senses for a few hours only to wake with a massive headache and my horse long gone. I walked home to find the whole village in hysterics. My horse wandered home saddleless and no one could find me. My mother had to be sedated with a special draught."

"Did he try again?"

"No. Trentham decided Father's petition was not urgent enough to set a precedent and rejected it. Orwin returned to simply making my life miserable."

"So you hate him?"

"Hate?" I considered the word. "No, I don't think hate describes it. Once father died, Orwin left Wisenvale. He became a yearly pest I dealt with after the first harvests when he came to claim his portion. I argued with him every year. He always won. There wasn't much I could do beyond yell. He was the earl and I was a nobody."

"You were still a gently bred lady."

I laughed. "He only saw the girl in braids who shamed him in front of his gang when he was fifteen."

"What did you do then?"

"He called my mother a horrible name. I gave him matching black eyes."

He considered it all for a moment. "It sounds as though you would need some pretty strong incentive to assist him in any way."

"He could offer nothing that would make me even consider it."

"Title?"

"I outrank him already. Tomas is an earl and the

king's favorite."

"Through Orwin's arrangement. Some might say you owe him." He lifted his eyebrows at me.

"He sold me body and soul to save his own neck from the noose."

He studied me. I ignored his scrutiny.

"Reevaluating your conclusion about my loyalties?"

"I grow more certain that nothing would persuade you to assist him in any way. But I am at a loss to prove it to the king. We can only pray that Orwin didn't know of the plan to implicate you and eliminates all doubt himself."

"I hate the thought of depending on him for anything." I shivered.

"The more I know of the man, the more I agree."

Tomas appeared at my other side. Dentin greeted him with a question.

"Are we slowing to accommodate the king?"

"We are separating. Our company will travel ahead and the king's will follow." Tomas grimaced.

"The advanced guard encountered Orwin a mile or so ahead. The King's men took down one of his companions but didn't they gain any information from him before he died."

"So, Orwin might be heading for Kyrenton." Dentin turned to me. "Does he know Sir Jorndar well?"

"I have no idea. He knew the previous Lord Irvaine well enough to be blackmailing him so I suppose he might know Jorndar."

Dentin lapsed into silence.

Tomas spoke a moment later. "Once we arrive, we will assess the situation, evaluate the best way to lay siege, and begin building siege works. The king expects to assault the walls in a week's time."

"Ambitious." Dentin adjusted his grip on the reins.

"Perhaps not. We are all experienced at this sort of thing now. Also, we will have plenty of resources. The forest around Kyrenton is plenteous enough to build siege works for a dozen vargars."

"Then it will come down to resources."

I spoke up. "Then best prepare to winter in tents." Both men frowned at me.

Dentin took the bait. "Why?"

"Kyrenton vargar has food enough to feed themselves through two winters."

Tomas groaned. "What we prayed for has now come to haunt us. They shall feast and we shall starve."

# Chapter Twenty-Four

The camp for the night was infinitely more luxurious than I was accustomed to after the days spent on the trail between Wisenvale and Kyrenton. Tomas' tent offered privacy and relative security from the curious eyes of the men. Between Wisenvale and our first camp, the cot became a bed wide enough for two sleepers. I made a mental note to find out who to thank for the switch.

However, I quickly discovered not everything had improved. I remained with Dentin when Tomas needed to meet with the supply master. A few moments later, Dentin was called away to mediate an argument between two of his men. I was once again fetching my own dinner.

I set off toward the mess tent hoping meat was on the menu. I hadn't eaten since breakfast. Passing through the dimness between the fires, I fell into wondering how Loren and Elise were doing on their first night together. Quaren probably wished he could be there as well.

"Did she really ride through the battle lines?" A young man's eager question caught my ear.

I stopped and looked around. The nearest campfire was beyond a copse of trees and brush.

"She nudged past me, hair wild and skirt hitched up so she could ride astride like a man."

I stepped off the trail toward the trees in time to see the second man, fair haired, rub his sword's edge with a whetstone. The sound sent my skin into goose bumps. He continued to stroke the metal as he spoke.

"I have never seen a woman look so focused. She didn't even flinch when the charge sounded."

"Bold, that one is." A graying soldier commented from the far side of the fire. He rubbed oil into the leather of the saddle across his knees. The strong smell of liniment stung my nose despite being ten feet away.

"Too bold perhaps." The blond man spat into the bushes. "Makes one wonder who is the master in that mating."

My cheeks warmed. I had shamed Tomas.

"Hush your mouth, Bitden. You will gain yourself a reprimand with that kind of talk." The older man smacked the fair one with a cloth. "Irvaine is master enough to show her what is what should it need explaining."

"She seemed compliant enough at their wedding," the young one pointed out from the shadows opposite the gray one.

"You won't catch my wife parading through battle lines," Bitden muttered. He paused to check the edge of the blade with the pad of his thumb.

"Your wife don't do nothing beyond bearing children and demanding money and you know it." The old man groaned as he shifted his saddle to work the other side. "A strong woman doesn't mean her husband's weak. It

242

means he knows how to show respect where respect is due."

They ceased talking. I turned to continue toward the mess tent and jumped in surprise. Tomas stood in the shadows only four feet away. His frown was so deep I could see it in the dim light from the men's fire.

I opened my mouth to explain, but he shook his head sharply. Grabbing my arm, he half-dragged me back to our tent. He barely paused to untie the flaps before pushing me through them. Following and pulling the canvas closed behind him, he then rounded on me with a glare.

Sudden awareness of his size hit me. He weighed two of me, was mostly muscle, and lived by his reflexes. Still fully armed and partially geared for the battlefield, he towered over me with anger contorting his normally controlled features.

"Where is Dentin? Why isn't he with you?"

"There was an argument over sleeping arrangements. He had to mediate."

"So you wandered off?"

I straightened my shoulders out of habit. "I was hungry. Last time you told me to fetch my own dinner."

"Last time you weren't accused of treason. I don't know what Dentin was thinking. If it happens again, find one of us."

"I cannot be trusted alone?"

"Not if you are going to do such foolish things as obvious eavesdropping."

Shame flooded my face with heat, but I ignored it and fed my rising indignation instead. "I was listening to a gossipy conversation about me, hardly a state secret."

The anger in his eyes didn't even flicker. "I know that. You know that. There is no guarantee a king's agent who spots you lingering in the shadows will report that detail along with your suspicious behavior."

I hadn't considered that. I closed my eyes and took a deep breath. "I am sorry. I wasn't thinking that way."

"You better begin."

I winced at his tone.

He closed his eyes as he labored to slow his breathing. Gradually his fingers relaxed and his head fell forward so his chin lowered toward his chest. He still didn't open his eyes. "You scared me."

"You feared I was a spy for Orwin after all?"

His eyes opened, dark and vulnerable. "No." He stepped close so that I had to look up to meet his gaze. His bare hands slipped up to bracket my face, calloused palms brushing my cheeks and fingers lacing through my rioting hair. "I feared losing you." His thumb stroked the tender skin beneath the corner of my mouth. My senses focused on the delicate pressure. Warmth infused his gaze enticing an answering heat in my cheeks.

I was at a loss as to how to respond. "I am sorry."

He leaned in and kissed me. My hands found his forearms as my balance shifted.

"Where have you two been?" Dentin demanded as he swept the canvas aside. He strode into the tent, pulled off his gloves and tucked them in his belt. "I thought you said you were going to keep the physical affection to a minimum."

Resting his forehead against mine, Tomas took a deep breath. "This is our tent." He released my face and stepped back to confront Dentin. Apparently unwilling to completely break our connection, he pulled me up against him with a possessive hand on my hip. "What do you want?"

"I was dealing with an issue among my usual troublemakers when a messenger from the king arrived with a missive for you. I figured you would want to know about it." He tossed a thin parchment packet on the table.

Tomas released me to pick it up. He tilted it toward the lantern to read the address better before opening it. As my husband read the contents by the light of the lantern, I grew aware that Dentin was eyeing me.

Once he had my attention, he nodded toward the space outside the tent opening. "The men nearby were leery of disturbing you two because it sounded as though you were having a marital row a bit ago. I was surprised to find you two so pleasantly engaged."

"Not that a fight would have stopped you," I pointed out in an effort to avoid the question. It wouldn't help matters to drag my foolishness out before Dentin. I doubted he would be as forgiving as Tomas.

"I wasn't about to wait all night to find out the contents of that." He nodded toward where Tomas was frowning at the letter.

"Messages from the king aren't expected?"

"Not personally addressed to Tomas with the king's personal seal."

Tomas muttered what sounded like a curse. "Dentin, read this and tell me it doesn't say what I think it does." He shoved the three pages of parchment into Dentin's hands. "He can't be serious."

Dentin moved to stand in the light so he could read

it. Tomas began pacing. I suspected it had something to do with me, but I wasn't inclined to wait.

"What do you think it says?" I asked as Tomas strode past.

"Mendal wants me to have you under constant guard between here and Kyrenton, and in chains when left alone."

Dentin grimaced as he flung the letter onto the table. "He will grow as paranoid as Trentham at this rate. She is accused of collusion not attempted assassination."

"I will not chain her. She has done nothing wrong."

Dentin nodded. "I recommend you bring in the irons as though you intend to comply and don't use them."

"And the guard within sight at all times? Does he not trust me?"

Dentin smirked. "He does not trust you with her. He knows your weakness. He suspects you do not see beyond your marriage oath to her and hers to you."

"What does he want me to do? Forget I am married to her? Forget that our informant's word is suspect? Forget that she has proven her loyalty repeatedly?" Tomas' strides grew swifter with each query.

"Her loyalty to you, not the king." Dentin's voice was almost a whisper in contrast to Tomas' rising tones

Tomas rounded to confront his friend. "In my mind it is the same."

Growing weary of being discussed in my presence, I spoke up. "The point is that it isn't the same in his mind and he is the king.¬¬"

Two surprised faces turned my way. As I suspected they had forgotten I was there.

"I am willing to submit to the king's instructions."

Tomas opened his mouth to protest, but Dentin

246

spoke first.

"The chains will be here in an hour. There is no need to use them within the tent walls. I will see that my men guard your tent. You will not be disturbed and the king cannot accuse you of disobedience if my men vouch for your compliance." He turned to Tomas. "But, whatever happens, don't let her leave your sight."

He stalked out through the canvas flaps without a word of farewell and began calling for his second-in-command. As Dentin's voice faded into the distance, I turned to find Tomas watching me with weary eyes.

"You shouldn't have to do this."

"Life is full of shoulds and shouldn'ts, but fighting for them to become reality isn't always the wisest course. I prefer to pick my battles with care. This is one I choose not to fight."

He ran his hands through his hair and massaged his scalp. "Are you going to insist on wearing the chains?"

"No."

He crossed to claim my hands. Running his thumbs across the inside of my wrists, he gazed deep into my eyes. "Good. I am not sure I could tolerate you in chains."

"My Lord Irvaine?" a male voice queried from outside.

"What is it now?" Tomas muttered as he turned away. He pressed through the flaps.

Mindful of my new status of prisoner, I retreated toward the far corner where my gear had been slung. Suddenly all I desired was food and sleep. The memory of falling asleep in Tomas' arms brought warmth and uneasy anticipation. I ignored the inevitable awkwardness to come and focused on checking my

247

gear.

Anise and Loren had assumed the responsibility of preparing my kit while I was being presented to the king. Three tunics, sturdy woolen leggings and a choice of two solid colored surcoats burst free from the leather satchel. They fell across my lap in a mass of burgundy, navy, and cream, Loren's favorite colors. I recognized the lace I gave her five years ago carefully stitched to the flared sleeves of the burgundy tunic. Her best clothes sacrificed for a rough journey. "Oh, Loren, you shouldn't have," I whispered. My throat swelled with unshed tears so it hurt to swallow. Stroking the cloth's edge, I vowed I would replace them with garments twenty times better.

"Lord Dentin ordered our dinner be brought to us." Tomas slid a heavily laden tray onto the table. "The other items will arrive in an hour or so. They have to find them." He began unloading the crocks and jugs. "Are you hungry?" He turned in time to catch me wiping away an escaped tear.

Without a word he crossed to me, dropped to his knees, and pulled me into his arms. The gentle caress of his rough hands as he guided my head to his shoulder brought more tears flooding forth. I pressed my face into the solid warmth of him and released weeks of pent up homesickness in a deluge of tears.

I could never go back. Loren had a family of her own now. I was married to Tomas. Loren and I were both ruled by duties, commitments, and separate lives. Now our treasured moments sitting together before a winter fire, exchanging laughter and girlish confidences, would become only cherished memories. Could a countess and a commoner relate over such confidences?

My struggles with treason, politics, and marriage to a powerful man with complicated loyalties seemed so different from our old worries of weather, getting harvest in before the rains came, and conserving every last drop of each bottle of father's wine.

"Hush." His lips brushed my forehead. "You don't even have to see them. I'll hide them under the bed. You won't even know they are there."

"No." I pushed away so I could see his face. "It isn't the chains. I am just homesick for a simpler time." I swiped at the tears still slipping down my cheeks. "It didn't seem so simple then, but I wish I could go back to when my greatest worry was the gophers or whether the wheat would come up in the spring."

He caught a tear as it dripped from my chin. "I wish for the days when all I focused on was besting Brevand in our next bout, a far cry from my concerns of the past few years."

"Brevand?" I blinked away the last of the moisture. My face felt bloated as it usually did after crying.

Tomas smiled. It transformed his face. Lightening his usual brooding stare and giving me a glimpse of what he might have looked like in younger days. The likeness to Darnay was astonishing.

"In the beginning Brevand had the advantage of early training. I only possessed an unquenchable desire to prove myself. Everyone looked down on me because my mother refused to identify my father. Sir Fortwin saw beyond my birth and treated me as though I was of equal worth as the rest of those in his service. I strove to be worthy of that regard.

"In the first bout, Brevand trounced me so badly I ached for days."

I wondered at the transformation of his features as he told his story. I kept getting glimpses of a young boy desperate to prove himself worthy of the potential Sir Fortwin saw in him.

"He didn't stop after you went down?"

"I refused to give up until I couldn't stand and lift my sword. Three days later we had our second face-off. He defeated me again. By the second week, he still whipped me in the practice yard, but I actually got a score in once in a while. It took me three years before I finally won a match."

"And now?" I asked.

"I don't know. We haven't faced each other over crossed weapons in a long time." Sadness clouded his eyes as he seemed to recall the betrayal that now stood between them.

"Brevand saved the women's lives when Orwin set fire to the lord's hall."

"He was still there?"

I nodded, avoiding Tomas' suddenly hopeful gaze. As much as I wanted Brevand's contrition to be a sign of complete repentance, I doubted it. I recalled that flare of anger in his gaze when we first met. A man who despises the good fortune of his friend is not a friend.

"I had Captain Eirianware confine him to one of the cottages until your return. I don't know what happened after that. For all I know, Eirianware left him there."

"I will check with him tomorrow. Eirianware is a good man. I am sure he secured Brevand."

"Won't Mendal want to determine his fate?"

"Possibly, but I would prefer dealing with him myself. Mendal, when he is in this mood, would sentence him to death without much thought."

I frowned at his wording. "Mendal has been like this before?"

"Right before he started his campaign to take the throne, even the most mundane things became secrets. He lived in fear that something would be discovered before the time was right to move openly against the other feuding nobles. Ironic, isn't it? Now he fears someone will do the same against him."

"Why did you support him?"

His brows lowered and he avoided my gaze. "Foolish idealism and a touch of desire to change the world."

I took a deep breath and asked the question that had been burning in my head since I met Mendal. "I don't know much about either king, but I am curious. Do you think Mendal is better than Trentham?"

I expected him to brush off the question, avoid it, or change the subject. Instead, he answered me.

"Then, I believed Mendal would be better. Now, my perception isn't as simplistic. Trentham was a good king until he went sick with paranoia, killing at random for nonsensical reasons. He left no sons or daughters so the succession was bound to be tumultuous even if the rebellion hadn't toppled him first."

I didn't realize how bad the government had been. Tucked up in the northeast, Wisenvale was isolated from the political gossip. "So Mendal didn't begin the rebellion?"

"I wouldn't have supported him if he had." Tomas focused on tucking a trailing curl behind my ear. "Trentham's favorites, the elite ranks of nobles he began executing randomly, tried to seize control. They would have succeeded if they could've agreed on a leader."

251

"So Mendal stepped in after the chaos began."

Tomas nodded. "I still believe Mendal can be a good king. Up until now he has proven to be wise and practical, but this recent plot and its aftermath shook his confidence in his allies, friends, and his ability to judge character. He must have believed Lord Wisten's drivel more than Dentin and I suspected."

Suddenly my position appeared even more hopeless. "How am I going to convince Mendal I am not a traitor if he is questioning everyone's loyalty?"

Tomas stroked the back of his fingers along my cheek, tracing my jaw. "Dentin is working on it."

"You are putting a lot of trust in Lord Dentin."

"Yes, I am. He is worthy of it." He caught my chin, guiding it so we were almost nose to nose.

I frowned and refused to lift my gaze to meet his. I didn't appreciate my life depending on the skills of a man I only just met. For all I knew he was going to do nothing and let me die a traitor's death.

"Brielle, do you trust me?"

I resisted the temptation to pull my chin from his grip, but I still didn't look up. "To a point." I studied his jaw instead. Covered in the beginnings of a beard, I wondered how it would feel to my fingers.

"Brielle." He almost growled my name in frustration. "Look at me and tell me the truth."

Without thought, I obeyed. "I do trust you, but I don't like sitting around waiting for someone else to rescue me."

"Imagine how I feel."

My eyes narrowed. "What do you mean?"

His gaze fell to my mouth, where his fingers traced my bottom lip distracting me from my question. "I am entrusting him with one of the most valuable parts of my life."

Before I could figure out an appropriate response, he caught my mouth with his own and drove all thoughts from my head.

# Chapter Twenty-Five

Two and a half days later we arrived outside Kyrenton's outer wall. Over that time, Tomas and Dentin's men became a single army. Camping, eating, sleeping, riding, and training together, camaraderie formed among the ranks. The relationship among the leadership was a bit rougher.

"I have to do what?" Rathenridge demanded from just outside Tomas' tent door.

"I want you to send scouts into the city." Dentin's clipped tones cut through the canvas as though it was nothing.

I slipped to the door and lifted the flap slightly. In the center of the common area beyond the tent walls, the two men were standing on opposite sides of a camp table spread with maps.

Rathenridge glared at Dentin over his crossed arms and adjusted his stance slightly. "Why my men?"

"You have been in the city before." Dentin pronounced each word with precise care as though the reason were obvious. "Your men know the layout better than mine."

"My men are known by the inhabitants."

Dentin raised an eyebrow, his face showing none of

the weariness I would expect. "Not all of them. Surely some haven't managed to gain a reputation yet."

Rathenridge rose to the bait. "How dare you slur the good name of good men!"

"What is the issue?" Tomas asked as he approached. Exhaustion marred his face in dark circles beneath his eyes. Lack of appetite had eaten away at his cheeks leaving them thin. He leaned over the table between the men and studied the map between his supporting hands. He blinked it into focus while Rathenridge smirked at Dentin over his head.

"You missed a gate here and the postern gate there." Tomas pointed to two spots on the map. "I recommend the scouts enter by the western gate. We don't have the men to surround the city until the king arrives. I see no reason to block the traffic through there until then. Waiting won't change much considering their stored food. If anything, it helps. There will be fewer innocents to get in the way if they run first. Besides, it makes it a prime spot for infiltration."

"What! You are giving Jorndar an escape route." Rathenridge complained.

"We can watch from a distance and stop anyone farther out," Dentin pointed out. "If Jorndar wants to run, he can, but we will catch him."

Rathenridge scowled at Dentin. "There is still the issue of whose men go into the city on reconnaissance."

"Landry's," Tomas said as he straightened. "He sent seven men out before we broke camp this morning."

"And when did you plan on informing me of this?" Dentin demanded.

"When you two stopped arguing long enough for me to get in a word." Tomas met Dentin's glare with one of his own. "I don't see why you two can't get along."

"It is a personality issue," Rathenridge muttered.

Dentin looked at him. No emotion, no reaction, simply bland observation. "Yours?"

Ignoring their sniping barbs, I watched Tomas. The weary set of his shoulders, the way he fought to keep his eyes open, I feared he would collapse any moment. Between duty and worry, he had barely slept the past few days. When he did lie down, he was restless and dreamed fitfully. He looked up and met my gaze. I ached at the exhaustion in his eyes.

"You might as well come out and join us, Brielle."

Tomas' words stopped Rathenridge mid-sentence. All three men looked toward my position. I swept the canvas aside and stepped into the cold sunlight. The breeze whipping among the tents teased a few strands of my hair loose as I approached.

"Eavesdropping again?" Tomas' frown lacked conviction.

"I thought you wanted me out of sight."

"Whatever for?" Rathenridge demanded, turning to face Tomas. "It isn't as though the sight of her will stir up sedition in the ranks."

"Are you trying to pick a fight with me, Aiden?" Tomas rubbed his face. "I wanted her to stay out of sight so if we are watched, it will be clear that we are all doing our duty."

"A wise move considering the blacksmith behind my tent is working extremely slow in replacing the shoes on my horse." Dentin didn't turn his head. It took every bit of control I had to resist the impulse to look. Rathenridge felt no such compulsion though.

"I wondered if he was a novice," Tomas murmured.

"No, just dawdling." Dentin leaned over and pointed to the vargar on the map. "I want to know how you plan for us to get in there."

"I thought you were handling that aspect of things."

Dentin frowned. "I can. When did you last sleep?"

Tomas' straightened to his full height. "Last night, same as you."

"How long?"

"Six hours."

"Three," I corrected him. "He slept three."

Dentin's frown deepened. "Go to bed."

"And toss and turn?" Tomas gestured toward our tent. "It isn't as though I can fall into bed and fall asleep. I am restless and plagued. You know how I get before a battle."

"This battle is a few days off, Tomas. You have to sleep or you will be worthless." Rathenridge twitched a bit uncomfortably. "I don't like agreeing with Dentin, but he has a point. You need sleep."

Dentin began clearing the maps from the table. "We will move our meeting. I will send Muirayven with a sleeping draught."

"I don't need it."

Dentin paused long enough to skewer Tomas with an intent stare. "I know you aren't a drinking man, Tomas. I am not about to press wine on you against your wishes, but I need you alert. You need sleep. I am sending over a bottle of wine or Muirayven with a sleeping draught, your choice."

Tomas closed his eyes in acquiescence. "Send the wine."

Dentin nodded sharply, picked up the bundle of maps and stalked off in the direction of the edge of camp. Rathenridge gathered the satchel of documents, nodded to me, and trotted after Dentin.

"I hate battles." Tomas rotated his shoulders and then winced. "I would rather be caught unawares than deal with the waiting, plotting, and nerves."

He allowed me to guide him inside. He sank onto the edge of the bed with a groan. "I feel like I could sleep for days, but every time I close my eyes and clear my mind nightmares and memories come flooding in to fill the void."

I knelt to pull off his boots. He tried to push me away, but I persisted and unlaced the first one. He didn't even attempt to dissuade me as I started on the second.

He closed his eyes. His last boot fell into my lap. "I hate sieges," he muttered before rolling over. By the time I placed his boots next to his gear, he was asleep.

In an effort to intercept Dentin's bottle of wine, I slipped outside. Dentin's man on duty outside the door nodded to me, but made no move to stop me.

"My lady?" Antano approached, a leather flask in hand. "I thought you were supposed to remain inside unless accompanied by Lord Irvaine."

"That is true, but he has fallen asleep without the assistance of that." I gestured toward the flask. "I stepped out to intercept you. The guard is here to account for my whereabouts."

Dentin's man nodded to Antano before resuming his tense stance.

"All the better that he fell asleep." Antano handed me the flask. "He makes a lousy drinker."

"Violent?" I had seen my share of violent men, more than I wished.

"His past sins come back to haunt him and sharpen his tongue." Antano grimaced. "Regret, if fed, can consume all hope of the future. At least when sober, Irvaine knows the wisdom of not feeding his regrets. I am surprised he requested it."

"Dentin insisted he sleep. He gave Tomas a choice of wine or a sleeping draught."

"It sounds as though he has made the best choice, neither. Keep that far from your husband."

"Then take it back." I offered the heavy container.

Antano waved it away. "No, if you take it, I can truthfully claim I delivered it."

He strode away. I retreated to loneliness of the tent and my softly snoring husband. Tomas slept for three hours without stirring.

The heavy pounding of an approaching horse woke me from a half-doze in the chair next to the bed. I cautiously straightened.

"Tomas!" Rathenridge called from just outside the tent door.

Tomas sat up, instantly awake. Rolling off the bed, he crossed to the door before I had done more than gain my feet. He lifted the canvas.

"Movement at the gate."

"On my way."

The horse galloped away.

I met Tomas at the door with his boots and sword belt. Our joint efforts had him out of the tent and mounting his horse within minutes.

I turned back to hide once again within the canvas walls, but Tomas had another plan.

"Come with me." He extended a hand down to me.

"I thought–"

"Seize the opportunity. I have to go. You can stay or—"

I took his hand and swung up behind him with a grimace. His healing rib still bothered him. He didn't wait for me to settle before setting heels to the horse's flanks. We plunged forward. I grabbed at him, catching hold of the front of his fur-lined overtunic while my heart thundered in my ears. Beneath his overtunic, his padded jerkin shifted. Only then did I realize he had left his breastplate, chain mail, and helmet at the foot of our bed.

We whipped by men clamoring for their horses in various stages of dressing for battle. Fear pricked my skin. *Please don't let this be the battle yet, Kurios.*

Suddenly, we burst forth from the crowded camp into the open fields. Tomas drew our horse up to a stumbling halt for a breath before whirling us off again along the line of tents. I could see nothing beyond his shoulders, so I contented myself with pressing my face to the center of his back. Then, just as before, he pulled back and our horse came to a messy stop among a group of other horsemen.

"What is the situation?" Tomas demanded.

"You brought her with you?" Dentin demanded.

"Obviously he did," Rathenridge retorted.

I managed to look around Tomas' shoulder in time to catch the loaded glare the men exchanged.

"Well, look for yourself." Dentin gestured toward the walls.

The gates looked much the same as they did the day we first arrived, except the massive gate was closed.

"Where is the portcullis?" Tomas asked.

"They drew it up." Rathenridge earned a glare from

Dentin.

"When did the white flag appear?"

I had missed the white flag, but when I looked it was there. Small and limp, it hung from one of the slits above the gate. Whoever hung it clearly intended for it to be seen.

"Shortly before I sent Rathenridge for you." Dentin shifted. "We have been watching the inner gate ever since."

"Lord Dentin." One of the heavily armed men straightened to attention. "Movement, sir."

Even as he spoke, a small square of light winked into being in the black façade of the gate. A figure appeared, outlined for an instant against the light beyond the gate, only to disappear when the door closed again.

I blinked and narrowed my eyes, hoping to identify the person slogging through the mud toward us. Silence fell across the men as they all did the same.

"I believe that is Horacian." Rathenridge frowned as he announced his conclusion.

"It is." Tomas sounded no less concerned. "Why in the world would Jorndar be sending my steward out to me?"

"Perhaps he seeks to negotiate surrender." Dentin's voice betrayed his disbelief that the steward came on such a mission.

"Should we send someone to meet him?" We all turned at Landry's query. "It is a long walk."

"Let him walk." Tomas nodded toward our army still assembling along the crest of the hill. "It will give us time to prepare should this be a prelude to an attack. Dentin, do you have the Southern gate covered? This might be a trap."

Dentin's frown grew even more terrible. "Captain," he called toward the men gathering behind us.

"Yes, my lord?" A heavy set young man straightened in his saddle.

"Take a platoon and march to the southern gate. Send news of the status when you get there."

The man saluted and then began yelling orders. A group of men detached themselves from the main group and started forming into ranks, as they rode west. I watched them until they disappeared from sight. When I turned back to check on Horacian's progress, I was surprised at how far he had come.

As he navigated the last bit of muddy field to reach us, I couldn't help comparing his approach to the first one. His shoulders stooped and his head hung lower this time. With his muddy boots and leggings, he looked decidedly less proud than that first day. Unlike then, he knew exactly whom he wanted to see.

"My Lord Irvaine." He fell to his knees with a wet slosh. "I have come as a petitioner to offer the terms of surrender of the town of Kyrenton."

"Why does Jorndar send you, old man?" Dentin demanded. "Does he hope we will not slay you out of respect for your age?"

Horacian's face paled, but his voice remained steady. "I represent the people of Kyrenton, not those of the vargar."

"How did this come about?" Tomas asked.

"Sir Jorndar took control of the vargar by force–"

"How many men?" Dentin leaned forward intently.

"Thirty, my lord. I voiced my objection."

"How many dead?"

Rathenridge didn't wait for Horacian to answer

before nudging his horse into Dentin's forcing him to steady his beast. "Will you just let the man finish answering the first question before you start pestering him for details?"

"Yes, please, Dentin." Tomas gestured toward Horacian. "I want to hear what happened."

Dentin's impassive features flinched for a blink of an eye as he curbed his eagerness.

After a nod from Tomas, Horacian continued. "In deference to my status as his father-in-law and Rolendis' delicate condition, he spared me from the sword. Instead I was turned out into the town. The town council–"

"Wait!" Rathenridge was the one to interrupt this time. "Father-in-law? Rolendis married the treasonous brute?"

"Two days ago." Horacian looked more dejected than I thought possible.

"She is more of a lack-wit than I thought."

"Aiden, please." Tomas' exhausted plea brought Rathenridge to silence. Turning to regard Horacian again, Tomas nodded for him to continue.

"The town council accepted me. They asked me to be their spokesman in their efforts to petition separately from Jorndar."

"Why do they wish to do that?" Landry's voice took everyone by surprise again. For such a large man he was very quiet. "Sir Jorndar is a capable warrior and an adequate administrator."

"Hardly, Sir Landry. He is known among the people as a harsh master. He values the land more than the people's wellbeing. He has cut off children's hands for crimes as petty as sleeping in his fields."

Tomas tensed, Dentin frowned, and Rathenridge glowered. I shivered. The thought of maiming a child for something so accepted by others chilled me to my core. Men, women, and children frequently slept during the mid-day break during harvest and planting. Some nights, I had even slept with the harvesters when we were rushing to beat the rain.

"Dentin, which of us is making decisions here?" Tomas asked.

Dentin considered the question for a moment. "Regarding the security of Lady Irvaine and those things concerning the king, I outrank you. When dealing with your title, land, and vargar, I defer to your commands."

With a curt nod, Tomas turned to Horacian. "Your request for peaceful surrender is accepted."

"The terms?"

"No conditions. Sir Jorndar, not the town of Kyrenton, defected. I see no reason to penalize the people for the foolish actions of a foreign invader."

"Thank you, my lord."

"I do have a request, though."

"Speak it and I will do my best to see that it is fulfilled."

"I request a search and seizure of Lord Wisten. He is a fugitive of the crown."

"Consider it done." Horacian rose clumsily to his feet and bowed. "Would you also like free passage of the army through the town as well?"

"Does Sir Jorndar know that the council is defecting from his leadership?"

"Not yet. There has been little activity beyond the walls of the vargar, and no communication save demands for supplies."

"Then, I would like to request we keep up the ruse for as long as possible. There is no need to alert Sir Jorndar."

"What are you planning Tomas?" Dentin was watching Tomas warily. "You have that look in your eye that suggests you already have a plan of assault."

"It depends on whether or not Wisten is found outside the vargar." He turned back to Horacian. "How might I get in touch with the council regarding our future plans?"

"Send word to the Leaping Hart in Lorinder Court. I have taken rooms there."

Tomas nodded. "Your faithfulness will be remembered, Horacian."

"Thank you, my lord." Horacian bowed and trudged back the way he came.

Dentin signaled his nearest man. "Sound the dispersal. We aren't going to fight today. War council in my tent or yours?" he asked Tomas.

"Yours." Then without signaling me, Tomas pulled us around. Again I was left grabbing at his overtunic and holding on as we plunged back in among the tents.

"It wouldn't hurt to give me some sign we are about to ride next time," I commented in his ear.

His reply was lost to the wind, but he shifted both reins to his right hand and laid his left one over mine. Squeezing my fingers, he pressed them more firmly against his chest.

"None of that now," Dentin protested as we all slowed to a walk.

"Oh, leave them alone, Dent." Rathenridge pushed his mount to the front. Dentin's mouth tightened in displeasure.

"One day he will go too far," Dentin muttered as he watched Rathenridge join Landry.

"He enjoys getting a reaction out of people," Tomas commented.

"I don't think he will enjoy the reaction I shall give him when he crosses the line."

"Remember he is one of my oldest and closest friends, Dentin. Allow that fact to temper your reaction."

"I might," he muttered.

# Chapter Twenty-Six

The king's party arrived that evening, throwing the whole camp into chaos as everyone rushed to prepare his entourage's living quarters and settle him into the elaborate canvas structure already made ready for him. I witnessed only a small sample of the flustered rushing of servants and couriers in Tomas and my brief journey between our tent and Dentin's to resume the planning meeting. It had been interrupted by the king's arrival.

With the king in the camp, Tomas didn't want me out of his sight. With the grip he kept on my hand, I might as well be chained to his arm with the manacles we left hanging from the end of our bed.

"Any word from Kyrenton?" Tomas asked the moment we stepped beneath Dentin's roof.

As large as our tent, his shelter obviously had a different primary purpose. Seven chairs of various designs were scattered about a wide collapsible table strewn with maps, parchment, measuring tools, quill pens, and an inkwell set, currently capped. Rathenridge and Dentin bent over the far end of the table, studying a curling parchment bit between them. Rathenridge's flamboyant hair contrasted starkly with Dentin's muted brown and unassuming manner.

"Lord Wisten is in the vargar."

"Allied with Jorndar?" Tomas asked.

"Read for yourself." Rathenridge handed Tomas the parchment. Curious, I stood on tiptoe to read it when Tomas pulled the parchment flat enough to see clearly.

*Wisten spotted in outer bailey. Source inside says he met with Jorndar. No developments yet.*

"They don't know and neither do we."

"You two know Sir Jorndar best." Dentin glanced from Tomas to Rathenridge and back. "Will he listen to Wisten?"

Rathenridge crossed his arms over his chest as though considering whether or not the décor worked. "It matters what his story is."

"No, it matters what he can get out of him." Tomas sighed. "Jorndar does nothing unless there is something in it for him."

Dentin frowned at me. "What are Wisten's strong points?"

"Persuasive arguing and blatant lying with ease."

"Weaknesses?"

That one I struggled to enumerate. There were so many. "He likes women, expensive pleasures, money, and the easy life."

"Does he care for power?"

"Not as much as the physical pleasures."

"So he would be seeking money."

I nodded.

"But Jorndar doesn't have money, does he?" Dentin asked Tomas the last bit.

"I have no idea. I didn't have time to inspect my treasury before I was called back to Wisenvale."

I spoke up. "Jorndar could easily hand my cousin

twice what he was extorting already from the late Lord Irvaine." All three men frowned at me. "I did get a chance to inspect the treasury."

Dentin's eyes narrowed. "Who was extorting money from Kolbent?"

"Lord Wisten."

"So your cousin uses extortion to gain wealth." Dentin began pacing the length of the tent.

I opened my mouth to point out Orwin sold me to Tomas to save his skin, but Tomas' hand on my arm made me hesitate.

Tomas leaned over to whisper. "Give him a moment."

Rathenridge, however, didn't read the cues. He flopped into the nearest chair, propped his feet on the table and asked, "What does all this have to do with our plans to retake the vargar?"

Dentin closed his eyes and came to a complete stop in the center of the tent.

"Know your enemy, Rathenridge."

"Lord Wisten is weak, spineless, and manipulative. So?"

Dentin leaned over the maps and charts, eyes scanning them. "Sir Jorndar is grasping, egotistical, and selfish. He will use Wisten to the point that he is useful and then discard him."

"Jorndar is not a fool, though." Tomas tapped the diagram of the interior of the vargar. "Whether or not the people of Kyrenton are behind him, he knows he is trapped."

"The question is what will he do?" Dentin pulled the diagram to the top of the pile.

"Run." Rathenridge leapt to his feet. "He will take his greatest assets and run to cause trouble another day."

"He married Rolendis." Tomas leaned over the plans, resting his weight on his fisted hands. "He controls Kolbent's wife and possibly Kolbent's son. Even if he escapes with only Rolendis and her pregnancy intact, he can return to cause trouble for me another day."

"If the child is a boy," Dentin pointed out.

"Even if the child is not," Rathenridge replied, "he can replace it with a boy babe. Someone he can mold into a weapon of revenge."

"So, when he realizes that the people of Kyrenton have already defected, he will use Wisten's skills to escape." Dentin pointed to the garden. "My lady, how many know of your route of escape?"

Before I could reply, the canvas flaps were drawn wide and the king's personal guard entered, followed by the king. Mendal scanned the room as the men bowed and I curtseyed.

"What is she doing here?" Mendal's pale glare drove a sliver of fear through my heart.

I lowered my head in respect and to avoid his unspoken accusations despite the anger rising in my chest. Tomas showed no such restraint. He straightened beside me, readying for a fight.

Dentin beat him to the first punch. "Contributing. As Irvaine and Rathenridge know Sir Jorndar better than I, she can offer me insight into Lord Wisten's motivations and possible actions."

Mendal's gaze narrowed, but he didn't confine me to irons so I counted my blessings. In an attempt to not cause more trouble for myself, I kept Tomas between us at all times. I also clasped my hands before me and kept my eyes averted in the classic position of submission.

"You have located Lord Wisten?" Mendal strode to

272

the table and scanned the documents on it.

"Yes, sire. He has taken shelter under Jorndar's protection within the vargar."

"Storm the city walls then. We will hang them both."

Tomas stepped forward. "I must protest—"

Dentin cut him off with a sharp shake of his head. "My liege, the people of Kyrenton have defected from the traitor and thrown themselves upon your mercy. In your name I assured them no retribution, dependent on their further cooperation in capturing the traitors and relinquishing the vargar back into Lord Irvaine's care. I hope you find this satisfactory."

Mendal's clear gaze met Dentin's masked one. "I suspect you are protecting someone."

"I serve only you, my king. You know that."

"Aye, I do, or I would wonder at the subterfuge."

"Part of my line of work, I am afraid, my liege. Do you wish to know the plan?"

"Yes."

Dentin outlined his proposal for retaking the vargar. "Our scouts and inside man report that besides Lord Wisten and the former Lady Irvaine, Sir Jorndar retains only ten to twenty men inside the vargar. In order to minimize destruction of the vargar gate, walls and the surrounding buildings of the town, we propose infiltrating the vargar with a small force. They will overwhelm the guard on the gates and let in the rest of the army waiting in the streets outside the vargar. Then the greater force, led by Sir Landry, will secure the fortress."

"It sounds like a wise plan, Lord Dentin. I recognize the obvious hands of both you and Lord Irvaine in its formation. My congratulations. You have my blessing to proceed and my troops' full support." He turned to leave only to look my way. "I require only one change."

All three men tensed, though none of them moved. I held my breath, unease tightening my throat.

"What change would that be, my king?" Dentin asked in a tone that could have been used to request more cheese be brought to the dinner table.

"She accompanies you inside the vargar."

Tomas' clenched fist shook. In an effort to still it, he pressed it to his stomach. His face remained impassive though.

"My king?" Lord Dentin asked. "Surely you don't mean to send a gently-reared lady into such a situation."

"If she wishes to prove her loyalty, I do require it. Lift your eyes, Lady Irvaine."

I obeyed. The cold calculation that met my gaze chilled my heart. "I live to serve you, my king."

"Strong words from the lips of a traitor's cousin."

"I am not my cousin, my liege."

"As you keep saying, my lady. I cannot risk accepting such a claim solely upon your word. Your honor is unproven. I will, however, consider believing if your words are supported by action. Your husband has proven his loyalty to me in battle. I ask the same of you. Are you worthy of such a challenge?"

My senses whirled with the heady rush. He meant to send me into the midst of a battle? I shoved away the memory of Kyrenton. By will alone, I kept my gaze steady and my chin firm. "I shall endeavor to be."

"Then I accept your act of homage. Return with evidence of your cousin's death and I will be appeased."

Without waiting for my response, he turned and strode from the tent, his men scrambling to follow.

My knees gave out. I sank to the ground and hid my face in my hands. My lungs ached for air. No matter how deeply I sucked my breaths, I couldn't relieve the pressure of panic in the center of my chest.

Did he expect me to kill Orwin?

"No, Tomas!" Dentin's strident tone broke through my concentration. My attention snapped up in time to observe Tomas moving to pursue the king, with Rathenridge and Dentin blocking his path.

"Get out of my way, Dentin. He has gone too far and I intend he should know it."

"With your hand on your sword and murder in your eyes, you will be fortunate if you manage a word before his personal guard cuts you down." Dentin's normal cool demeanor frayed a bit at the edges. Every word from his mouth came out with a barely controlled snap. Muscles in his jaw moved even when he quit speaking.

"He cannot do this," Tomas protested.

"He can." Rathenridge's voice was the calmest of them all. "He is king, Tomas. We are his vassals. You swore to serve him."

"I swore to protect Brielle."

"The Kurios will hold you to both oaths," Rathenridge pointed out.

Tomas swore. It was mild, but it was enough to snap me out of my shock.

"I chose to rise to his challenge."

All three men turned their heads toward me. Tomas' mouth was already forming a rebuttal, but I didn't wait for him to argue.

"It is this or fear the taint of treason on both of our

names for generations. Orwin ruined any chance of my words of loyalty being enough to absolve me in the king's sight. I must prove my innocence. For me." I met Tomas' stormy gaze. "For you."

"For me? I don't require it. Only a fool–"

"Tomas," Dentin warned.

Turning away abruptly, Tomas groaned. Every movement and line of his body screamed barely controlled anger. He wanted to lash out, but he didn't. "Her oath should have been enough."

"It isn't, but there is a chance to earn Mendal's trust."

"And let her die in the process. No. I will not sacrifice her life."

"It wasn't your choice." Rathenridge's uncharacteristically flat tone cut through the tension like no blustering could. "The decision has been made and the terms accepted. Now it is time to focus on making it possible."

"Is it possible?" I asked, scanning their faces for hope. "I can handle a sword."

"You are not a soldier," Tomas snapped.

"I know." I scrambled to my feet in a flood of anger. In some part of my detached self, I realized the anger wasn't really for him. "I don't claim to be one. I am, however, willing to fight. You once told me you wanted a wife who could stand beside you, not behind you. I am your wife, Tomas, and you are going to have to let me stand beside you."

The war of emotions in his inky-black eyes tore at my resolve, but I held firm. I had to do this for him, us, and our children.

He turned away. "I was wrong."

I blinked. Did he mean he regretted marrying me?

Or that I was a fighter?

Rathenridge cleared his throat to catch Dentin's attention and then jutted his chin toward the exit. Dentin nodded. They both left in a hurry.

Tomas didn't move. Lantern glow painted the canvas behind him gold and threw him into shadow. At some point during our arguing the sun had set. Despite the shadows, I could still read the strain in his shoulders. The stillness of his face scared me. I knew it didn't reflect what was going through his thoughts.

"It is the only way, Tomas." Sudden tears pressed against my eyes, but I willed them back. This wasn't the time to cry.

His shoulders lowered with a heavy sigh. "I know." He held out a hand toward me.

I ran to him. As his arms closed around me and his mouth found mine, I savored the illusion of safety. Within his embrace, relishing the warmth of his touch and savoring the thrill of desire flooding in its wake, I could envision a future of children and love. Clinging to him, I attempted to banish my dread of the morning in the fantasy of the night and the security of my husband's arms. For tomorrow the dreams would be gone. The reality of the task before me would demand its due.

If Kurios was gracious, I would only forfeit my inner peace for the nightmare memories of battle. If not, he might demand my life. I shied away from considering a third possibility—widowhood. I feared that outcome the most.

# Chapter Twenty-Seven

The morning of the vargar breach dawned with a multi-hued sky. Tomas rose before the sun, forcing me from the bed to prepare. Choosing my heaviest tunic, he cut it off at my knee. Heavy woolen leggings followed. My walking boots clad my feet. As soon as he was geared up, with my assistance, and I was decently covered by my heavy cloak, we left the tent in the direction of the armory.

There he found chainmail made for a squire small enough for me to wear, but we couldn't find a breastplate that would fit me without restricting my movements too much. We were arguing over the necessity of armoring me from the waist down when Rathenridge arrived with his wife's padded jerkin.

"I see you two have made up." He glanced between us a few times. Tomas glared at him, but my cheeks warmed beneath his teasing grin.

"Thank you for the jerkin." I began pulling it on over the mail. I felt as though I carried double my weight in gear already. Thankfully the jerkin weighed less than I expected. I was struggling with the tapes when Tomas approached with a helmet. I eyed the thing warily.

"Must I?"

"If you want to keep your head, you will."

"Are you going to lop it off for her if she doesn't wear it?" Rathenridge asked as I put the metal can over my head. "That monstrosity is too large for her. She won't be able to see a thing and we will spend half our time stopping her from running into walls. Here–" He tossed a smaller and lighter helmet to me. "This one is functional and fashionable. I hear it is all the rage to wear helmets like these in the capital this winter."

"Leave off, Aiden. That thing won't stop anything. It is too light."

I ignored him and exchanged the helmets. As I hoped, Rathenridge's choice didn't obscure my vision nearly as much.

"I prefer this one."

I expected Tomas to protest. Instead he demanded, "Why?"

"Visibility, and the weight doesn't hurt my neck. Besides, it fits the shape of my head better."

He frowned, but took his choice from where I had set it. "If a head blow kills her, Aiden, I am hunting you down."

"If a head blow kills her, I suspect you will do more than that," Aiden replied with surprising severity.

"Where is Dentin?" Tomas asked as he walked over to inspect the selection of spare shields.

None of the metal plates looked like a good fit for me, but I kept that thought to myself. Tomas had let me choose my helmet. I should let him choose my shield, within reason.

Rathenridge picked up a sword and put it through a few practice swings. "I passed him on his way to the blacksmith's to have the sword sharpened. He should be here soon."

"Good." Tomas approached with a shield for me to try. "Pick out a knife for her, will you? Her current knife is ill-suited for this."

I slid my left arm through the straps on the back of the shield. Tomas let go. I expected it to be heavy since it was hardly the smallest in the collection, but it wasn't. I moved it about, blocking an imaginary opponent and found it would work.

"Lower it a bit like this." Tomas guided the shield down three inches. "Now tuck your head."

"That helmet is too light," Dentin declared as he ducked beneath the canvas roof.

I didn't wait for Tomas to respond. "I do need to see, my lord. All the other helmets are proportioned for a man and my eyes don't match up. Besides, they are too heavy and make my neck ache."

Without acknowledging my protest, Dentin extended a sword belt and sheathed sword to me. "Put it on."

After freeing my arm from the shield, I accepted them. Before donning the weapon, I paused a moment to appreciate the workmanship of the sheath. Deceptively simple at a distance, the metal and leather work of the belt and sheath enticed one to examine it closer. I couldn't help rubbing a thumb over the intricately etched metal and leather.

"It once belonged to a formidable warrior."

I frown at him in confusion. "But this is a woman's weapon." Behind him Tomas and Rathenridge were arguing over knives.

Dentin nodded to the weapon in my hands. "She

wore it well and fought with honor and courage. I expect you to do the same."

"I will try to be worthy of it." I pulled the belt around my waist.

"Just stay alive." He walked away before I could assure him I intended to do just that.

"Here, try this one." Tomas held a knife hilt out to me before I finished cinching the belt.

"Who wore this before me?" I took the knife and tested its weight.

"He never told me. I just know that it is always with him no matter where he is. Will the knife do?"

"It is a bit dull."

He nodded. "We will stop by the blacksmith's on the way to practice." He turned to hail Rathenridge. "Meet you at the field."

Both Rathenridge and Dentin nodded.

Tomas threw my cloak over my shoulders and led me out into the sunshine again. Despite the nerves fluttering in my stomach and constricting my chest, I couldn't squash the occasional stray musing about the original owner of the belt and sword at my waist. If I survived this, I intended to persuade Dentin to tell me the story. Something about the fleeting emotion in his eyes hinted at something deeper than simply the respect of one warrior for another.

After a brief stop at the blacksmith's tent, we arrived at the practice yard. The yard of one of the small houses I had spotted on our first approach to Kyrenton served as a space for the men to warm up. The hard-packed dirt hadn't succumbed to the snow melting as much as the roads or fields.

In the meadow bordering the cottage guarded by tree

skeletons, scattered pairs of men sparred. Others drilled through exercises alone. An angular man passed amid the chaos and mud, leaning heavily on a twisted staff. Spotting us, he made his way toward us.

"My lord." He bowed quite easily. I tried to guess at his injury, but could find no visible clues beyond his obvious dependence on the wood for balance. "My lady." His bow to me was equally low.

"How are you, Lolathen?" Tomas respectfully lowered his head in greeting.

"We will have rain before nightfall." Lolathen tapped his thigh.

"I am sorry to hear that. Have you told Lord Dentin?"

"When the sun rose. He mentioned a night battle. The men have been drilling extra hard today."

Tomas nodded as he scanned the men around us. "Did you receive the selection requirements for our point crew?"

"Aye. Worand, Yerns, Polaner, and Eirianware will serve you well." Lolanthen pointed out each as he said their name. I almost didn't recognize Eirianware coated in mud from head to toe as he lunged at his opponent.

"Tell them to be ready at dusk and meet us at the sentry point south of camp. We will leave from there."

Lolathen acknowledged the order with a half bow. "I understand you are including Sir Rathenridge and Lord Dentin in your party as well." A tone of concern edged his voice, but it was subtle enough to be ignored should Tomas wish.

"You don't approve?"

Lolathen tilted his head slightly to the side, eyes measuring Tomas' expression with keen interest. "Their constant bickering is becoming the talk of the camp."

"Shame on you for listening to gossip." The right corner of Tomas' mouth twitched.

The old man shrugged. "There is not much else I can do comfortably, my lord." His grin sweetened the bitterness of the words.

"I suppose there are worse things to gossip about."

"Indeed, the verbal war has distracted the worst gossips from dwelling on other things." Lolathen's sharp gaze flicked my way briefly. "Though, the general consensus among the men is the lady is innocent."

"I am glad to hear that."

Someone yelled an oath. All three of us turned to look in that direction. I didn't recognize the man, but Lolathen tensed in disapproval.

"Pardon me, my lord, I need to speak with one of the men."

Tomas dismissed him with a nod. After bowing to both of us, the old man hobbled swiftly away.

"Now, let us see how skilled you are." Tomas lifted my cloak from my shoulders and flung it onto the pile of others hanging from a nearby tree. "How much training have you had?"

"Three years of study in my teens." I drew and swung my weapon. It was lighter than my father's old practice sword. The grip fit my hand better than the hilt of the old relic had.

"Have you practiced since?"

"Daily until three months ago." I practiced some of the footwork my father had taught me.

"Why did you stop?" The worry in his voice brought my attention to him.

"We had to get the harvest in."

"And after that?" The creases between his eyebrows

grew as he watched me.

"Preoccupation with finding a solution to the coming hunger crisis." I lowered my arm and glared at him. "I know I am not good."

"I could cut you down in moments."

I lifted my chin. At least he was being honest. "Then teach me so I can lengthen my life by a few more minutes at least."

The pain in his face took my breath away.

"I need to do this, Tomas."

He drew in a shaky breath and donned his helmet. "First, keep your guard up." He tapped my shield into place with his blade. "That shield is your best weapon. Use it." He walked three steps away. Whirling in place, he faced me, his features set and hard. "This is your last moment to prepare yourself."

I lifted my sword, adjusted my shield, and nodded.

The following minutes passed in a blur of adrenaline pumping reaction. He drove at me with a rain of thrusts, jabs, and lunges. I barely knocked aside most of them. At least thrice he missed my head so closely his sword whistled in my ear. Finally it glanced off my helmet, making my ears ring.

"Have I dissuaded you yet?" he asked.

I shook my head to dispel the ringing. "I gave my word to the king."

He strode over, discarded his helmet, and plucked my helmet from my head, releasing the crazy mess of sweaty hair beneath. "You can offer an alternative act of homage."

"I doubt he would accept it." Staring up into his taut features, I could feel him willing me to back down. "I gave my word, Tomas. I would never ask you to go back on your word. Why do you keep asking me to do something which you would not do?"

"Because I would rather you live." Dropping his sword in the dust, he reached for me and then stopped mid motion. He pivoted on his heel and turned half away. "War isn't orderly, Brielle. Battles are chaotic. No matter how I try, I cannot guarantee you will survive. I have lost good friends, men more deserving of living long lives than I. Cut down next to me, only a handsbreadth from me."

"This is not a battle."

He frowned. "The same rules apply."

"Nothing you say will change my mind, Tomas. I have to do this."

"Not even my order?"

I closed my eyes. If he ordered me to stay behind, I would. But, I didn't believe he would. I looked up at him again. "You won't order me."

Our gazes locked. I refused to look away even as my aching stomach continued to tighten and my heart thundered in my ears. I wanted to give in yet I couldn't. It wasn't pride. If I thought it would work, I would plead on my face in the dirt at Mendal's feet.

The turmoil in Tomas' face tore at my resolve. Maybe he was right. There was another way. There had to be another way to earn Mendal's trust.

"My lord?"

Tomas' head snapped around. The soldier recoiled, but recovered enough to deliver his message. "Lord Dentin sent me to fetch you. We just received more details from your steward."

"Where is he?"

"Lord Dentin?"

Tomas raised an eyebrow.

"His tent, my lord." The poor man's face pinked.

"Tell him we are on our way."

The man bowed quickly and ran back toward the camp.

"We will finish this later."

Tomas fetched my cloak while I claimed our discarded helmets. We met again in the middle. Tomas settled the heavy fur and fabric around my shoulders. Instead of claiming his helmet that I offered, he claimed my head. Hands in my hair, he kissed me fiercely and quickly. Withdrawing as swiftly as he came, he claimed his headgear from my lax fingers.

He strode five steps before I realized he was leaving. I ran to catch up.

# Chapter

# Twenty-Eight

We never finished our argument. Dentin kept Tomas planning until midafternoon. Then he sent me to bed so that I would be fresh for our assault. He woke me at dusk, mere minutes before we were to rendezvous with the rest of the team. I scrambled into my gear. Tomas produced two oilskin capes. They didn't offer much protection from the cold, but they would keep rain off.

Once he checked to make sure I had all the armor and weapons I was supposed to, he led me out into the deepening darkness. The sky hung almost black in the east, and the gray-yellow glow of an overcast sunset faded slowly in the west. It wasn't raining yet. A frigid wind whipped through the camp from the north. As my teeth started chattering, I hoped the sacrificed insulation was worth it.

I shouldn't have wondered. True to Lolathen's prediction, the rain arrived as a fire circle marking the sentry point came into view. The random drops of water spit and hissed in the flames. Eirianware stepped out of the gloom and bowed.

"How many have arrived?" Tomas asked.

"Worand, Yerns, and Polaner checked in, my lord."

"Sir Rathenridge show yet?"

Before Eirianware could speak, the man himself stepped out of the gloom. "Just waiting for you to arrive."

"Dentin?" Tomas asked.

"Coming. You should have time to make introductions, assign roles, and clarify orders before he shows."

Tomas turned to Eirianware in time to watch Worand, Yerns and Polaner join us in the light of the smoking fire.

"Men, this is my wife, Lady Irvaine. You may refer to her for the duration of this mission by the name Rell. We don't want them to know who she is. Upon completion of our mission that permission is revoked."

The men nodded.

"Brielle." Tomas checked that I was attending. "Captains Worand, Yerns, and Polaner will make up the rest of our party. They respond best by their last names, just like Eirianware, whom you already met."

Each man dipped their head in turn as their name was mentioned. I couldn't get a good view of Worand because he stood on the edge of the light, head tilted so his face fell mostly in shadow. His one obvious feature was a shaggy mane of medium brown hair.

Yerns was a thin man, wiry and lean, with alert eyes and still hands. I expected him to be a fidgety type with that intent gaze, but his hands rested on his weapons, relaxed and ready.

Polaner stooped and hunched to one side. Holding his left shoulder higher than his right, he appeared to be hiding his face like a shy boy when he nodded my way. He moved deliberately, as though thinking about each gesture. I wondered how he would handle himself in a fight.

I smiled at Eirianware. A familar face among these new strangers calmed my nerves a bit. After a startled blink, his features relaxed into an answering smile.

"The mission is simple in concept. Infiltrate the vargar and capture Sir Jorndar and Lord Wisten. The execution will be a bit more complex. The king has demanded that Lady Irvaine–"

"Rell," Rathenridge prompted.

Tomas glared at him before continuing. "Rell is coming with us. Your primary goal is to protect her."

All three men lifted their faces. I glimpsed Worand's heavy features and narrowed eyes before he hid his face in the shadows again. At least I had some idea what he looked like.

"Not the mission?" Polaner asked.

"Let Dentin, Rathenridge, and me worry about the mission. Her safety is of utmost importance, understood?"

The four acknowledged the order.

"Good, now for the details. We enter the city by the postern gate hidden on the south wall. Our escort will lead us into the vargar via an entrance prepared by our inside informant. From there, it is our task to find the two men. Questions?"

"How many armed men inside?" Yerns' eyes darted to the others as though counting our number.

"Ten armed guards, Lord Wisten, Sir Jorndar, and the lady, Rolendis."

"What should we do if we encounter the lady?" Polaner asked.

"Subdue, but do not harm. She isn't our focus."

"I am not happy with the plan, sir." Yern's sharp gaze studied Tomas' face without diffidence or guile. "A cornered animal is more dangerous than one with a way out."

"Sir Landry and the king's men will storm the vargar in five hours. We have until then to get inside, open the gates, find the men, and subdue them."

"Not kill them?" Worand hadn't moved, but his gravelly voice drew all of our attention.

"If possible."

"If not?" Yerns asked.

"You won't be reprimanded if they die once we have a confession," Dentin clarified.

All four men avoided glancing at me. Though from the awkward shifts in their gaze, I knew they understood the significance of the clarification.

"Ready to move out?" Dentin asked.

Everyone double-checked their weapons. Once Dentin received acknowledgement from each man, he signaled for us to fall into formation.

Dentin and Rathenridge took point, Tomas and I claimed second position, Eirianware and Polaner fell into third, while Worand and Yerns brought up the tail. Hoods up and heads down, we plowed through muddied fields.

The rain remained gentle until we approached the city walls. Out of the darkness a wave of pouring rain washed over us with a roar. The seething cold cut through the oilskin. I halted, my heart pounding frantically and my lungs straining for air. Eirianware plowed into me, driving me into Tomas, who caught me.

"Sorry," I whispered as I scrambled to find my

balance.

"Are you hurt?"

"No."

"Good." He squeezed my upper arms gently as he set me on my feet again.

We tramped to the wall. Dentin turned sharply to the left, away from the gate, and picked up the pace. The rest of us fell into a single file. Tomas walked behind me. I focused on trotting to keep up with Rathenridge's rain-glossy figure. Not sliding down the slick grassy mound while climbing it took more skill than I suspected.

About the time I wondered if Dentin truly knew where the opening was, Rathenridge stopped abruptly. I managed to follow suit. Tomas steadied himself on my shoulders when those behind him didn't stop in time. After a few moments of almost silent scuffling, and a muttered oath or two, they sorted themselves out.

A crack of pale gray light appeared in the blackness of the wall. Dentin and the man beyond exchanged murmured words. Then the crack widened to become a door and we filed through into the town.

"Horacian?" Tomas' whispered exclamation brought my attention to our contact's face. It was him. Armed, soaked, and looking more worn, he bowed elegantly despite his bedraggled appearance.

"I seemed the obvious choice. Besides, I wanted to plead on my daughter's behalf when the time comes."

"I am not sure what you will be able to say to stay her punishment." Rathenridge shook his cloak slightly so it fell correctly. "She has acted against her liege lord's better interests and colluded with enemies of the crown."

"Back to the issue at hand." Dentin broke in before Horacian could answer. "Which way is the vargar entrance?"

"This way, my lords." Horacian pulled his hood over his helmet and strode off into the dark and rain soaked streets. We fell into pursuit, dodging heaps of muck and plowing through puddles of slush that soaked through my boot seams and into my socks beneath. By the time we reached the outer bailey wall, I could no longer feel my toes and the sock beneath my foot was a solid lump of compressed ice. The temperature continued to drop, converting the rain to sleet.

Horacian led us straight to a postern door. Hidden behind a rough-edged buttress, it blended in with the wall of the tower above it and was only visible from one direction. We had to squeeze past a strategically placed copse of bushes and stunted trees to get to it.

"Who else knows of this door?" Dentin asked as Horacian fumbled with the key.

"The late Lord Irvaine showed it to me when I took on the duties of steward. He impressed upon me that no one else knew of its existence."

Rathenridge groaned. "Rolendis could have known."

"And told Jorndar." Tomas' gloved hand closed around my shoulder. He leaned down, nudging the hood aside so his breath traced eddies of warmth across my cold cheek. "Enter behind me."

I nodded.

The door finally jerked open with a groan that echoed somewhere beyond. Horacian struggled to pull the key from the lock as Dentin and Rathenridge pushed past him into the dark gap inside. Reappearing, Rathenridge waved the rest of us past him.

Beyond the door was a space barely wide enough for two men to stand abreast and four to stand together. To the right a stone stair rose twisting and steep, crowding out the ceiling. Tomas, sword already drawn, took the stairs at a sideways run with the confidence of a man with experience in tight and curving spaces.

I didn't even attempt his speed. My lungs burned. Panic rose. What if I stumbled? Eirianware and the others breathed heavily in the darkness behind me. I could not turn back. As though underscoring the finality of our course, the door below closed with a solid thump.

After an eternity of steps too narrow for my full foot, a shout from above sent my heart into my throat. I scrambled. Thomas needed help. I was in the way.

The top of the stairwell opened up into the center of a bastion. I tripped over the last stair and rolled out across the wooden floor. Crawling to the wall I climbed to my feet, dragged out my sword, and looked for the fight.

Eirianware engaged a swordsman. Beyond the open arches, I glimpsed Dentin and Tomas fighting two others on the wall walks. Distantly, a third man, ran madly through the rain. Yells from below turned my stomach cold.

"So much for surprise." Dentin stepped back into the shelter of the bastion as he wiped his sword with a piece of his dead opponent's shirt. "There were more than ten men running across the bailey toward the keep."

"You aren't going to faint on us, my lady, are you?" Worand's heavy-lidded eyes watched my face.

Mouth dry, I shook my head.

"Good, because there is going to be a lot more of that before the night is through."

I nodded again, not trusting my voice.

Spotting Tomas, my gaze shied away from his weapon. Instead I sought his face. He grimaced, but only in concentration.

"I suggest we split up. We can cover more ground that way." Dentin consulted Tomas. "Any idea where they would hole up once alerted?"

"Jorndar will run. He isn't one to stick around if he is losing. Horacian, best routes of escape?"

"Three. A hidden passage from the noble's bedchamber to a tunnel beneath the walls, the postern we just used, and the main gate."

"There was a tunnel?" Rathenridge's face tightened in anger. "Why didn't you mention this sooner?"

"Later." Dentin's sharp retort silenced even the murmuring between Yerns and Polaner behind me.

Horacian squirmed beneath Dentin's glare. "The access in the woods to the west is locked by a key only Kolbent carried. I couldn't get you in that way. Jorndar can only get out that way if my daughter has the key and gave it to him."

"Fine. So the chances are even he will try any of the three exits. How certain are you that those are the only exits?"

"They are the only three Kolbent told me about when I attained my position."

"Where is the tunnel entrance?"

Horacian glanced at Tomas as though asking permission.

"Just tell him."

"The second tapestry to the left of the fireplace

296

covers the door."

Dentin accepted this with a sharp nod. "Eirianware, Polaner, and Worand take the front gate. Rathenridge, Horacian, and Yerns stay here. Tomas and Rell with me."

It took me a split second to remember I was Rell.

He started trotting along the wall walk toward the keep. I followed. An arrow whistled past my head. I dropped behind the nearest turret, fear cutting into my air supply.

"Rell!"

Tomas crouched one turret to my right. Once he gained my attention, he signaled to stay down. "Tell Dentin to draw attention."

Dentin squatted three turrets away to the left, too far to yell without giving away the message. I shook my head at Tomas.

Tomas signaled to someone on his right. When he turned back to me, he grimaced. "We have to draw fire so Yerns can disarm the archer."

I nodded.

"I am coming your way."

I waved him back. "No. There isn't room."

"I am not about to let you do it."

He wasn't in a position to stop me. I pulled my cloak from my shoulders. Half-frozen sleet sluiced through my layers. Gasping, I clamped my teeth together against the instant shaking. Working within the confines of my cover, I propped the hood on the tip of the sword. Bracing against the slick stone at my back, I lifted my makeshift decoy with shaking arms. Once it creasted the turret's edge, I pulled it down again. The archer didn't respond.

The crack of wood on stone reverberated through the air. I glanced past Dentin in time to see three swordsmen jostle from the tower door.

Dentin squatted, obviously readying for a fight despite being pinned behind a stone half his height.

"Don't be a fool!" Tomas hollered.

"He doesn't have a choice." I yelled in response.

Dentin ignored us. The first of the three neared him.

I moved the oilskin so it looked like I was peeking out the side toward Dentin. An arrow glanced off the stone, startling my breath from my lungs. I clenched the rain-slick hilt, flexing my cramping fingers. I had to do this. Dentin wouldn't hold out long. I took a deep breath.

Another teasing peek out of the shelter brought another arrow, this one closer. My teeth chattered and my arms shook. My ribs ached.

"One more time," I whispered.

The rhythm of battle began.

Shoving aside my rising fear, I braced my quivering arms on my knees and jabbed the oilskin out farther toward Dentin.

The force of the arrow hitting my sword knocked it from my numb hands and over the edge of the walk. My heart fell with it. Metal clattered distantly on the stone in the bailey below. Shuddering silent sobs gripped my chest.

The archer's cry of triumph morphed into a shout of anger. He cursed fluently.

Dentin yelled in pain. His opponent lunged in for the kill only to have his shin split by Dentin's sword and shoved from the wall by his shield. The heavy thud of his body striking the stone turned my stomach.

Dentin's relief didn't last long. The next combatant took the first's place. I couldn't decide which was better to die quickly by three to one odds or this slow death by attrition.

Just as I debated sticking a hand out, anything to spare Dentin, Tomas called out. My head whipped around in time to see Tomas running toward me.

"On your feet." Catching my upper arm, he half dragged me along with one hand. When I gained my feet mid run, he let me go.

"Stay behind me."

Dentin drove his opponent backwards to where the walk widened where it joined the tower wall. The remaining combatant dodged Dentin's shield and lunged at Tomas.

A deadly test of balance and agility commenced. Tomas blocked a blow aimed for his chest only to be caught in the head by a shield. He stumbled back, teetering for a moment on the edge.

Suddenly uncoiling at his opponent, Tomas lashed out with sword, catching the man unawares and drawing first blood. The gash along the man's forearm looked deep.

Connecting blade to blade, Tomas forced his opponent backwards in a sudden show of strength. The man stumbled, scattering pebbles over the edge.

Tomas followed him. Sword moving faster than my eyes could follow, he pressed the man backwards.

My skin prickled. Someone was breathing behind me. Heart stuttering in fear, I pivoted on my left foot and raised my shield in a clumsy attempt at an old training move.

Nothing prepared me for the force of his blow. I

almost dropped my only defense. His blade slid off of the metal rim.

I fumbled for my knife. At only nine inches long, it was a platry offense against a sword, but the best I had.

Instinct brought up my shield arm to meet his next blow. The downward force of his blow brought me to my knees. His blade bit deep into the metal rim. Wood groaned.

He brought it down again. I shoved back against the blow this time. The rim of my shield snapped off with a twang.

The next blow nearly cleaved the wood in two. The tip of his blade stopped inches from my arm. He braced his feet to heave his weapon free, and I saw my opportunity.

He pulled and I let go. Staggering backwards, his heel missed the edge, coming down on air.

For an eternity, he hung there, frozen on the verge. Then he was gone.

A groan drew me to the edge of the walk. Far below, a broken body on the bailey cobbles, limbs twisted unnaturally. My stomach turned. With my heartbeat thundering in my ears, I swallowed back the acidic taste of bile.

"Rell?" Tomas joined me at the edge.

He looked past me at the remains. Then wordlessly, he searched my face.

I found I couldn't face his scrutiny no matter how sympathetic. I focused instead on my shaking hands. Only a minute ago, that mess on the ground below had been a living man. My chest grew cold.

"I killed a man." The words tasted bitter.

"He wanted to kill you." The sharp edge to Tomas'

voice brought my chin up. The understanding in his eyes counterbalanced the coldness of his voice. "We need to move." He gestured toward the tower door.

I turned to obey his unspoken order.

One body lay sprawled on the walk next to the door. Dentin stood over him.

"I lost Dentin's sword over the edge."

"We will claim it later." He handed me the dead man's. "Can you manage with that one?"

I wanted to throw the heavy thing aside. "Any sword is better than none."

Acknowledging my acceptance with a nod, he stepped over the corpse's legs. Yanking the tower door open, he gestured for us to enter ahead of him.

Tomas took the lead. With shield before him and sword drawn, he started down the steep stairs.

Dentin followed.

We met no resistance. The door at the base of the tower opened without protest. Despite our caution as we emerged, no one stepped forward to confront us. We ran along the inner bailey wall toward the keep.

My stomach threatened to empty when we passed the remains of the men from the wall, but I willed it back into place.

The rain slowed as we entered the inner bailey. Our running feet echoed in the eerie silence.

When we crossed the opening into the practice yard, Dentin came to an abrupt halt in the center of the archway.

Three corpses lay in the center of the yard. Arrows jutted from of the backs of two of them. The third lay face up in a puddle of his own blood. I couldn't see how he died, but I recognized his ash-white hair and red beard in the light from the open stable and armory doors that spilled across the yard.

I averted my eyes in time to see Dentin's fingers tighten around the hilt of his sword. He adjusted his grip on his shield straps.

"Revolt?" I asked.

"Eliminating witnesses, more like." Dentin met Tomas' gaze over my head. I didn't catch the message in his expression, but I heard Tomas grunt his reply.

My stomach soured with the thought that Orwin was capable of such brutality. Then in light of his recent activities, it didn't seem as far-fetched. After arranging my life and others for his benefit without regard for our safety, health, or happiness, taking a life to save his own would have been a small step.

Dentin changed course. He ran for the nearest entrance to the keep, the door I had used the day I left. I kept up, barely. His legs were longer than mine and more accustomed to running in full gear. My lungs ached from the icy air and exertion. I was so thankful he slowed to pull the door open.

Immediately inside another body blocked the entrance, sprawled on the stairs as though he had been climbing for the door. Sheathing his sword and bracing himself against the wall on either side, Dentin hurtled the distance, landing hard on the stairs beyond.

"Move aside." He motioned for me to get out of the way.

My legs wouldn't move. I couldn't take my eyes from the dead man's face. The features were familiar in the way a servant's were. Seen perhaps dozens of times and still not completely recognized as an individual's face.

Tomas pushed me to one side, gently, so I braced the

door. Grabbing the feet and hands of the body, the two men hauled it down the passage and into the first room.

I followed, careful to avoid stepping in the blood trail. Some distant part of me screamed at the injustice of so many deaths. Another part urged me to wake up from the nightmare. However, the functioning parts of me kept moving forward, following Tomas and Dentin through the undercroft, across the great hall, and up the main staircase.

We passed three more dead. A trail of burning torches, broken furniture, torn tapestries, dripped wax, and occasional blood smears led us up the main stair, right to the door of the lord's bedchamber. Dentin stopped on the top step and signaled for silence. Tomas turned to relay the message from his perch a few steps below Dentin. I forestalled him by folding my lips around my teeth, clamping my mouth closed, and nodding.

Someone was crying. The soft whimpers and shuddering breaths filled the silence between another person's pacing treads.

"Oh, stop sniveling!" Orwin's voice echoed out into the corridor through the open bedchamber door.

"They didn't have to die." Rolendis yelled back and then burst into loud sobs.

"Would you rather we die? Those rats were threatening to hand us over to that army out there. I doubt Lord Irvaine would reward you for your part in our schemes."

A loud sniff came from the room. "I have done nothing wrong."

"Releasing a prisoner of Lord Irvaine and taking his vargar by force are hardly nothing, woman. If you didn't carry the heir to the title of Irvaine, Jorndar would have killed you too despite your pretty face."

"He can't. He swore to protect me. It was part of our vows."

"Naïve child, that hasn't stopped men before."

Her desolate wail cut across my nerves. Dentin flinched and Tomas cringed.

Orwin's foot falls retreated from near the door.

Dentin took advantage of a momentarily clear shot and dashed across to the other side so that he and Tomas now flanked the doorway.

"Cease your wailing. We might be able to help each other." Orwin lowered his voice.

"Take your hands off my wife, worm!" Jorndar's anger echoed around us, bouncing through the open doorway, off the empty corridor walls and the cavernous space above the stairs.

Tomas and Dentin exchanged frowns. We couldn't see from where he had come. I could only guess he emerged from the secret tunnel.

"I was merely keeping her company." Orwin's voice dropped into subservient tones.

"I don't share, Wisten. You touch and you pay, with limbs."

"Is the end of the tunnel open?"

One of them spat. Something metal skittered across the floor.

"Never reached the end. The middle caved in decades ago. By the look of it someone did it on purpose." Jorndar cursed. A great crack of something striking wood heralded a deafening crash of pottery. A metal bowl rolled out the open door, wobbled in a circle, and then settled on its bottom.

Dentin flattened himself against the wall. Tomas and I did likewise. Swords at the ready, we listened in the tense silence that followed.

"What do we do now?" Orwin whined.

"Bargain."

"With what? We have no money. She isn't worth anything until she births the boy-child. What do we possibly have to bargain with?"

Jorndar laughed. "You." The scrape of a sword coming free of its sheath filled the silence.

A second sword was drawn.

"You are mad!"

"Maybe so, but I am not wanted for treason and you are." Someone shuffled their feet. "The king arrived yesterday. His banner waves over the camp now. Rumor is he wants the architect of the invasion, the mole. You."

"But what about..." Orwin was cut off by the whistle of a sword cutting the air. He scrambled and fell.

Jorndar laughed. "Yes, I picked a fight with his favorite, but that is insignificant compared to your transgressions."

"There is another way." Orwin's voice cracked.

"Do tell."

"There is a tunnel under the wall in the garden."

"That will only gain us entrance into the town. How do you propose we get past the walls?"

My cousin rushed to explain. "I know someone who will get us out...for a price."

"How much?" Jorndar's incredulous tone sent chills up my back. He wasn't buying into Orwin's plan.

"A few gold nibs should do it. Nothing much."

"Do you have a gold nib?"

"No." Silence.

"Then we are back to my plan."

"But..."

Another whistle ending in a cry of horror from Orwin.

"I suspected as much. You are a coward."

The clash of metal grating against metal set my teeth on edge.

I still wasn't in the clear. Orwin had admitted to nothing. If he died before confessing my innocence, I would be as good as dead as well.

Dread filled my chest. My cousin was not a skilled swordsman. I debated the wisdom of storming the duel. If we did, we could possibly save Orwin from dying and taking me with him.

"Fool, you cannot run from me!" Jorndar yelled.

Orwin emerged from the room at a run only to be propelled back inside again by Dentin's shield.

"He has a point, Wisten. There is only so far one can run." Dentin stepped into the bedchamber. Tomas and I followed. "Close the door, Rell."

I bolted the door and stationed myself against the wall next to it. I wished I could have placed myself on the other side. I was useless either way.

"Who are you?" Jorndar sneered at Dentin. His gaze flickered briefly over me to Tomas. His scorn hardened into hatred.

"Tomas the mutt, have you come to beg for your castle back?" He adjusted his grip on the hilt of his sword and drew the knife at his waist. "I will finish you this time."

Dentin's sword whipped up to derail Jorndar's lunge. Sliding his weapon the length of Jorndar's blade,

Dentin stepped between the childhood adversaries. He forced Jorndar to scramble backwards, barely missing Orwin's prone form.

"You forgot me."

Jorndar's gaze lost a bit of its mad glitter as he focused on Dentin again.

"You do not interest me."

The two of them exchanged blows, testing.

Dentin nodded a bit. "You, on the other hand interest me greatly. I understand you want something."

Jorndar's eyes narrowed. "Who are you?"

Orwin, taking advantage of Dentin's distraction, scrambled to his feet and backed toward the strangely silent Rolendis. She remained perched on the edge of the bed, apparently frozen in surprise. Only her eyes moved, following Dentin.

"Your wife knows."

Orwin froze as attention shifted to Rolendis. I couldn't see Tomas' face, his back was to me, but I did see him tilt his head ever so slightly.

"Who is he, Rolendis?" Jorndar demanded.

Her lips moved, but no sound came out.

Tomas took a smooth step to the left, out of Orwin's direct line of vision.

"He is Lord Dentin, you fool." Orwin smirked. "You are crossing swords with the man responsible for the safety of the realm. Now would be a great time for a confession."

"What are you babbling about?" Jorndar's sword dipped as he half-turned to glare at Orwin.

Dentin leaned in and neatly sliced through Jorndar's jerkin and tunic to the skin beneath. Jorndar cursed and dropped his knife to clamp his left hand over his right forearm. "I wasn't looking."

"Never been on the battlefield, I take it." Dentin punctuated his question with a hard stroke. "I don't take kindly to knights who have never seen combat, especially in view of the conflicts of recent years." Two more strokes and a half-hearted lunge pressed Jorndar back a step.

"I served."

"Which side? Are you of Trentham or Mendal?"

"Mendal, of course."

"Then why is there record of your knights on Trentham's books?"

"I fought at Manowing."

"I wouldn't consider hiding in your tent fighting. Are you a coward as well as a traitor, Sir Jorndar?" Dentin timed a thrust and whipping lunge at Jorndar's head to match the final question.

Jorndar ducked and deflected, but only barely. "I am not the traitor here!" He lunged madly at Dentin. "I fought at Manowing under Mendal. I have supported him from the beginning."

"You lie." Dentin cracked Jorndar on the side of the head with the flat of his sword. His opponent fell like a rag doll.

Rolendis screamed, but the sound was cut off abruptly.

Orwin held Rolendis against him, bending her awkwardly over his paunch. His knife tip pressed against the underside of her jaw. "No one move or she dies."

"You are assuming we wish her to live."

Dentin's cold response provoked a flicker of fear in Orwin's darting eyes as he tried to keep all three of us in sight at once. An impossible feat since Tomas now stood next to the far left wall and only two strides from the pair.

Sometime during Jorndar's confrontation with Dentin, Tomas sheathed his sword. Behind his back, hidden from Orwin but not from me, he held a knife. He glanced at Dentin. Some kind of communication flicked between them.

With a yell, Dentin raised his sword and lunged. Despite the sword tip still being feet away from him, Orwin jumped backwards. Rolendis fell forward, whimpering. I expected Orwin to dive to recover his human shield. Instead he clutched his throat and crumpled to the floor, Tomas' knife stuck in his chest.

# Chapter Twenty-Nine

Sleet whipped at my helmet, each ping echoing strangely in my ears. Around me, the outer bailey filled with armed men, returning servants, and former residents who had fled Jorndar's coup. The baker yelled at his assistants as they guided an overloaded cart toward the kitchens. A commander called out assignments to three ranks of armed guards bearing Irvaine's crest and colors.

Their neat tunics and clean armor contrasted sharply with Tomas' and my own appearance. Blood from Orwin and others stained his knees and tunic. Mud crusted his leggings, boots, and sleeves. I knew I didn't look any better, more likely worse. The commander kept glancing our way as though he wanted to come over and reprimand me for my sloppy kit.

I stepped closer to Tomas and Antano.

I didn't attempt to follow Irvaine's list of questions and orders as he and Antano bounced words back and forth. I felt like a drowned rat. My teeth kept chattering if I didn't clamp them closed. I welcomed the cold, though. It distracted me from the horrible dread coiled in my stomach, like a cobra ready to strike if I looked its way. Still, I couldn't ignore it forever. Eventually I was going to have to face the fact I was going to be tried for treason. A shiver gripped my spine. I shied away from the inevitable and focused on Tomas' voice.

"...Search the city for any of Jorndar's men. Twenty are still missing." Tomas bit his blue-tinged lips as he closed his eyes as though to gather his thoughts. Antano's brows tightened in concern. "I am forgetting something." He rubbed his face with his gloved hand.

"What are you two still doing here?" Dentin strode across the bailey from the direction of the armory. "The king is going to want a report. You both need to change."

My stomach growled. "And eat."

Tomas signaled for a horse before turning back to Dentin. "Are you returning to the camp?"

"I have a few people I need to speak to, but I will be there. Get your wife out of here. She looks frozen through."

The horse arrived and we rode through the waking town. Our passing was noted by wary eyes from child to blacksmith, a sad indication of how life for the residents had been over the past weeks. We slowed as we approached the town gate. The guard came out from the shadow of the gatehouse to greet us. Suspicion tightened his gaze and mouth.

Tomas drew us to a halt at a respectful distance.

"Where do you think you might be going in such a hurry?" He circled our horse as though evaluating it for sale.

"The camp beyond the wall. I am returning from duty."

The man peered up at Tomas' face. "Commanding officer?"

"None, I am Lord Irvaine."

The man laughed.

I couldn't blame him. Tomas looked worse than the time I first met him. Plain armor, no livery, no insigna of rank, and looking worse for wear, he could have been anyone, friend or foe.

"Hold the reins." He wound the leads through my frozen fingers. Unbuckling the chin strap, he pulled his helmet from his head, tucked it under one arm and began peeling back his mail hood. Digging around his neck, he produced a thick chain. Pulling it forth, he caught the end and pulled it over his head. "My signet ring," he said as he dangled the heavy ring on the end before the man's widening eyes.

"My apologies, my lord." He bowed so quickly that I feared he would fall over. "We feared one of the madman's brutes would escape. I was ordered to question everyone seeking to get through the gate."

"Rightfully so." Tomas tucked the chain and ring beneath his breastplate and proceeded to redon his helmet. He fastened the strap and nodded to the gatekeeper. "Just bring a companion out when you inspect. Any fugitives will be desperate and more than willing to run you down in a run for the gate."

The man grinned enthusiastically. "Just let them try." Turning to face the gate, he waved at the archer slits above. "All clear," he yelled. He turned back to Tomas with a cocky shoulder shift. "My son, one of our best archers, is up there. He can shoot the hat off a minstrel at twenty paces without disturbing his hair."

Tomas looked up at the slits and nodded. "I believe it.

Keep up the good work." He urged the horse forward only to stop it again and swing it around. "What is your son's name?"

"Pip Huntsey, my lord."

"If you son is ever interested, there will be a place in my service for him."

"Thank you, my lord."

We left him behind, bowing us out with great flare.

"That was very generous, Tomas."

"Nonsense. I meant it. If his father proves to be truthful as well as bold, we will use Pip."

The horse ate up the distance between the gate and the edge of camp in silence. The sentry waved us past.

I didn't recall ever feeling as grateful to see a tent before, but the sight of our tent sent tremors of exhaustion through my limbs. I wanted sleep so badly my eyes watered. Tomas lowered me down with one arm. My knees barely managed to support me. I started toward the tent door. Shedding gear from the door to the bed, I was about to sink into the offered softness, when Tomas came through the canvas flaps.

"Don't! I ordered a bath for you. It should be here within a half hour."

I suddenly wanted to cry. My knees shook. I didn't fight them. Sitting unceremoniously on the ground, I pulled my helmet from my head and let loose a sob.

"Brielle?" Tomas knelt before of me. "Beloved, what is wrong?"

His large hands caught my head in the familiar hold. His fingers laced through my sweaty, tangled mess of hair, thumbs brushing at my tears. I only released more to replace them. I couldn't stop them despite my closed eyes.

"I am going to hang."

"What?"

He tilted my head up so we were face to face, but I couldn't open my eyes. My heart ached so that it hurt to breathe. I feared what I would see in his eyes when I said what I must.

"You killed Orwin before he could clear me." Suddenly more afraid of not knowing than knowing, I opened my eyes.

Blackness. I forgot how limitless and strange his eyes were. I couldn't interpret the swirling change in their depths.

"I won't let them kill you, Brielle."

"But you won't be able to stop them." I shoved his hands from my face and turned away. "Don't you understand? In the king's eyes I am a traitor."

"You aren't."

I rounded on him. Was he being deliberately obtuse? "Orwin's toady said I was and only Orwin's word that he was the only architect was going to free me. You killed him!" I screamed my frustration at him.

His face remained as frozen and expressionless as the first time we met. I couldn't even read emotion in his opaque gaze. The slump of his shoulders and the dead weight of his arms hanging at his sides only spoke of exhaustion. I could discern nothing more.

"I killed him, Brielle, because he was going to kill Rolendis."

"You valued Rolendis' life higher than mine?" I stared at him. I felt as though a knife had torn through my gut.

"No. I killed Orwin for the child Rolendis carries, the life guiltless of its parents' sins. I did it for that child

315

and because we already had enough. Mendal will not convict you of treason."

"Why? What has changed? Why did we go through this charade of me going with you on the assault if Mendal won't convict me of treason?"

"Because I won't let him. The king is summoning us now. There are still a few pieces that need to be put in place. You have to trust me, Brielle." He caught my hand, folding it over his and pulling it up to his mouth. Hovering a breath from my fingers, he locked gazes with me. "I love you. I will not let anyone take you from me." He pressed his lips to my skin.

My heart raced, flooding my limbs with liquid heat. His words brought tears to my eyes. I already knew he cared for me. His actions demonstrated his affection from the moment we spoke our vows. Despite my lack of doubt, hearing those precious three words from his mouth made my heart swell.

Even as I came willingly into his arms when he tugged me closer, a part of my brain still protested that he wasn't invincible. He was only a mortal man.

"I love you." I traced the curve of his jaw with my fingers. "And trust you. I am not sure I trust Mendal."

"You and me both." He caressed my knuckles with his thumb. "That is why Dentin is following up leads to the real culprits. I obeyed his order to take you with me because it strengthens our case."

"It does?" Between exhaustion and the warmth of his touch, I grasped at my thoughts. They slipped beyond my reach.

The bath water arrived and the moment was gone. We bathed and fell into bed. He slept heavily, snoring. I rested uneasily, terrorized by worries and phantasms that twitched me awake only to greet me when I fell asleep again. After what seemed like eternity, Dentin arrived to deliver the summons to appear before the court.

Tomas rolled to his feet, alert and ready for a fight. I crawled reluctantly from the bed, dragging the covers half off with me. I ached worse than when I laid down. Only Dentin's presence prompted me to keep moving despite the siren's call of sleep.

"Is all ready?" Tomas asked as he pulled on his fur-lined tunic.

"As it can be." Dentin rested his hand on the hilt of the sword strapped to his hip.

"That bad?" Tomas reached for his sword belt.

I frowned as I glanced between them. "What are you two talking about?"

Dentin ignored me. His naturally neutral expression gave nothing away. However, the coldly efficient way he handed Tomas a sheathed throwing knife set my instincts afire. Suddenly completely awake and alert, I grabbed Tomas' arm. "What are you two planning?"

Tomas avoided my gaze. "Finish dressing, Brielle. It will all become clear."

"No."

Tomas stopped in the middle of reaching for his boots. Straightening, he drew in a deep breath.

Dentin rested a hand on my shoulder. "Brielle–"

"No, Dentin, I will handle it. Go."

The men exchanged a look. Dentin swung around, strode to the table, deliberately placed a wrapped bundle on the top, and strode out the door.

"Brielle." The weary tone in Tomas' voice brought my focus to him.

Looking up into his familiar face, I realized how much I wanted him to be right and how much I believed he wasn't.

"Promise me you won't do something foolish," I pled. "I am not worth it."

The right corner of his mouth quirked.

My hand rose of its own accord to touch the twitch.

He kissed the tips of my fingers. "Darling, I have survived this long by taking risks. Calculated choices are part of life. Marrying you was a risk. Accepting the title brought benefits, duty, and danger. Every time I ride into battle, I know there is a chance I will not return home whole. Unlike then, this is a sure bet. And even if it doesn't work, I do not regret my choice. You, my love, are worth every risk."

I was torn between joy and fear. The love in his eyes invited me to believe, hope. My heart wanted to step out on faith that it would work out. However, my head kept listing all the reasons I shouldn't and all the possible ways this could go wrong. The worst being that he died.

*Please, Kurios, show me what to do.*

He was my husband. I trusted him more than I trusted anyone, except perhaps Loren. All we had experienced together in the past month of marriage proved him a skilled soldier, great leader, and a wise man. Above all he had been a friend who had yet to lead me wrong.

"Go get dressed, love. We need to leave." He brushed my hair back from my face.

I obeyed. Twisting my hair into an acceptable form, I tried to keep my worries at bay by counting all the ways Kurios had delivered me in the past. He wouldn't fail me now.

*Please keep us safe*, I prayed.

As I adjusted the most ornate girdle about the waist of a deep navy blue tunic, I turned to find Tomas bent over Dentin's parcel of paper. His dark brows bunched over his nose, but when he finally finished reading, he nodded as though satisfied.

"Presentable enough?" I rotated for him.

"Radiant. No one would believe you were playing a warrior only a few hours ago. Come." He held out his hand to me while tucking away the packet beneath his overtunic with his other hand. I grabbed my lined cloak and drew the hood up over my hair. We plunged out into the noontime sun.

Melting sleet crunched beneath our feet the whole way to Mendal's camp.

As we passed through our camp, men appeared and fell in behind us. Antano, Eirianware, Yerns, Polaner, Kuylan, and Muirayven the healer were among the faces I identified when I glanced back. By the time we reached the edge of camp and crossed the narrow gap between camps to enter the king's camp, we were about thirty men strong. The cacophony of crunching echoed along the spaces between the tents.

Sentries ran after us before we reached the center of camp.

"My lord, you can't march into Mendal's presence as an army," the first man protested, his panic evident in his flailing hands.

"The king summoned my wife and me to a trial. These are merely witnesses I wish to call." Tomas' calm demeanor and even tones did nothing to soothe the man's agitation.

"But, my lord."

Dentin appeared at the sentry's side, tucking away something into the front of his jerkin. "I vouch for their peaceable motives, Ret."

The man sputtered for a moment. "Very well, Lord Dentin."

He bowed and trotted back the way he came as fast as he could. Perhaps he hoped if he put enough distance between him and us, he wouldn't be blamed should Dentin prove to be lying. The others disbursed as well.

"You are late." Tomas cupped my elbow and propelled me forward again.

Dentin fell in step with us on my other side. "Jorndar was more trouble than I expected."

"You got what we needed, right?"

King Mendal's personal guards blocked our way into the great open space at the center of camp. Similar to the one his camp formed outside of Wisenvale, it was large enough for a small army. A single tree grew on a small rise at one end. Behind it, so that the skeleton branches canopied the opening, the king's pavilion staked a large portion of the field. In any other season it would have been almost picturesque. However, in my current state of mind, I thought it looked as though the tree were the king, grasping for the sky as well as his domain on earth.

Dentin spoke quietly with the captain of the guard. He returned to our side.

"The three of us may approach the tent, but the rest must stay here." Silencing the murmurs of dissent among our escort with a glare, Dentin offered me his arm. "My lady?"

I glanced at Tomas. As much as I trusted Dentin, I

didn't want to walk into the lion's den without Tomas' support.

"I will be right behind you," Tomas assured me as he laid my hand on Dentin's sleeve.

Dentin stepped forward and the personal guards parted for us. He led me out into the center of the square to a circle marked in the dirt. He guided me to the center of the circle and positioned me to face the entrance of the king's tent.

"Say nothing unless required and follow Tomas' and my lead."

I glanced at him, but he was staring straight ahead, his face a mask of indifference. Striding a short ways away, he turned to face the entrance of the pavilion as well.

I stood alone. Lifting my chin, I straightened my back and pulled back my shoulders.

"Well done." Tomas' voice made me jump. I began to turn, but he stopped me. "Face forward. Here he comes."

The canvas rolled up and the court poured out. The few women among the men looked very uncomfortable despite their fur lined capes and headdresses. Their gaudy robes and stiff dresses were woefully out of place among the austere surroundings of the camp. The men didn't appear much better. I recognized a few of their faces from my last summons outside of Wisenvale.

Finally the king emerged, warmly dressed and obviously more comfortable in his attire than his court was in theirs. He still leaned on a cane. Two pages followed him carrying a chair. He whipped his cane out to point at where he wanted the chair to go. The lads hurried to comply and then retreated. A third appeared with a footstool as the king eased down onto the cushioned seat.

My knees ached as I watched him settle on the very comfortable looking pillows. A few of the courtiers' expressions slipped into envy as well.

"Begin the proceedings." Mendal waved to Lord Dentin. But then he spotted Tomas standing behind me. "Lord Irvaine, please join your peers." His rings flashed in the meager sunlight as he gestured toward the courtiers surrounding him.

"I humbly refuse, your majesty."

"What?" Mendal's eyes narrowed as he leaned forward to peer at Tomas.

"I wish to stand with my wife."

"She is accused of treason!"

"She is innocent and my wife. I stand with her."

Mendal's face stilled except for his intent gaze snapping from me to Tomas and back. Then his jaw tightened. "I am your king."

"You are." Tomas' voice carried firm and clear, but the clipped words hinted at the tension underneath. "I am at your mercy."

Mendal's eyes glinted and for a moment I feared he would press the issue further. But he didn't. With obvious effort, he eased back in his chair. "I accept your argument. A husband should stand with his wife if he chooses." Lifting a finger, he signaled Dentin.

"As ordered by our sovereign king, I have investigated the accusations against Brielle Dyrease, Countess of Irvaine and Wisenvale."

"What evidence have you found?"

"I have discovered nothing to support the informant's accusations and plenty to undermine the validity of the accusations."

Mendal frowned. "I expressed my wishes very clearly at Wisenvale regarding this matter and Lord Wisten's fate."

"You did, sire. You wanted Lord Wisten's full confession and him in custody. Circumstances did not provide opportunity for us to capture Lord Wisten."

"I understand he is dead."

"Yes, your majesty."

"At your hand?"

"No. It was done at my order."

Mendal's face tightened as he peered at me. "Did Lady Irvaine kill him?"

"No, your majesty, I did." Tomas' calm confession banished all my hopes of him remaining free of blame.

The king blinked. "You, Tomas?"

"Lord Wisten threatened to take the life of a woman with child. I chose chivalry."

Murmurs passed through the gathered courtiers. A few of the men smiled in satisfaction. They most likely hoped the king's favorite, Tomas, had gone too far.

"I expect nothing less of you, Irvaine." The king's pursed lips spoke of displeasure despite his words.

One of the nobles standing at the king's left hand leaned forward. "What do you wish done about Lord Wisten's title and lands, sire?"

"Thank you for reminding me, Cilnore." Mendal leaned toward the clerk, but his voice carried so the whole gathering could hear. "Hold Lord Wisten's lands in trust to the crown until a suitable time when I feel inclined to award them to a deserving party." He stressed the word deserving.

Cilnore flinched as though stung, and half of the

other nobles shifted uncomfortably in their shoes.

"Lord Irvaine, might I assume that the woman you rescued was your wife?"

"It was not, my king. It was Kolbent Briaren's widow."

Mendal's eyebrows rose. "He left a widow? Who's the child's father?"

"Briaren is, I believe. I would like to petition for guardianship."

The king's face grew stormy. "That is a matter for another day, Tomas. Beware. I will not be distracted from the issue at hand. I will not look well upon any attempts to divert me."

Tomas fell silent as my gut tightened like a lute string. Dentin and Tomas intended to push the king much farther and he was already voicing warnings. This boded ill for my fate.

*Please spare Tomas,* I prayed.

The king continued questioning without pause. "Lord Dentin, did the knight provide any further information when you questioned him?"

Dentin summoned one of the pages with a single finger. He handed the lad the bundle of pages that he had tucked away when he met us and indicated they were for the king. "Sir Jorndar bragged of taking Kyrenton vargar with only a handful of men and wishes to lay claim to the title and lands of the noble title of Irvaine upon his marriage to Rolendis Briaren, widow of Kolbent Briaren, late Earl of Irvaine. He claims he was not party to the plot to invade. That piece of foolishness, he professed, was completely of Lord Wisten's making."

The king skimmed the pages and then handed them

324

to the man beside him, who noted every word spoken. "No mention of Lady Irvaine?"

"None."

"Fine." The king nodded and waved a hand at the scribe. "Note that Sir Jorndar's claim has been denied. Draw up an execution order for my signature, death by hanging. I can't have knights riding about causing trouble with peers of the realm."

Unwieldy silence stretched as the scribe made notes. Not even the nobles stirred.

"Back to the matter at hand." Mendal cleared his throat and gripped his cane. "I see no reason to spare the Lady Irvaine. You have spoken no evidence in her favor, Dentin."

"You have not given me opportunity, my king." Dentin pulled a completely new bit of parchment from under his over tunic.

One of the courtiers cleared his throat pointedly. "If you keep pulling documents from your clothing, Lord Dentin, we will be led to believe you are nothing but rustling paper." A few around him laughed uncomfortably with furtive glances in the king's direction.

"Be wary Doritane, lest your name appear on one of his lists," another man responded.

Again the courtiers shifted and murmured.

Dentin waited without reacting until the rustling ceased before speaking. "My lord king, I have collected a host of witnesses who can speak to Lady Irvaine's actions and companions over the last month. I, myself, can swear to her movements since our meeting in Wisenvale. Before that, I have corroborating sworn testimony from two or more witnesses as to her

325

location and actions from the moment Lord Irvaine's company entered Wisenvale until this moment."

"All on that piece of parchment?" Mendal tilted his head and lifted his eyebrows in obvious disbelief.

"No, your majesty, this is simply a list of the witnesses and the periods they witnessed. I have the detailed statements under lock and key. I have arranged for a sampling of the strongest witnesses to be available, should you wish to question them yourself."

The king motioned for one of his pages to fetch the parchment. "Is that the army of men that escorted Lord and Lady Irvaine into my presence?"

"They are a sampling of my witnesses."

The king frowned over the list. "Most of these are Irvaine's own men."

"Yes they are, your majesty."

"Might they be stricken from the record based upon their corruptibility? He is their superior."

"Have you ever known Irvaine to choose a traitor to serve in his ranks? He demands complete loyalty to you as the primary requirement of service in his ranks."

I could think of a traitor from Tomas' men. Brevand's mutinous face danced before my mind's eye. Tomas had chosen unwisely in selecting him. Seeing his childhood friend, he had employed a traitor. I tried to keep my features neutral as Mendal studied first Dentin's face and then Tomas', directly over my shoulder.

"You vouch for this woman, Tomas?"

"I do."

Mendal's scrutiny fell on me. I met his gaze for a moment, then lowered my face and waited.

"Fine." Mendal grunted to indicate it was nothing of the sort. "I clear her of the charges."

My head snapped up in surprise. I was free. I felt as though a great load had fallen from my shoulders. My body was suddenly so light I wanted to fly. However, one glance at the king's frown rooted my feet in the ground again.

In the king's mind, I was not clear of suspicion. For now, perhaps forever, I was compromised in his mind, a woman of dubious lineage. My cousin plotted against him. He believed I would do the same, given the chance. Strange considering how he overlooked Tomas' lack of a father.

But, it did explain why Tomas kept his true parentage a secret. Should Mendal discover Tomas was sired by a western baron, the king would never trust my husband again.

While I worked through the implications in my head, the court formalities wound down. Tyront's sentence was announced, death by hanging, and King Mendal declared his intention to break camp come morning and return to the capital. Now that there were no more signs of revolt, he perceived no reason to stay.

Finally, he withdrew, signaling the end of the gathering.

The courtiers and court staff disbanded in a hurry.

Dentin left after a swift bow to me and Tomas. I hoped I would see him before he left.

I turned around to find Tomas standing closer than I thought. His dark eyes drew in my gaze, relief in the midst of exhaustion.

"Come, wife." The corner of his mouth twitched. "We have sleep to catch up on."

"No kiss of celebration this time?" I widened my eyes in false innocence.

He laughed and caught me up in his arms, spun me around. Finally setting my feet on the ground, he didn't pause to let me catch my breath before lacing his fingers through my hair. "I love you, Brielle," he whispered before kissing me so that I clung to him for balance.

# Epilogue

"Mother! They are here!" Darnay ran into the great hall, his new puppy at his heels and barking so that the ceiling echoed with the ruckus. Sliding the last few feet and colliding with my legs, the boy wrapped his arms about my waist in an effort to keep upright. The grasp quickly morphed into a hug. The dog danced about and continued yapping.

"Hush, Samson!" I freed a hand to signal the dog to sit. As the puppy's wiggly hind end lowered to the floor, tail whipping the rushes every which way, a wail rose to replace his yapping.

"Linora." Darnay released me and dashed to the cradle only a few steps away. "Sh. It is all well." Scooping his little sister from her nest of blankets, he smiled as she quieted to stare at his face and bat at his nose.

The instant attraction was reassuring to see. Even now, two years since my marriage to Tomas, I reveled in how Darnay's attitude had changed toward me. Linora's birth three months ago solidified our family in ways I had not expected. She was of the three of us, not a fragment of the past.

Darnay took to the role of older brother with joy and a seven-year-old's eagerness to help. The attraction between the siblings had been almost instant and mutual. Linora usually drank in his every word, laughed and smiled at his antics, and would soon be trailing him everywhere. As every older sibling does, Darnay did tire of sharing Tomas with Linora when he would much rather Tomas be outside teaching him to use a bow.

"Who arrived?" I asked Darnay as he bounced the now smiling Linora.

"I spotted Father and Lander coming through the outer bailey gate."

I splayed a hand across my middle as it tightened with anxiety.

"Don't worry, Mother, he will like you." Darnay smiled up at me with the confidence of a young man with little experience with disappointment.

"Like you liked me at first?" I smiled and ruffled his hair so he knew I teased.

"Mother, please stop. I don't want to look like a little boy." He handed me Linora so he could smooth his dark curls.

I pressed my face against Linora's soft auburn spirals and breathed in the baby scent of her. She tangled her fingers in my own escaped curls and tried to cram them in her mouth.

"We are home. Where is everyone?"

Tomas' voice brought my head around, yanking my hair and Linora's fist from her mouth. She protested with a mighty wail. Despite her angry noise, I couldn't tear my gaze from the welcome sight of my husband striding down the great hall.

"Father!" Abandoning his unruly hair, Darnay ran to his father. He was almost too tall to be swung about, but Tomas did anyway. Bracing for the catch and throwing his son up as though he were still five.

"Did you take good care of the women while I was gone?"

"Yes, I watched Linora while she slept every afternoon. I carried the linens for Tatin. And I played with Linora four times so Mother could nap, didn't I Mother?"

I nodded as I tried to ease Linora's fist open. "He was very helpful."

Darnay immediately launched into a story about his recent training with Antano.

"Whoa, just a minute, Darnay. Mother needs some help." Tomas set him gently on his feet and approached me with a smile.

Linora, spotting her father, reached both arms out to him and attempted to launch herself from my arms, my hair still in her fist.

Tomas laughed as he caught her. "You aren't supposed to be stealing your mother's hair, little one. You will grow plenty of your own soon enough."

With both hands available, I made quick work of freeing myself from my daughter's grasp. "How did it go?" I asked in a whisper as Tomas leaned in for a kiss.

He didn't pause to answer. Claiming my mouth and pulling me up against him with his free arm in a way that promised more delightful attention later, he worked a familiar magic on my senses.

"I missed you, wife." He drew back to kiss my temple before retreating. "I will fill you in on the details later."

The fleeting grimace on his face indicated enough

discomfort to make me concerned, but I pushed my worries away when he turned to face the far end of the hall. There, standing in the shadows and looking as though she wished the floor would swallow her, was a tall young woman carrying a thin, toddler boy.

"Come and greet my family, Gelsey." Tomas beckoned the girl toward me. "Brielle, this is Gelsey, an orphan who has been rearing Lander for Rolendis."

Gelsey came forward and dipped an awkward curtsey before offering a shy smile.

I made a point to smile warmly in return.

"Welcome to our home, Gelsey."

"And this–" Tomas placed a gentle hand on the small head of the boy in Gelsey's arms. "–is Lander, son of Rolendis and Kolbent Briaren."

I approached slowly. The boy's wide blue eyes watched my movements from beneath a thick fringe of very straight brown hair. The hair and eyes looked nothing like Rolendis, but the almost pretty form of the boy's face reflected his mother.

I offered a hand. "Very nice to meet you, Lander. I am Brielle."

Lander regarded my offered fingers with suspicion. Then he turned away, pressing his face into the hollow of Gelsey's narrow shoulder.

"He is hesitant of strangers, my lady."

I nodded. "I would be too if I was just taken to a new and strange place. Is there anything he particularly likes? Any favorite foods?"

"He loves white bread and butter."

I smiled at the mention of the delicacy. "I am sure we can find you some white bread and butter."

"I will get it." Darnay disappeared in the direction of

332

the kitchens.

"Do you have any preferred foods, Gelsey?" I asked.

"Me, my lady?"

"Of course, you must be hungry too. Come, let the three of us go to the kitchen and see about feeding you both. Then I will have Tatin show you two to the nurseries. I assume you won't mind sleeping in there with the children and their nurse for the first few nights until Lander adjusts."

As I spoke, Lander slowly eased his face from Gelsey's shoulder. "Gelsey stay?"

I smiled into his fair eyes. "Yes, Gelsey can stay."

His small mouth lost a little bit of its petulant firmness. "Bread?"

"Yes."

"Let me show them, my lady." Tatin had appeared in her usual, efficient way. I nodded my agreement. The expression on Tomas' face indicated he wanted me to himself. Taking Linora from Tomas, Tatin led the way toward the kitchens. As the door closed behind them, I heard the girls exchange introductions.

"Now, wife, I have plans for you." Tomas' strong arms enfolded me, pulling me backwards into his warmth. "I have missed you, and I intend to take advantage of our temporarily childless state by whisking you away."

I turned in his arms so we almost brushed noses. "What makes you think I don't have similar plans, my lord?"

# Acknowledgments

When I was about four or five years old, I was admitted into the hospital for eye surgery. While there a friend of the family came to visit me and he gave me a bear with a t-shirt that said, "Consider yourself hugged." This is my first time including acknowledgments in one of my books. That said, I realize I am not going to be able to thank everyone by name who has helped in the creation of this story. If I miss mentioning you, please "Consider yourself thanked."

Abigail, thank you for the spark that set fire to this story. I hope it lives up to your expectations for the opening line. Also, I owe you greatly for the selection of Brielle's name. Your comment prompted me to look at the name twice.

Thank you, Elizabeth, for offering the other opening line that I used in the first chapter. Your contribution fed the story and gave me a place to begin with Brielle's character.

Alyssa and Joanna, thank you for naming Brielle. Once she had a name, her personality and past opened for me. She wouldn't be the same to me if she bore the name Susan or Kay.

Thank you to my wonderful and supportive husband for letting me disappear on random evenings to write. Without you, this book would have never been written. Most of all, thank you for your love.

To the wait staff of our local restaurants, thank you for your patience with the odd woman with the laptop who would show up late at night, ask for a booth, and type like mad. You were unfailingly kind and generous.

My children, you contributed equal parts motivation,

inspiration, and distraction when I needed it. To my oldest son who planted the seed of Darnay in my mind, I hope you are pleased that you did, when you are old enough to understand.

Lovely ladies of Iridescent Inklings, thank you for your feedback, support, and chatting with me about writing and other various topics. Your encouragement saw me through the rough spots when my characters weren't cooperating or when I grasped for a new plot idea on the fly.

Not least, and certainly not last, Charissa, my sister of the pen and sister of the heart, you never fail to listen and give good advice, no matter the topic.

Ann, thank you for reassuring me that my scribbling has value despite my fears.

To all my beta readers, thank you from the bottom of my heart. You push me to improve. Without you, this book wouldn't be as polished as it is.

Finally, thank you, dear reader, for picking up this book. I hope you have enjoyed reading it as much as I enjoyed writing it.


- Rachel Rossano

Also from
Rachel Rossano

A Romany Epistles Novel

## An excerpt from WREN

I knew Wren would follow me. The sympathy in her eyes could only be born of similar circumstances. She had family, siblings, but she hardly ever mentioned them. However, before Kat left, I caught her watching us as though remembering something lost.

Snow turned the courtyard into a mess of slosh and muck. The space didn't welcome the kind of activity I intended. My hands itched to grasp a weapon and everything in my being screamed that I should destroy something. Not a safe state of mind for plotting logically or sitting still. I strode through the slush to the heavy keep door. The great hall would work perfectly for my short term plans, open area and shelter from the elements.

I turned back before opening the door. Wren was close on my heels.

"Care for a round of sparring?"

Her strange eyes cleared from worried brown to an amused amber. "Do you have an extra sword?"

I shook my head as I shoved the door. "I was thinking along the lines of staffs or cudgels, something that won't kill you if I miscalculate."

"Miscalculate? You should be a bit more concerned about me hurting you." The wooden door closed behind her with a muffled thump. "Do you want to be disturbed?" She indicated the repaired bolting system.

"Lock it. Let them wonder if we are killing each other."

The worn stone floor, spread with rushes, lay empty. An old trestle table dug out of storage rested against the far wall, and the newly-beaten tapestries adorned the walls. I ignored them. Now was not the time to dwell on the past. I needed to drive history from my mind, far from my mind. Exercising until I was too exhausted to think would numb the pain. It would distance the ache enough so I might progress beyond the inclination to kill the enforcer slowly with my bare hands. He killed my parents!

"Weapons?" Wren's voice cut through my thoughts at just the right moment.

"Take your choice." I indicated the rack of various implements next to the trestle table. Walking to the far end, I shed layers of clothing down to tunic and britches. "Are you sure you are up for this?" Discarding the last overtunic on the heap, I shivered in the frigid air. I welcomed the discomfort.

"Of course," she said from right behind me. "On guard."

A wooden club whizzed past my head. Striking the wall inches past my shoulder, it clattered to the floor. I stared for a second. Gone was the quiet, withdrawn woman I thought I knew. Hair wrapped around her head, stripped to her leather jerkin, shirtsleeves, and leggings, she moved like a sleek cat, feminine, yet deadly. Confidence radiated from her as she whipped another cudgel into her dominant hand.

"Remember what I do for a living."

She advanced and I retreated to the fallen weapon. Scooping it into my hand, I swung it up into a defensive stance seconds before she struck at my shoulder.

I retaliated with a series of strokes that should have reduced her to begging for leniency. Instead, she met me hit for hit, backing away into the center of the room. Although she gave ground, I grew wary. She was holding back. Fury boiled in my belly.

I changed my attack. After feinting to the left, I jabbed at her right. She took advantage of a small defensive weakness and landed the first blow, a hard jar to the ribs. I renewed my onslaught, taking a risk. She saw the move and sidestepped at the last moment, dancing out of my reach. Breathing hard, we faced each other.

"The point of this was for me to work out some

frustration."

"I know."

"This is hardly satisfying."

She laughed, a clear sound that echoed in the rafters. "I am not about to submit to a beating just to help your frustration level. I will help you wear yourself out, though." She leapt forward and attacked again.

Coming Soon

# Honor

Second Novel of Rhynan

Written by Rachel Rossano

# An excerpt from HONOR

## Lord Dentin

Even before I lifted my head, I recognized Elsa's voice. But nothing prepared me for the vision that I beheld. Her dark hair coiled around her shoulders in waterfall of waves, curls, and silvery gray ribbon. Her kirtle was simple wool, but the deep blue complemented her complexion perfectly. I noted the heightened color in her cheeks and her widened eyes before realizing I was probably the cause.

I returned to studying the craftsmanship of the goblet between my hands. "I am hardly fit company for a lady at the moment."

"You are not alone. Lord Irvaine looks positively livid."

I lifted my head long enough to glance at Tomas and Brielle locked in intense conversation across the room. Brielle shot me a stormy glare. This evening's meeting would not be pleasant.

Elsa shifted. "I don't think I have ever seen him so angry before. What did you say to him?" Then she blushed even deeper. "No. Don't tell me. It is none of my concern."

It dawned on me that I needed to know more about the child that I was about to take into my care. The woman overseeing his care, even temporarily, would be an excellent resource. "Actually, you could help me."

She studied my face. "I will do nothing to harm that family."

I smiled. "An admirable resolution. By helping me, you will be helping them."

"I don't believe you."

"Come sit." I rose.

She backed away from me. I could see she contemplated running. Where had the fearless warrior of that morning gone?

I pulled out the chair next to mine and offered it to her.

We stood close enough that I could hear the air hiss softly between her teeth as she took a deep breath.

I tried to smile warmly, but the movement pulled at my face strangely. "I won't bite."

She glanced at my face, disbelief raw in her gaze. But, she accepted my offering and sat.

I reclaimed my own place, occupying my hands with my goblet once again.

Avoiding looking her way lest I spook her, I traced the design in the metal with my thumb. "I need to know more about Lander."

"Why?"

"I am to be his foster guardian." I risked a peek her way. Her brows were gathered in thought. Her slender fingers traced the weave of the cloth on the table.

"Then the rumors were true." She straightened. "Will Darnay be fostering with you as well?"

I hadn't thought of that. "Possibly."

"What do you need to know?"

"His habits, likes, and dislikes. I know little about caring for children."

"Surely your staff will see to those things."

"I have made no arrangements." I glanced her way. Lips pursed in thought, she now leaned forward slightly. I had snagged her interest. I floundered for a way to keep her engaged. "I have never fostered a lad before."

"Then why are you taking on such a task now?"

I frowned. "My house is the safest of the choices."

Forgetting herself for a moment, she openly frowned at me. "If this isn't Lord Irvaine's choice and you are only taking on the fostering because your care is the safest, why is Lander being removed from Irvaine's household in the first place? From all I have seen, he is thriving and happy at Kyrenton."

"The king's decisions rarely take the happiness of his pawns into account."

Her eyes widened in understanding. Sitting back in

her chair, she lapsed into silence.

I set down the goblet without drinking the contents. "So, what can you tell me about the lad?"

She pressed her lips together for a moment. "You shouldn't take him away from the Irvaine household."

"I have no choice."

"There is always a choice."

"When it comes to a directive from the king, there is no contest between obedience and defiance for an honorable man, my lady."

"You consider yourself an honorable man?" Her challenge so innocently issued cut me to the quick.

"I take it from your tone that you don't consider me so."

She weighed her words before speaking which made them all the more devastating. "No, sir, I don't. A man who acts as a thug for a man of few morals is not a man of honor." She grew pale, perhaps realizing that she had just impugned the king's honor and insulted me in the same breath. "Pardon me, my lord, I seem to have lost my appetite." She rose and walked off the dais before I could gain my feet.

# Honor

*Second Novel of Rhynan*

**Coming Soon**

# About the Author

As a happily married mother of three small children, Rachel Rossano dreams of new stories among chaos. Then she writes as fast as she can during nap times and after the little ones are tucked in for the night. She draws from a long history as an avid reader and lover of books. Usually she writes non-magical fantasy novels set in medieval worlds, but she also dabbles in the science and speculative fiction genres.

**Connect with Rachel Rossano online**

Blog: rachel-rossano.blogspot.com

Twitter: twitter.com/@RachelRossano

Facebook: www.facebook.com/RachelRossanoRambles

Amazon: www.amazon.com/dp/B00BAI41RO/

Smashwords:
www.smashwords.com/profile/view/anavrea

Made in the USA
San Bernardino, CA
18 April 2016